Praise for

"...dark, erotic and dangerous..." **RT BOOKreviews**

"Loved this book.. HOT! HOT! HOT!" **Reviewer on Goodreads.**

"Great faced paced story that will [definitely] re-read again and will recommend to others." **Reviewer on Goodreads.**

"A dark, edgy romantic suspense..."
The Long and Short of It Romance Reviews

"...Captivating, mysterious, suspenseful, and hot!...a great romantic suspense debut!!" **Among the Muses**

Circle of Desire

The Circle Organization

Carla Swafford

Ebook ISBN: 9781386619796

Paperback ISBN: 9781956518023

Hardcover ISBN: 9781956518146

Chapter One

O livia St. Vincent typed the ammunition data into the keypad on the sniper rifle and then nestled her cheek against the stock's custom-fit pad. She waited for the information to be processed and her target to come into view.

Keeping her attention on the boardwalk outside the open window, she caressed the silencer attachment and sighed. Powerful and lightweight compared to others, the rifle was her favorite and the only one of its kind. She wasn't sure how The Circle got their hands on the prototype, and she knew better than to ask. She'd used it twice in the last eleven months and had no complaints.

She inhaled the fresh salt air coming in and watched the few early joggers trotting along the boardwalk next to Elliot Bay. Almost the whole length was visible from the empty fourth story apartment. A strong wind picked up and splattered water off the windowsill onto her hands and the rifle even though she sat a good three feet from the opening. She grabbed a soft cotton cloth and stroked off the liquid. It had rained for ten days straight since she'd arrived in Seattle, and only twenty minutes ago had it stopped. To the north, a break in the clouds showed deep blue sky. A miracle. Good grief, she couldn't wait to get back home to Atlanta.

One moment, she was running her fingers across black metal, enjoying the bumpy finish. In the next, she was aiming at her target, taking a deep breath and then releasing it, relaxing, holding her trigger finger steady. He'd crossed the street and started down the boardwalk. Five foot eleven with a well-proportioned torso, he always wore the same dingy sneakers with orange Day-Glo stripes.

She squeezed her eyes shut for a few seconds and inhaled. Time to concentrate on the job. The Circle had given her orders to eliminate him, and she was programmed to follow. Later she would hear he was a child molester or a killer like herself. Why she should care one way or the other, she wasn't sure. Maybe knowing helped her sleep at night. Not that it would matter otherwise; she was a killer and good at what she did. She never really had a choice.

She waited as he'd jogged a little past the half-mile mark. His feet pounded in a steady rhythm as the early morning light glistened on shifting muscles. Like clockwork every day, he hit the pavement at sunrise, jogging down the same area. Only thing about predictability, it could be deadly.

The area around him was clear, no one nearby. He turned down a short pier. Only a few feet more and he would be at the mark. She cleared her mind and inhaled, holding her breath for the fraction of a second. She squeezed the trigger. The jogger's body continued straight ahead, propelled by the bullet's trajectory, and then he toppled off the edge of the pier and splashed into the water as his god-awful shoes tumbled across the boardwalk. Perfect shot. That was why they sent her.

Once she pressed a couple buttons on the gun's micro-computer, she scooted away from the tripod and stretched with arms up, bending her back, getting the kinks out. Her back popped. After an hour in one position, it was no wonder her body protested, no matter how much she worked out. She shook her head when the image of the body landing in the water tried to resurface. Think of the good she carried out. Her job eliminated those who preyed on the weak. She performed as a tool for the greater good.

Yes. That was it. She was a lethal tool.

Thinking of tools, she smirked at the gun. The usual brutal recoil dampened by the hydraulic system always surprised her. The rifle worked like it should with little firing signature, a thump of air and only a small amount of flash at the end of the barrel. The suppresser did its job. Unless someone stared directly at her open window and caught the small flare, nothing gave away her location.

Damn! If she'd been a man, she would have a hard-on now. She loved her gun. Objects she could control. People were a different factor.

As she closed the window, a warm breeze caressed the fine hairs on her arm. She shivered. Yeah, she was ready to relieve the pressure that had been building up inside. Playing the waiting game and finishing the job always sent her seeking the only outlet from all the tension. Others used alcohol or drugs to forget for a little while what they'd done. Sex with an anonymous handsome stranger was her drug of choice. Someone clueless about what she did for a living. Someone who held her as she used them for release.

She looked out the window at the crowd gathering at the end of the pier. She jerked her gaze away. Concentrate on anything but the finished job. Think of the gun she loved to control. Think of the power she held. Think about sex. A strong, hard, hot male body always helped. Think about getting away and planning the next job.

She reached out and caressed the two marks she'd made on the butt of the rifle. *Time for a third.* Her fingers shook; tears threatened her composure. Drawing her hand into a fist, she took a few deep breaths and then with well-practiced precision broke down the rifle and placed the sections into her luggage. Another tremor started at her hand and vibrated down her torso, before she knew it her whole body shook. Why couldn't her body cooperate? She'd done worse, been worse. Taking several more deep breaths, she closed her eyes and imagined a swing on a long porch, pushing against the wooden floor with a bare toe. Back and forth. Finally, the shaking stopped, and she swiped at her forehead, surprised by the sweat she found there.

She glanced at her watch. Time to get her act together and pick up speed. By the time the authorities responded to a passerby's 911 call, she needed to be on the road, heading to I-90 and Denver. Unless someone noticed the spray of blood before he landed in the water, they would be clueless that he'd been hit by a sniper until they dragged the body out of the water.

Inside ten minutes, she sauntered out of the fingerprint-cleaned apartment, pulling a rolling safari-chic suitcase behind her while clutching a large tote on her shoulder. The black linen pants, tailored black silk blouse, and auburn hair piled on top of her head shouted business trip.

The clouds in the blue sky had separated allowing the sun to peek between the breaks. Emergency vehicles zoomed by and their echoing sirens bounced off the buildings. They headed toward the boardwalk further down the street as a small crowd pointed at the water.

About the time she walked the block and half to the

parking deck and threw the luggage into the trunk of her rental, her cell phone vibrated.

"Yes, sugar booger." She loved irritating the hell out of her handler.

Jason Kastler thought he was God's gift to women, and she took every opportunity to remind him his good looks were good only for one thing, to play a Romeo, an operative who seduced women for information. Whenever he walked into a room, women watched his every move as if he was a walking sex toy. He hated it when she reminded him that men stared too. With his sun-kissed blond hair, vivid blue eyes, and six foot six frame, he needed someone carving off his massive ego.

"Sugar booger? Christ, woman, can't you be the least bit respectful?" His growl revved her engine.

Good looking *and* an orgasmic-inducing voice. It really was a shame. She could use him at the moment, though it would never happen. He liked to be the one in control. One thing about her, she always relished being the one on top.

"Respect is earned, doll. The job's done, and I'm heading to my next assignment's location. I already have a plan. Should take me a couple months to set up. I just need to scout the area," she said, ready to move on.

She tossed her purse to the passenger side and then slammed the driver's side door. Wasting no time, she had the cell phone plugged into the radio's speakers before cranking up the car. The state of Washington had a hands-free cell-phone law and ironically, considering her job, she followed all the traffic laws. The last thing she needed was to be pulled over for a minor infraction and be caught with the sniper rifle and numerous other weapons hidden on her person and in the rental.

"Change of plans ... Theo wants you to return to the

office. We have a ticket waiting for you at the airport." He was smiling. That light tone shouted his enjoyment in frustrating her.

She shut her eyes for a moment, anxiety curled in her stomach; he knew how much she hated flying. Not counting the up and down of the plane, the arranging for her arsenal to be shipped across country without her was a pain in the ass. The roar of the plane's engines didn't help the defenseless feeling.

Being ordered off an assignment by Theo was a bad sign. She avoided any face-to-face with him as much as possible. Hell, she'd worked hard for her freedom and for the last couple of years he rarely required her presence. So this meant something bad. Last time he'd made the demand, it had taken her a week to recover. He wasn't an easy man to please, and she no longer cared about satisfying his perversions. From the orphanage to the streets to Theo's control, there was always somebody waiting to use her, to take advantage of her. No more. She wouldn't go back to being that girl, begging for kindness and love. She squeezed her eyes closed, blocking out the images. No more. She dreaded being that needy little girl again. Tears welled up, threatening to spill.

Inhale. Exhale. Worrying wouldn't help. She struggled to regain her usual calm, steady façade. She took several more deep breaths, hoping it stopped the feeling of panic engulfing her. Pressure applied by her fingertips on the corner of her eyes pushed back the tears.

Olivia knew it was useless to argue. Operatives never won arguments against Circle handlers; disagreeing too much could be unhealthy. People had been known to disappear.

"Okay. Tell me which airline." She took another deep breath.

As he spit out the instructions, she turned the car toward a local UPS store and made her plans. Two hours later she boarded the plane, and all her weapons, including her gun, were on their way in several parts to her home in Georgia.

She settled into her first-class seat. After questioning the flight attendant, she learned the plane was full for the nonstop flight to Atlanta. She hated it when the seat next to her was used. No elbow room. Not that she was tall¾a mere average height of five foot five¾or big¾roughly a hundred and twenty pounds. She didn't like strangers rubbing against her and often took the window seat, not for the view since she usually pulled down the shade, but so she could lean against the wall of the cabin, putting as much distance between her and the next seat. First-class seats were wide enough she could even pull her feet up beside her, but she always loved more room.

Pretending to stare out the window, she waited for the rest of the plane to load. One drawback to first class was having every man and woman file by, staring at those seated in the more expensive rows. Bloody hell, wouldn't they hurry up? She hated the closed-in feeling, the helplessness, the sitting and waiting, the curious looks. Couldn't the freaking flight attendants help the tourists place their handhelds into the overhead compartment, so everyone would quit staring at her?

Closing her eyes for a few seconds, she mentally shook herself. What good was it to be short tempered, bitchy? Sure, crowds made her uncomfortable. Too many people pressing in, too many staring, guessing at what she did for a living. Was murderer written on her face, her clothes? She hated feeling like this. Add in her unexpected meeting with Theo, and she was certain she would go crazy.

When she was about to scream in frustration, the last person walked through. Whoever had the ticket for the seat next to hers hadn't arrived yet. Maybe she'd be lucky, and the seat would remain open. She rarely slept well the night before a hit, and it would be wonderful to stretch out.

The attendant pulled on the door and stopped when someone shouted from the walkway.

Olivia dug her nails into the armrests. Shouting always grated across her nerves. She always expected the worse. Had she screwed up and the local yokels or the big boys were after her? When she heard laughing, she realized whatever happened didn't involve the law. People rarely laughed when the authorities showed up.

"Sorry, my flight was late coming in. I almost didn't make it," a deep voice said.

She looked up. Oh, yes, this was what she needed. The man was a good six-one, possibly two, and the Armani suit showed off his wide shoulders perfectly.

He glanced toward the empty seat the attendant pointed to and then he looked at her. Those mysterious dark eyes punched the breath out of her. Set in an angular face with a small dimple in the chin, his eyes appeared almost amber, glowing with such a life force. His lips etched full but still masculine and begged to be licked. Oh, she liked the look of those lips. His nose was manly, not crooked from fighting but not a picture-perfect narrow one either.

Yeah, she liked the package in front of her. Now if she could remove the wrapping to see what lay underneath. Her body had been humming ever since she'd completed her mission. With those gorgeous eyes and his athletic body, she was more than willing to put him through his paces.

Maybe being stuck on a plane for five hours wouldn't be so awful after all. This stranger she wouldn't mind touching or have him touching her. She reached out and introduced herself.

"Hi, I'm Olivia Roth."

"Joe Murphy." He held her hand for a second longer than necessary.

Her grin spread wider. Oh, yeah, this was going to be a whole lotta fun.

By the time the tires bounced and rolled on the tarmac at Hartsfield-Jackson Atlanta International Airport, Olivia already had Joe inviting her to dinner that evening. She felt primed and ready to give her new friend a good time. Since taking a stranger home with her was out of the question, she worked her wiles until he told her he was staying at the Marriott Marquis.

Then she remarked, "Isn't that a coincidence? I'm staying there too." She liked how his eyes glimmered when she said that. To him, she was a lone woman on a business trip, easy pickings for a one-night fling.

She ducked into the women's restroom at the airport and called reservations. The Marquis happened to be her favorite hotel, and they had room. When she stepped out, her gaze zeroed on Joe, leaning against the wall nearby; his eyes drank in every inch of her. Oh, yes, he was exactly what she needed.

They shared a cab, laughing and talking all the way to the hotel's check-in counter. As they walked toward the elevators, he mentioned wanting to visit one of the restaurants below street level. She smiled.

They would never make it. Though she detested strangers brushing up against her, she didn't mind using one to release her tension, to forget what her job entailed. Her body using his throughout the night until he fell exhausted from her demands. And she had many demands.

Oh, yeah, a beautiful thing about being a phantom in the world of assassins, at the end of a mission she could enjoy a little downtime with a good-looking man. No one in the world knew what she did except her handler and Theo. She'd always been careful.

Leaning against the glass wall of the elevator, she stared as the lobby became smaller. A few more years and she'd kill Theo and disappear.

One corner of her mouth lifted as she looked from beneath her eyelashes at the man next to her. "I'll be waiting for you at seven-thirty." She felt like the spider waiting for the fly.

<<<>>>

The knock came at seven-thirty on the dot. She liked how his amber eyes flared when she opened the door and waited with one hand on her hip. Her deep sigh brought that burning gaze to her breasts.

She'd dressed—better yet, undressed—specifically to push all thought of food from his mind. The lace-and-mesh deep ruby nightgown brought out the red highlights in her hair that flowed down her shoulders and made her skin appear a creamier white. Her full breasts tested the strength of the well-placed lace. Masterfully applied makeup emphasized the green of her eyes and the fullness of her dark red lips. Her bare toes peeked out beneath the edge of the gown and a fragile tinkle rang from her anklets, drawing his attention to her long, long legs as the slit at the side opened and closed with her every movement. She knew how to rein in a man's interest.

10

"I like a woman who knows her mind," he said in a low voice. His lips lifted, allowing only a flash of white teeth.

She stepped back and without hesitation he walked in.

"And I like a man who knows what he wants." She closed the door and leaned against it. With deft fingers, she locked it with a double click behind her.

"So no dinner." One dark eyebrow lifted.

"A man who picks up on the subtleties."

His body grazed hers as he moved closer and looked down, a grin flitted across his lips. "You look beautiful," he murmured. "Damn, you smell good." He inhaled, his eyes half closing as he brushed his thumb across her bottom lip. "You feel good too. Smooth, soft, hot."

Though she enjoyed being called beautiful, she knew better. Makeup and clothes could hide many defects and she was an expert at it. Yet she appreciated a man who would lie to get what he wanted, especially when she had done the same.

"For you. Hot for you." Her eyelids heavy, she leaned toward him.

He slid his hands down her arms. His gaze traveled a burning trail across her breasts. "Luscious."

"What a sweet talker." Her nimble fingers pulled at his tie and worked the knot loose until she had the silk material in her hand and tossed it over her shoulder. Then she started on his shirt.

His hand clasped her wrists before the second button made it through the hole.

"Wait," he said softly.

Her shoulders drooped. She wanted to forget about what she did today. Hell, to forget what she did for a living just for a few hours, to immerse all her thoughts in a hard male body. She took a deep sigh, causing her breasts to lift high enough to catch his attention again and remind him of what waited. Did he really want to chitchat? Patience wasn't one of her virtues.

She hoped to survive her nine a.m. meeting with Theo tomorrow and still go on assignment. And that could be anywhere, maybe Denver as she'd been originally scheduled, or even somewhere on the other side of the world, far, far away from Theo. What a lovely thought.

Anyway, the memories she made tonight would help her live through the time she spent with Theo or at the least make them bearable. She puckered her lips and looked up at him beneath her eyelashes, pretending to pout.

His heated look confirmed it worked.

"I have to taste you," he whispered, his lips brushed her cheek.

"Yes, sir," she teased. Before she could raise her face, he wrapped his arms around her waist and lifted her to his mouth. His tongue thrust against hers, tasting, stroking until her fingers dug into his back.

Whoa! The man knew how to kiss.

He lifted his head.

She liked how he tasted of whiskey and male heat. She wanted more. She tried to push him away but he grabbed her arms.

Who did he think he was? She preferred to be the one in control. Before she could show him how she felt about his manhandling, his lips fanned small bursts of hot air against hers as he said, "I couldn't resist a sample. I wanted to see if you're as spicy as you look."

Her skin heated and stretched so tight she thought she would burst from need. The man did have a way with words.

"And?" She rubbed her breasts against his hard chest.

"Another taste. Just once more." His mouth covered hers. He sucked in her bottom lip, and then his tongue dove into her mouth, taking what she offered, taking all he wanted. Whenever she tried to meet his tongue with her own, he thrust harder, opening her mouth wider, dominating the kiss and her response, showing her what he liked and giving her an idea of what else he expected from her. He decided on the rhythm of their kiss and she was surprised by how much she enjoyed letting him have the lead. Her body softened as he took her breath away.

His fingers gripped her butt and pressed his groin to hers. She leaned into him, letting him hold her weight, letting him have control. For a little bit.

Yet his kisses weren't enough. She wanted to see and touch every inch of him. Despite how wonderful his mouth felt against hers, she pinched his hard abdomen. Not enough to hurt. Just to draw his attention away from the kiss for a second.

"Bed?" she suggested with hope in her voice.

Her libido was on overdrive, and his kisses had been like gasoline on a smoking fire. That was her excuse for letting him get away with caveman tactics so far. She always liked being in control, but there was something about the way he held her, kissed her, touched her, made her want more. He dropped one wrist and held the other, leading her deeper into the room and toward the bed. She followed, taking in his broad shoulders and the way his hair curled at the back of his neck.

Happy that he was finally getting down to what she wanted, she purred.

She stepped in front of him and reached for his shirt. "Let's take some of your clothes off. You're overdressed in

13

my opinion." She wanted to see what was hidden beneath his expensive suit.

Without a jacket, would his shoulders be as broad? Would he have defined muscles? Exotic tattoos? Scars? How far down did his tan go? How big and hard was he? She rubbed a hip against his groin. Oh, yes, he was hard. Men were easy to manipulate when sex was involved. And she was grateful.

He stopped in the middle of the room and looked at her. His face turned brooding as his eyes darkened and searched hers. The hot kisser from a few seconds ago had vanished. She wasn't sure what he was looking for, but she shivered in excitement. She liked being the center of his attention. The businessman had disappeared, and in his place was a dangerous and lethal man. Danger proved to be the strongest aphrodisiac. She knew that for a fact. He looked ready to throw her on the floor and fuck her to death.

Death by sex? Now that would be the way to go. Lust slapped her libido into higher gear. She stepped back to recover her breath. At the same time, he clutched a handful of material at her shoulder and with a flick of his wrist tore the gown in two.

She gasped. "You son of a bitch!"

Chill bumps popped along her arms and across her chest. She wanted to believe the tingling was from the cool room. She knew better. She liked it rough, only that gown was her favorite and an original. With a fluid turn, she brought her leg up and he caught it, stopping her dead. Uncertain of what he was up to, she knew she needed to think fast, as only an expert in martial arts could stop her kick. Going with the momentum of her leg, she twisted her body midair and brought him down with her.

Instead of knocking him out or at least dazing him, he

smoothly flipped her onto her back and seized her wrists, pulling them above her head. She kicked and bucked, trying to loosen his hold as he dragged her onto the bed. His knee jabbed her stomach, and she lost her breath. Before she could recover, something cold and hard clicked around her wrists. Handcuffs? He'd handcuffed her?

She blinked. "What the hell?"

"Shhh, Olivia. It will be over quick," he whispered in her ear.

With his knee still in her stomach, he held her cuffed wrists with one hand while the other unbuckled his belt.

"No you don't, asshole. There's no way I'll let that happen now," she said in a steady, angry voice. At the moment with her hands useless and his body pinning her down, her words were all hot air, but she wasn't about to give up.

He chuckled.

Heat flooded her cheeks. He actually thought she was funny. She bit the inside of her mouth. He may control her body, but she needed to rein in her emotions. She needed to think clearly about the situation and a way out.

"Un-cuff me," she demanded.

He placed a finger on her lips and shook his head. "Don't raise your voice. I would hate it if you forced me to neutralize any unwelcome visitors."

She would never endanger an innocent, no matter what he thought. Too many variables could go wrong. First rule she learned in The Circle was You're on Your Own. Second rule, Protect the Innocent. She could handle this man and anything he dished out.

Wait. What did he say? Neutralize? Well, crap! No regular Joe off the streets talked like that. Who did he work for? She needed to know and sex was one way to soften him up.

She peeked at the door.

And then she would find a way to escape.

Whatever he did was nothing compared to what Theo could do to her.

Normally, she could protect herself as she had enough experience to keep the upper hand. But by the way this guy talked and handled himself, he was different from the others she'd picked up. His toned body appeared to come from more than regular gym push-ups or daily runs. Few men could stop her like he had. Well, damn, she'd picked on the wrong one this time. Her recklessness had finally caught up with her, all because she wanted him so much. His soft voice and perfect manners had blinded her to what was beneath his gentlemanly facade. Maybe deep inside she sensed it. She did enjoy a challenge. So why not see how far he'd go. She had no problem going all the way to get her answers. A little pain turned her on.

She tilted her head and watched as he fastened the handcuffs to the bed frame with his belt. No hesitation. As if he did it every day. He shook her arms to test the hold. She was as good as stuck until he unlocked them or she found a way out. He acted as if she was merely a job. Was she?

"Who are you?" she asked.

He ignored her as his gaze traveled a heated path to her chest. Resting a knee on the edge of the bed, he straddled her thighs, keeping her legs flat on the bed by using his weight. His hands rested on her collarbone for a second and then skimmed down, dipping and massaging areas as if he was searching or maybe testing for something. When his palms cupped her heaving breasts and he squeezed, she groaned, hating how good it felt. Unable to resist, she arched her back, wanting more of his firm touch.

He dragged his calluses over her sensitive nipples before traveling down her waist; taking his time as his eyes savored every inch of skin, his fingers continued with their examination.

He was examining her!

Was he looking for a locator maybe? Only another operative would think to look for one. The Circle embedded the device beneath the skin of those considered unpredictable. Luckily, she'd been deemed trustworthy, a small benefit from being Theo's former mistress. Then again, she never understood how they could use that as a gauge, considering how much she hated him.

Could he be a former operative? Well, that explained a lot.

He lingered a moment at her hips, brushing his fingers across her shaved mons and then continued to her knees as he slid down and resting his weight on her feet. Her body bowed, trying to stay in contact with those strong, rough hands.

Why not tell him the truth? He would realize it soon enough. But then again his hot gaze tempted her to lie and suggest a certain wet place to look.

"Damn you. I don't have a locator on me."

She'd never been as turned on in her life. He moved onto the bed and jerked her legs apart, and she gasped. Open and wet, she throbbed in answer to his stare.

She kicked and he quickly clasped her ankles. His gaze returned to her mons. She wanted to tell him to go to hell, yet his hungry look sent heat skimming over her body. Her nipples hardened. She wanted his fingers in her. She wanted more of his attention.

"And you would never lie to me," he quietly said.

She ignored his sarcasm. Deep inside her sex-hungry brain, his hands had slowed during the examination and wandered into areas less likely to hide a tracking device. The change told her he was rethinking his strategy. He attraction had grown despite his original intentions.

His fingers dipped and traced where she'd hoped he would venture. They retraced their path, returning to her breasts to pinch the aching tips. She gasped again. The electrifying tweak brought a flood of moistness between her legs. His fascination in her body was appreciated by her own. She couldn't catch her breath, and she didn't want him to stop.

"Obviously you're a man who won't take my word for it." Unable to catch her breath, the words emerged nearly indistinguishable.

The handcuffs rattled and began to cut into her wrists. For heaven's sakes, they weren't even fur lined. He needed to learn no one treated her this way, even if it did turn her on. In the end, if she escaped, she would find him again, he would learn not to mess with her in this way. She would stake *his* life on that fact.

She looked down and noticed the nice long bulge beneath his slacks. Good. She hated to believe he possessed more control over his body than she did.

Why wasn't he doing anything more? Tuned and ready, she wanted everything. She licked her lips and released a long moan.

Hurry.

He was pissing her off. What was he waiting for?

"Ah, come on. No need to play around," she said. If he released one of her hands, he'd be waking up in the Chattahoochee River. "Let me go, and I promise you'll be surprised. I can take you places you've never been...." She fell silent.

If she'd been standing, she'd stomp her foot. Not a blink or look from him to indicate one word had registered. No longer did his hands probe and test but instead heated and rubbed to bring pleasure. His eyes followed every inch he touched. He mounded and then squeezed her breasts with the right pressure. She inhaled deeply. Then panting, she groaned and arched into his touch again. Lord of Mercy, his hands felt so good. She wished she could control her reaction. The man wasn't human; not a drop of sweat touched his forehead, while she wanted ... no ... needed him badly. Her fingers dug into his belt as her body moved with each stroke. She hated feeling powerless.

He ignored her as his eyes remained on her heated body. Then he looked away for a second. When his gaze returned to her, she caught the conflict burning in their depths. He wasn't sure what to do next. Nice to know he was human after all.

Her own flaw of needing to be touched had brought her here. What about him? What did he really want?

Being angry and still aching for him drove her crazy. He thrilled her, excited her with the unexpected. Yet a part of her wanted to kill him.

He finally moved back. Seconds passed as his gaze remained on her. Like a bird caught in a cobra's stare, she stared back. His hand reached down and adjust the elongated bulge in his pants.

"Fuck it," he said in that deep, soft voice as he yanked off his jacket, tossing it to the other bed, and then rolled up his sleeves.

Her heartbeat picked up speed again. The sleek

muscles on his arms showed how strong he was without being bulky. Just the way she liked it.

Then she noticed where his gaze lingered, radiating enough heat to scorch her, and she forgot everything. His stare centered on the vee of her legs. In a graceful move, he stretched out at the foot of the bed, and his arms wrapped around her legs before she realized what he intended. He pushed her heels almost to her buttocks, opening her wide, and then his mouth covered her.

Her back bowed off the mattress. His wicked tongue dove into her and licked the taut nub already throbbing for attention. His teeth scraped sensitive skin as he moaned with her. Two thick fingers jabbed into her wetness and worked in tandem with his tongue.

Each firm thrust of his fingers and tongue wound her body tighter. When he sucked on the knot of nerves, she gasped. There wasn't enough air in the room. She couldn't breathe. She'd never had a man go down on her like she was a honey jar, and he wanted every last drop. The sounds of his sucking and licking excited her as much as the act itself. Her hips rotated and thrust against his expert tongue and fingers. Her nipples hurt from being stiff for so long.

She squirmed, wishing she could free her hands to soothe the aching tips. As if he'd read her mind, a broad hand moved up and rolled and tugged one nipple and then the other, pushing her over the edge. She released a long high-pitched moan. Oh, hell, she'd never climaxed so fast or so hard. Limp, she opened her mouth and took gulps of air.

He moved up just enough to rest his cheek against her stomach, his stubble caused her muscles to flinch. His heartbeat throbbed against her thigh as his short breaths tickled her sensitive skin. Good. His treatment of her had pulled him in too.

She waited for him to take her. Though he'd done a good job bringing her to the better side of satisfaction, she still felt a light humming in her body. She knew that meant she needed more.

Then his tongue glided from her belly button to her clit. Her hips reached for his mouth. Holy crap! It was as if she'd never climaxed. Her body hit second gear with the needle in the red. She wasn't sure if she could take another one like that. Wasn't he ready for the real deal?

He shoved himself off the bed and stood, shrugging his shoulders, pulling them back as he rotated his head. She heard joints popping. He stretched as if he'd finished a job and wanted to get the kinks out. Then he wiped her off his chin and looked her way with glittering eyes.

She groaned. Oh, shit, he was so damn hot.

He turned away from her.

Shock sent a shiver through her. Was he finished? She admitted his technique was different and a little constraining for her taste, but she wanted more. She'd gotten a glimpse of his groin. Hell, yeah, she hadn't been the only one wanting more. The impressive bulge against his trousers promised he had the right equipment needed to do the job. But first things first, he needed to let her go.

"Okay. You've had your fun. Un-cuff me." She jingled the handcuffs.

He picked up his tie and slipped it into his jacket as he sat next to her on the bed.

"No. I don't think so. Not yet," he said in his usual soft soul-sucking voice.

Heat traveled down her torso and centered on the area now tender from his enthusiastic treatment. She liked how he didn't raise his voice. She'd liked it on the plane, though she'd thought it was from wanting to keep their polite conversation private. But she now realized it was normal for him, if she could call him normal in any sense of the word. What man didn't take what was freely offered?

"What do you want?" She narrowed her eyes at him. "You never said who you're with."

When he kept quiet and lifted his chin, she kicked out. In a lightning quick move, he caught her ankles and then threw his torso across her knees. In seconds, he had her feet fastened together with his tie. A snap of his wrist brought a sheet off the other bed, and he wrapped it around her feet. If she'd planned to kick him again, the cushion would make it no more than a nudge.

"Enough already," she protested. "Who are you?"

He continued to ignore her. Her stomach tightened, and she swallowed to keep the fear down. Was he out for revenge? Had she killed a friend or a brother of his? Which organization was he with? Blinded by lust, what had she missed?

"Who do you work for? Who are you?" she asked once again.

Those eerie amber eyes caught hers. "I'm your worst nightmare, Ms. Olivia St. Vincent."

A chill swept her body. He'd called her by her real name.

Chapter Two

He'd called her by her real name, as much of one as a child found in a trash bin could own.

She looked at him again. Nothing about him appeared familiar. So he wasn't a previous mark. Those never walked away alive anyway. Without further thought, she decided having the hotel staff find her naked and bound was better than whatever this fellow planned, she opened her mouth to scream.

"We can't have that," he said, and in a split second he'd shoved a white handkerchief into her mouth, tying the ends of another one tight behind her head.

Pissed, royally pissed, she felt stupid too for allowing herself to be taken so easily.

He stood and pulled a small medicine bottle out of his pocket. Flipping off the top, he shook out a tiny white pill and walked into the bathroom.

What? Had she given him a headache? She rolled her eyes. Now wasn't the time to do anything but find a way out of the predicament she'd gotten herself into. While she listened to the water running, she struggled with her bind-

23

ings. Her wrists and ankles bound tight refused to budge. She'd have bruises tomorrow when she made her appointment with Theo. That was, if she lived. But she wasn't about to panic yet. She'd been in scarier spots before.

Hoping the bed frame had a rough edge, she sawed the belt back and forth, uncaring if the leather belt would take forever to split. She had to try something. Unbuckling the damn thing hadn't worked as he'd positioned the clasp beneath the bed somehow. As she worked, she replayed every word they'd said on the plane. Were there any clues?

Nothing. He'd said he was on a business trip and worked for an engineering firm planning high-end communities. She'd used her usual cover of being a buyer for a women's clothing chain. Men never asked questions about her job as they were certain to be bored with anything but taking her clothes off.

Jesus H. Christ! Why was she thinking about clothes? She was losing her mind. The only clothes she should be thinking of were those she would place on her body after she marched over his dead one when she was free.

He walked out of the bathroom and she stopped working the belt. His eyes flared amber again as he took in her naked body stretched out before him. Her skin felt tight. What was wrong with her? She'd never, ever acted so needy. Dammit, she wanted him and at the same time, she wanted to kill him. The latter was more like her old self. Whatever he had planned for her, she planned to do it twice as bad to him.

She still didn't know who he was and from the way he handled her, she doubted he worked with a branch of the government. That left only one organization known to be a thorn in The Circle's side. The Onyx Scepter, better known as the OS, was a former faction of The Circle and had split away ten years earlier. Their goal was to eliminate anyone not working for them. She always guessed the OS was probably a bunch of hard-headed pricks who'd left The Circle because they hadn't gotten their way. From this guy's example, she was probably right.

The mattress shook as he sat next to her, placing the glass on the nightstand. He bent over to his ankle, and when he straightened, he placed a snub-nosed revolver next to the glass. Well, how old-fashioned of him. A revolver, huh? He'd been a busy boy before coming to her room. She'd screwed up big time. She blinked slowly to collect herself, enough of the self-pity.

Out of the corner of her eye, she watched him drop the white pill into the half inch of water. With a finger, he pressed the tablet until it dissolved. That better be for him, as she refused to open her mouth. Gritting her teeth the best she could with the cloth in her mouth, she waited to see what he would try.

"Now, no screaming. Otherwise, you won't like what I do to silence you."

Did he really think she was intimidated by what he'd said? As soon as she felt the handkerchiefs leave her mouth, she took a quick, deep breath to scream. No more than a squeak emerged before his hand muffled the sound. He pressed a thumb beneath her jaw to make certain she couldn't bite. And at the same time, his other hand covered a cool breast and twisted her nipple. Her body shuddered from the pain. No tweaking for pleasure this time.

"Bastard!" she said, though his hand garbled the word.

"I warned you. Make one sound above a normal level and I'll show you what else I can do that's even more painful. So keep quiet. Now drink this. It'll help you relax. We don't have time to figure out another means."

Another means to kill her? Shooting her *would* be messy.

He raised her head and placed the glass to her mouth. She glared at him and kept her jaw locked.

"Come on, Olivia. Time's a wasting. Be a good girl. We can do this the easy way or I can have the pleasure of showing you others." He brushed his thumb across her cheek.

Had she seen regret soften those amber eyes? He touched her swollen lips. She pulled away. Hard to believe those same hands had given so much pleasure only a few minutes ago.

His brows rose as if he couldn't believe she refused his touch. Another try with the glass soaked her hair and the pillow. He glanced at his watch and then his cold eyes returned to hers. "I don't have time for this. I knew you would be difficult, but I didn't have time to pick up a needle and¾"

A knock on the door had him moving quickly. He dropped the glass back on the nightstand. Pushing up her chin until her neck arched from the pressure, not allowing her a chance to scream, he had the handkerchief back in her mouth and the other one tied. Her jaw throbbed. She was certain her chin, along with her body, would be sporting several more purple bruises.

For a couple heartbeats she didn't hear anything; she guessed he was checking the walkway through the peek hole. A double click and then she heard whispering but couldn't make out the words.

He walked back in and tossed a sheet across her torso. She almost released a sigh of relief at his offhanded gesture. Two men dressed as EMTs followed. One of them sniggered when he saw her tied up and obviously naked beneath the thin cloth. A look from her captor hushed the man, and they began setting up a gurney.

So that was how they would take her out of the room.

"We can't move her until she's out," the taller EMT said. "People'll be suspicious if she has a gag, and the hotel will insist on calling the authorities if we bag her."

Yeah, she could imagine how seeing a body bag going out of the hotel would raise questions. Without bagging her, she would look merely out of it, like from a heart attack or an overdose. Maybe that was why he hadn't killed her. Then again, what stopped them from killing her and leaving her body in the room? Maybe they needed her alive for now.

"It won't be long." He studied her and then stepped into the bathroom and returned with another glass.

She almost wanted to laugh. Did he think she'd refused because the other glass looked dirty?

He pulled out the bottle with the small white pills again and tapped two out. Then he placed them in his mouth.

Was he crazy? She wasn't a child waiting for an adult to try it first. Sitting next to her, he leaned over, yanked off the gag, and grabbed her chin, digging his fingers into the area where her jaw connected and squeezed. The pain shot across her mouth and down her throat. She gave in and parted her lips.

His mouth covered hers. The unusual tactic shocked her, and she forgot to fight for a second. That was all the time he needed. He spit the pills down her throat. She choked. In the next moment, he had the glass next to her lips and nearly drowned her as he poured the water into her mouth. Water sprayed out of her nose. Sure that she would die from choking, she did the only thing she could. She swallowed. The pills slid the rest of the way down. He pressed up on her chin, causing her neck to arch, not giving an opportunity to scream.

"Give us a minute," he said in his soft voice. He grabbed a corner of the pillowcase and wiped her mouth. He watched her as his hand smoothed the wet strands of hair from her face.

She glared at him. Her throat ached.

Was it poison? Was she wrong and they'd decided that explaining a dead body was worth the trouble? Whatever he decided wouldn't matter to her soon. Being blasé about death came easy in her line of work. She'd dealt it out often enough.

A languid feeling came over her limbs.

In his own bizarre way, he'd been kind. Most poisons caused spasms and excruciating pain. She blinked. Her lids closed in slow motion and then opened just as slowly. His handsome face remained detached.

She was a job to him as so many had been to her over the years. Yet no one would mourn her passing. She'd always considered herself living on borrowed time anyway. Cheating death over and over again from the time she was a child.

Tickling along her temples made her aware she was crying. She tried to stop, yet the tears continued to stream into her wet hair. Never had she imagined dying from a woman's weapon. She'd refused to use poison herself—she always liked the direct approach—but he apparently had no such qualms. It would be less of a mess to clean up.

He looked at his watch and nodded. His thumb moved and her sore neck relaxed and her head rested on a pillow.

Was there only one more minute left? She was as good as dead. So she might as well go out with a little dignity. She closed her eyes and waited.

<<<>>

"Ms. St. Vincent, it's time to open your eyes."

She heard his soft voice. Had he followed her into hell? She didn't want to open her eyes. She ached all over.

She'd been merely asleep.

And for the first time in years, she'd slept without dreams. No, not dreams. The word *dream* conjured up fairy castles and drifting clouds. She never had those. Whenever she'd slept, night-terrors visited with regularity. The type where she woke up screaming, clawing at the sheets, sweating from being tortured by those who controlled her.

Whenever on assignment, she wouldn't allow herself to fall asleep. Catnaps at night and, if time and place allowed, a short doze in the late mornings were plenty to keep her going for a week or two. Then she would arrive home, falling into exhausted sleep, unable to stop the night-terrors from returning. Without neighbors, no one heard her screams, her pleads.

Her arms felt like lead weights, not responding to her command to move.

Wiggling her fingers and toes, she realized straps held her wrists, knees, and ankles to the bed. Parts of her body stung like someone had pressed needles into every square inch of her skin. The brightness on the other side of her eyelids told her a light shone directly overhead. She inhaled. The smell of antiseptic confirmed she was in a medical facility. Had they brought her back to life? Why kill her to bring her back?

She guessed she missed her appointment with Theo. He was going to be rather irritated. What an understatement. Then again, she had a good excuse.

Who would've thought she still possessed a sense of

29

humor? Like Theo ever accepted an excuse of any kind. Maybe believing she'd died and then waking up in the enemy's bed, so to speak, had gotten to her.

"I know you're awake. Look at me."

If she had a hand free, she would tear out his throat. She lifted her eyelids. The stinging caused her to close them again.

"Dim the light or turn it off." The words came out hoarse since her dry throat felt swollen.

"Jennifer, get that switch and wait outside," the deep voice ordered, the sound mere inches above her head.

With a click and buzz the fluorescent light went off. She blinked several times and opened her eyes. Her kidnapper—jailer? whatever he was—pushed a button on a lamp next to her hospital bed, giving the room a muted glow. She blinked a couple more times to clear her vision.

"How do you feel?" he asked.

"Like shit." She tried to rub her achy throat but was quickly reminded of her immobile hands. "Any chance you'll undo the straps?"

"Soon."

He checked the Velcro fastenings and took his time returning his gaze to her face. Heat spread from her groin to her neck with every inch he'd examined. Lifting her head, she looked down and was relieved to see someone had pulled a thin white sheet over her chest.

"When are you going to tell me who you really are and who you're working for?" She rested her head on the pillow and watched his expression, watched for lies.

"I'm Collin Ryker." His cold eyes revealed nothing.

"Ryker, the head malcontent of the OS," she stated. Coldness spread from forehead to chin as all the blood drained away.

Even with her rudeness, not a flicker of emotion showed on his face. Further proof the rumors might be true about his merciless elimination of The Circle's operatives.

"So why am I alive?" she asked.

"You're too valuable."

When he didn't elaborate, she asked, "How's that?"

No one could call him a motor mouth. He towered over the small hospital bed, watching her, always freaking watching her. She dug her nails into the mattress.

"You have certain skills we can use." Arms crossed, he looked as if he was more likely to send her off to be executed. "I imagine you know many things that we would find most useful at the OS."

Her gaze drifted down his fine body. He'd changed clothes and wore stylish black slacks, a new leather belt, and a light gray shirt stretched across broad shoulders. The sleeves folded to his elbows showed off nice masculine arms and hands. Ironically, regret weighed her down as she realized she hadn't seen him naked. What a crazy thought. Once he tortured the information he needed out of her, he'd surely kill her.

"And what makes you believe I'll help you?"

He leaned close to her ear. "I have no doubt you'll cooperate."

What the hell did he mean by that? He wouldn't have anything on her. Then again, he may not need anything. Only in the movies did the hero or heroine bluster about how they would never do what the bad guys demanded. Life had taught her real bad guys became quite dangerous when pushed and their reprimands immediate and most painful.

Besides, she wasn't heroine material. Yet she considered

herself honorable and committed to The Circle's goal of removing the most dangerous filth from the world.

Her heartbeat picked up speed. A floating feeling spread down her body. She felt like she was seeing everything happening from a distance. Helplessness and fear were no strangers. She'd endured Theo's fierce punishments. Her eyes closed and then opened. The noise around her sounded tinny.

True to form, Collin merely stared at her for a moment and then turned away, strolling through the open door.

She squinted at the beautiful blonde dressed in scrubs who stopped him in the doorway. The woman held out a chart and said something Olivia couldn't hear as she tossed her hair over her shoulder. Collin replied and the woman laughed. A big smile broke across his face. Handsome even while somber and grim, his smile showed how dangerous he could be if he half tried. She fisted her hands. Her desire to strangle the blonde confused her. Why should she care who he talked to? Then she recognized the heavy clenching in her chest¾jealousy.

Her heartbeat sped up. Jealousy? Ages had passed since she felt that emotion. Last time she'd been only a kid, watching families in the park across from the foster home she'd been placed in one summer.

That was why she made it a point to not visit parks or any place where families congregated. She hated the feeling and avoided entanglements for that reason. One-night stands helped her evade the tender emotions and the more powerful sentiments that could get someone killed. Never had she felt anything but hatred or lust for a man. The only solution to stop feeling this way was to pull her wits together and find a way to escape.

Her eyes drifted closed. She took several steady breaths,

in the nose, out the mouth. Her heartbeat slowed and the unwanted feelings eased up.

She pressed her toes against the hospital bed footboard, pretending it was a wood plank. With all her being, she listened for the bobwhite's call in the trees as the wind rustled the leaves. Her swing gently rocked back and forth. The smell of bread baking drifted out of the screened door as she heard a woman's laughter. Another deep breath and the clenching in her chest eased up a little more. Her little exercise worked like always. Thank goodness she still controlled part of her emotions.

"How's my patient this morning?" The blond woman peered over the chart at her with finely plucked brows raised.

Olivia looked toward the empty doorway. Her stomach churned. Was Collin planning to let this woman interrogate her?

She returned her attention to the blonde.

"Be kind enough to loosen the straps. You've cut off the circulation to my toes and fingers."

All she needed was a little wiggle room beneath the straps and she'd be out of there in sixty seconds flat.

"Better, I see," the blonde said.

Was she deaf? Before she could tell the nurse how she truly felt, two large men dressed all in white stepped into the room. Looking a little closer she recognized them as the EMTs from her hotel room.

"Dr. Shelton, Mr. Ryker said to help you if she gives you any trouble," the shorter one said.

So she was a doctor. Blondie shook her head.

"I'll be fine. I need to examine Ms. St. Vincent and she doesn't need you watching. Tell Jennifer to come and help."

"You don't understand who you have here," the taller EMT warned.

"Collin filled me in." The doctor looked at Olivia. "You're not going to try anything, are you?" Not giving Olivia a chance to answer, the doctor turned back to the EMTs. "I plan to check her vitals to make sure the dosage of Twilight Sleep he gave her didn't have any lasting side effects." She shooed out the EMTs. "So now go."

Twilight? It was a fancy name for a combination of morphine and scopolamine. A knockout drug. Only wimpy men who wanted to take advantage of women in bars used stuff like that.

That son of a bitch! What did he do to her while she was out? That was playing dirty for sure.

Olivia eyed the blond doctor as the woman pulled down the sheet and examined the bruises on her side. Immediately chill bumps covered her from arms to ankles and were followed by waves of heat as she blushed. She squeezed her fists. Bad enough a stranger was touching and moving her from one side to the other as she lay there helpless. She hated being treated like a piece of meat.

"A dry throat and a little bit of dizziness are common symptoms along with hallucinations. I've been told some see little people." The doctor laughed and leaned over, pulling Olivia's eyes wide open and shining a light in each pupil.

"Doc, throw the sheet back over me," Olivia said between clenched teeth.

"What? Oh. Don't worry, as my grandmother used to say, only us chickens in here." The doctor laughed, but lost her smile when Olivia continued to glower at her. "Sorry. Sure." She tossed the sheet over her body. "Call me Anne."

Olivia turned her face to the wall. She didn't need a friend.

"Dr. Shelton, you need my help?"

Olivia turned to see who entered. A small brunette in pink scrubs with tiny cupids stepped through the doorway.

After a quick and humiliating examination, they took a couple vials of blood, swabbed her mouth, and even pulled a few strands of hair. Olivia fumed as she waited for one of them to make a mistake by loosening the fastenings, allowing her to make her escape.

Then her opportunity came. The doctor left the room after telling the brunette to get fingernail clippings. They were determined to leave her without even a shred of dignity.

"Please relax your hand. This won't take long." The little nurse pulled at her hand.

"Could you loosen the strap? When I relax my hand, the edges pinch my skin. It hurts and all the circulation has gone," Olivia said in her most pitiful tone.

"Oh, I don't know." The brunette's gaze darted to the door and back to the hospital bed.

"I'm not asking you to untie me, just loosen it a bit." She could only hope her helpless act worked.

"I guess loosening it would be okay."

The nurse reached for the strap on her wrist and took her ever-loving time pulling up the top Velcro strip.

As soon as Olivia felt the tightness give, she thrust her arm up and grabbed the nurse by the neck and butted her head.

The nurse hadn't expected the move. Dazed by the hit, the woman slowly sank to the floor, holding her head. Olivia yanked off the other fastenings and jumped over the railing of the bed. She stumbled. In seconds, her weak legs found purchase and her training kicked in as she worked without mishap.

In seconds, the nurse was strapped to the hospital bed with a piece of gauze stuffed in her mouth and held in place with a tape from a nearby tray. The woman shook from terror but Olivia made sure not to bruise her. The poor woman had been only doing her job.

What a shame the nurse was too small to donate her uniform. Olivia wrapped a sheet around her torso. It would have to suffice until she came across someone closer to her size.

She peeked around the opened door into the hallway. About fifteen feet away, Doctor Blondie stood with her back to Olivia and beyond the doc a green exit sign glowed. Jumping the doctor was an option.

No. Not really. Hostages created trouble and only got in the way of escaping a bad situation. Grimacing, Olivia looked toward the other end of the hall. Several open doors and a large window at the end of the hall offered a way out.

Hmm. The window would be doable if not for being visible to the doctor. Maybe there were windows in the rooms on the other side of the building. After a quick check on the doctor, who hadn't moved, Olivia darted into the hallway. Several long strides brought her to the last room on the left. She glanced out the window and judged she was on the third floor. Without waiting a second longer, she stepped into the room.

No windows. Well, shit!

Okay. The empty room looked a lot like the one she'd left.

She took a quick look down the hallway. The doc was gone. All clear. Waiting any longer would narrow her chances of an escape, so she darted toward the exit. She slid to a stop. An adjoining hallway with a nurses' station stood between her and the stairway exit.

No one was there. The brunette probably belonged to that station.

Olivia zipped past and pushed open the door. In seconds, she was leaning against the stairwell wall gasping. Damn! Her knees and hands shook. The drugs played havoc with her system as her energy fell to almost nil.

Listening for shouts or footsteps, she remained still, trying to control her breathing. First, she needed clothes and shoes, and then a way out and to The Circle headquarters. She eased down the stairs and stopped on the second floor. Pressing her ear to the door, concentrating on identifying the sounds, her gaze traveled up the wall. All the air left her lungs.

A camera. The red light blinked like crazy at her. Fucking cameras were everywhere nowadays. In her line of work, she used them to her advantage but she still hated them.

She took a deep breath and concentrated on finding a way out. Just because cameras pointed her way didn't mean someone watched at that very moment. Yet chances were that her ass was on prime time.

She turned the lever and pulled it open. Across the way another door stood ajar. From what she could see, the office had windows and in one corner stood a rack with a long black trench coat waiting for its owner. No sounds of fingers clicking on a keyboard or shuffling of paperwork came from the room. Perfect.

After looking up and down the hall, she dashed into the office. Empty. The computer monitor showed a chart with a rainbow of colors instead of a screen saver. Had the owner just left for a break or planned to return in seconds?

Wasting time worrying wouldn't help. She left the door cracked, dropped the sheet, and scurried into the coat. It brushed her toes. The guy was a giant.

Her fingers thumbed the buttons closed all the way to her neck and then she flipped up the collar. The fabricated air in the building was a little on the chilly side. She inhaled. A man's cologne clung to the cloth. Nice scent.

Time to get out of there. Shoes would be nice but she wasn't pressing her luck. Probably seven minutes had passed without an alarm. Not bad so far.

She checked the windows. Who in their right mind designed a building with windows that wouldn't open? For only a fraction of second did she consider wrapping the sheet around her hand and busting the pane. Pressing her cheek to the glass, she looked down at the ground and noticed how the windows interlocked with the outside wall in a smooth finish.

No toeholds. This side of the building looked over a courtyard, revealing two more floors below street level. Closing her eyes for a few seconds, she sighed. She was roughly forty feet up. That meant the only way out was through a street-level exit.

She scurried over to the door. No sounds from the hall-way. The building was one of the most deserted she'd ever been in. Maybe it was lunchtime.

Taking one step toward the door and stairs, she heard voices and footsteps echoing in the stairwell. Well, wasn't she lucky?

Gritting her teeth, she looked left and right in the hall-way. Not waiting to see if they were coming for her, she picked a direction and ran. The hallway curved and then turned into another wing of the building. She took the corner blindly. Then she slammed into a solid mass.

A broad chest flattened her nose. Without hesitation she hooked her foot around a leather clad ankle and kicked back as she shoved her fist into his hard stomach. The man stumbled but somehow held onto his balance as he reached out and grabbed her hair.

"What the hell?" a deep voice shouted above her.

She aimed for his groin, but he anticipated the move and hit her with an uppercut.

The bastard had a fist made of steel. Stars floated in front of her face.

Funny. Birds really do chirp above a person's head just like in cartoons.

Then everything went black.

Chapter Three

"Did you have to hit her so hard?" Collin glanced over to his best friend and second in command, Rex Drago. The big man stood to the side with his arms crossed, glaring at the unconscious woman strapped down in the hospital bed.

With a tender touch, Collin applied an ice pack to Olivia's swollen chin.

Anne was tending another patient and the dark-haired nurse, Jennifer, refused to come into the room. She was still shook up from the treatment Olivia had dealt her earlier. That the nurse still lived gave Collin hope for The Circle operative. Rumors were she wasn't known for her restraint.

He'd only found out what happened after they brought her back unconscious into the clinic, and within a few minutes of arriving in the room he'd realized no one would tend to her. The staff resented her treatment of Jennifer. Ordering them to take care of Olivia would be easy but he wanted to be near when she woke up. So here he was playing nursemaid, ice pack in hand, trying to reduce the swelling.

"You better be glad that's all I did. That slut deserves to die a slow and painful death." Rex actually growled.

The scar across his nose and the other one near the corner of his mouth met in a vee on his cheekbone, pulling his upper lip in a grimace.

"No one is certain she was the one who pulled the trigger. We've discussed this. It could have been someone else," Collin reminded him.

Rex had fallen in love with another operative who'd been killed by one of The Circle's assassins five years earlier. She'd died two weeks before their wedding. For his friend to lose his cool proved Rex hadn't recovered from her death. He shouldn't be here.

"It doesn't matter. She's brushed with the same filth." Rex's eyes glittered with hate for all things connected to The Circle.

"I believe it would be best if you returned to your office for further orders." Collin needed to find him a mission and soon.

Rex stiffened. The flicker of hurt in the man's light gray eyes almost had Collin relenting. They were at war with The Circle and the last thing anyone needed from him was sympathy. Sympathy could get someone killed.

"Fine. I need to go and throw my coat into the incinerator anyway. I would never get her stench out of it otherwise." Rex stomped out of the room.

"That's a shame. Nice coat," a hoarse voice commented.

Collin looked into eyes as green as the emeralds his dad had given his mom on their twenty-fifth anniversary. Their last to celebrate before the car bomb killed his family.

"How do you feel?" He tossed the ice pack onto a tray next to the bed.

How much had she heard? Her eyes searched the room.

Was she already planning her next escape? The woman fascinated him. Deadly with a hidden vulnerability she'd let him see for a fleeting moment in the hotel room. He doubted she even realized she'd done so.

Her gaze burned into his. "What's Big Foot's name?

He purposely ignored her question as he lifted the strips, releasing her. "They're bringing your dinner in about five minutes. You've been out for about ten hours. There are three guards outside your door. All trained in hand-to-hand combat and have instructions to match hit for hit times two. If you kill one of the guards, I can assure you I'll make your death a slow and painful one."

"I was out that long?" She rubbed her wrists, cutting her eyes to him. "You'll kill me yourself?"

"Yes," he bit off. Did the wheels in her brain ever drop below warp speed?

"Ha! You didn't have to think on that one, did you? Better men have tried." She smirked and flinched, lightly fingering the bruise on her chin.

Collin stepped back as the orderly walked in carrying her dinner. The fellow arranged the tray on the over-bed table and rolled it to her. Then he smiled, eyebrows raised, as he cranked up the head of the bed.

She smiled back. "Thank you." Sugar nearly dripped off her lips. The orderly leered at her and made a big show of arranging the small bowls and accessories.

Her sheet dropped to the tips of her breasts. The hint of coral areolas peeked over the edge. The orderly's eyes bugged and Collin couldn't take it anymore.

"Get out," Collin snapped, pointing to the door. Red-faced, the man scurried out of the room.

Though he enjoyed the seductive sight too, he needed

to get the woman a hospital gown or shirt, anything to cover her up. She was treacherous naked.

"You're terribly rude to your slaves."

No way would he respond to that. "Eat." He unwrapped the utensils and handed her a plastic spoon. "Don't think of using it for anything but food."

"I can't imagine why you don't trust me." She eyed the food with revulsion. "What is this?" Jabbing at the mashed potatoes, her spoon slipped and she knocked the small bowl of green Jell-O off the tray upside down onto her lap. "Bloody hell, it's alive!"

Eyes wide and her mouth stretched in a frown, she looked like a little girl spotting a frog in her pocket. He burst out laughing. She looked up at him and her expression changed from disgust to frustration. He couldn't help laughing harder.

She shook her head as she examined the mess. "I can't believe you laughed. Actually I wasn't sure if you knew how." She cut her eyes toward him, her distrust closing up her face.

Without thinking his actions through, he leaned over and scooped up the Jell-O and tossed it back into the bowl. Shoving the tray and over-bed table out of the way with more strength than necessary, he kept his eyes on it until the table hit the wall with a bang.

"I'll tell them to bring you another meal." He chuckled and returned his attention to her. His hand grabbed her wrist.

Frozen in midair, her hand reaching for the holster beneath his jacket, she met his gaze with a guilty one. The sheet was bunched at her feet as she was on all fours. Her full breasts swayed with the quick movement. He looked at the bare length of her back, all the way to the small dip above her buttocks—nice rounded ones perfect for cradling a man's stomach.

He released her wrist and grabbed her chin, forcing her back onto her haunches until they were eye to eye. The hardness between his legs begged for release, but he reminded himself that if he listened to his cock, the woman looking at him with such pretend longing would probably cut it off and feed it to him.

"What?" One wing-shaped brow lifted.

"I'll not warn you again. Any further attempts of escape or potential harm to others under the OS control will be met with harsh punishment." He released his hold and pushed her shoulders back onto the bed.

"What would you do? Threaten me to death?" she asked as her mouth quirked on one side.

Then he grasped what she was doing. The bravado in the woman's voice told him she was scared. She used sarcasm as a defense mechanism. The fear he sensed from her actions was like cold water. His lust cooled off instantly.

He strode over to an intercom on the wall. "Have someone bring the patient a gown." Collin bit off with impatience, "Now!"

She cupped her breasts and lifted them up. "Don't you want to play?"

Why hadn't he noticed before, whenever she thought she was losing control of the situation, she turned on the sexual charm? Like an abused little girl trying to put off her attacker until she could find another way to protect herself. The process of converting her to the OS mind-set was going to be a long and difficult one. The Circle was known for recruiting damaged souls who already knew the worst one human could do to another and then exploiting it.

They picked a prime one with Olivia St. Vincent.

Watching her desperate attempt to seduce him, he narrowed his eyes in concern.

He wanted her bad, wanted her on her back, legs spread and mouth open screaming his name. The little grin spreading across her face as she stared at his ever hardening groin warned him she knew it.

Was he about to contribute to her damage? Could he stop?

<<<>>>

What was up with him? Why was he staring at her as if he pitied her? She didn't need his pity.

She turned away.

Within minutes they brought her a puke-green hospital gown. She looked down at the faded design. At least she was warmer.

He even ordered them to bring another meal, one with real food, not that mushy crap. What had they thought? That no one had ever thrown a twenty-pound sledge-hammer fist into her chin before? Big Foot was an amateur compared to her foster mother's brother.

One fact was for certain, he would pay for hitting her. Just as her foster mom's brother did.

Who was Collin protecting by ignoring her questions? Her or Big Foot?

She rolled the over-bed tray to the side and folded her arms across her chest, hiding how her nipples pointed to the man she wanted badly between her legs.

She huffed.

Yeah, that was right. Strip her naked, handcuff her, dope her up, knock her out, and watch her libido go into overdrive for the man responsible. As she'd been told many times by those who knew her as well as she would let anyone, she was a sick individual. Obviously they were right.

"I'm all full." She patted her nonexistent tummy.

The man stared at her as if she was a fly pinned to a board. Wanting a reaction of some sort, she gave him her best come-here smile.

"Want to fuck?" she asked sweetly.

He didn't blink, not even a raised brow.

That was no fun. What did it take to get a rise out of this man? Her crudeness always brought a reaction from Jason. Though not as pretty as Jason, Collin was more masculine looking with the slight dimple in his chin and dark eyes filled with untold stories of going to hell and back. His dark brown hair cut in a stylish businessman length made her want to run her fingers through it, mussing it. Those masculine lips begged to be bitten.

"Tomorrow, you'll move into your room."

She really hated how hearing his soft spoken voice brought her concentration to a screeching halt, like she wasn't already focused on his kissable lips. Around him she lost her edge. She needed to get away before she did something really stupid.

"How about letting me out of here? Whatever you want to discuss can be done in the comfort of my home." She pulled at the hospital gown. "I could put on some decent clothes too." Sounded reasonable to her.

"We already have your possessions." He crossed his arms and shifted his weight to one leg, settling in for an argument by the looks of it.

"My possessions?" she asked.

How did they know where she lived? What about her art? Her stash of weapons? Some of them were antiques.

46

She treasured every one. Someone had gone through her things! Touched her stuff? Invaded what little privacy The Circle allowed? Enough was enough.

"You. Put. Them. Back." She pointed a shaking finger at him and then quickly pulled it back and stuck her hand beneath the sheet. *Show no sign of weakness.*

Her head pounded and her stomach bubbled as her mind shifted gears and tried to figure out how to escape. She concentrated on regaining control of her breathing. Otherwise, she might as well roll over dead. Or beg for crumbs of mercy.

Closing her eyes, she took long, slow breaths. Anything to regain control of her temper.

"Forget about your old life. They've received news you're dead now." He leaned over her, placing his hands on the pillow, his arms and body trapping her against the mattress. "Your life is with the OS and if you fight me on this, you'll force me to end your contract before it truly begins."

The way he said contract warned her he wasn't referring to anything truly written. The gist of his nicely worded threat was her life would end.

Think. She needed a little bit of time to figure her way out of this jam. No matter what was thrown at her, she was a survivor.

"Well, now. What good will I be to you if you keep me locked up?" She leaned close to his ear and whispered, "Unless you can think of something I can do to prove how valuable I really can be."

She fell back on the pillow and grinned. His eyes flared amber, the only sign he wasn't unaffected by her play. That was more like it. A man interested in the promise of a willing woman.

"You do have a one-track mind." He leaned in a little closer. The warmth from his body drew hers toward him. "You'll find we're looking after your best interests."

Her nostrils flared as she caught the scent of his cologne. The aroma was as intoxicating as the man. She wanted him more than she ever imagined.

How irrelevant was that?

Here he was threatening her life and instead of protecting herself, she wanted to rub up against him like a cat in heat. Every time he came close to her—hell, in the same room, her thoughts went haywire. He was right. It did appear she had a one-track mind.

He added, "Your chances of survival are greater with us."

"Ha! Let me pull on my waders."

While he'd spoon-fed his propaganda, she reached up and slid her hand across his cheek, letting it fall to the top button of his shirt and caress the opening with a finger. A slight hesitation was the only sign he gave acknowledging her brazen touch. She liked how hot his skin felt.

Leaning forward, her lips almost touching his moving ones, she half-closed her eyes. Her tongue licked her lips and brushed his at the same time. The hand not drawing circles on his chest slipped into his pants' front pocket, hoping to reach the cell phone she'd seen him drop in there earlier.

"Olivia."

"Yes." Fingertips touched the smooth metal surface.

"Get your hand out of my pocket," he said in a firm tone.

Her tongue traced the seam of his lips as her fingers changed course and traveled toward what leaned heavy and

48

thick against his left thigh. She grasped him through the thin fabric and purred. Oh, yeah. He felt good and hard.

Before she could give a good pump, he clasped her wrist and squeezed. Fire shot through her muscles until numbness took over. Refusing to release her hold and let him know how much it hurt, she absorbed the pain and used it as the emotion for her kiss.

His lips remained together for a few seconds, resisting her demanding tongue. Then he accepted what she offered and took control. He released her wrist and dug his fingers into her scalp, keeping her head still for his pleasure as his mouth covered hers. Each thrust of his tongue brought a mimicking thrust of her hand. When she became too involved in the kiss and forgot to move, he would remind her with a shift of his hips against her palm.

Tired of the juvenile heavy petting, she pulled her hands away and fumbled with his zipper. Only a millimeter from her goal, she opened her eyes as he jerked his mouth away. He grabbed her arms and pushed them above her head. His weight landed across her torso, holding her down. His face was above hers, but too far for her to reach and return to their kiss.

"Stop it." His face flushed with desire and the same measure of anger. "Dammit. What's it about you that makes me forget¾" He took several deep breaths, his lips drawn tight.

Oh, Lord, he was a fine-looking man. He needed a woman to challenge him, loosen him up, and she was the perfect one to drive him into a sexual frenzy. Until she could find a way to escape, she would enjoy tormenting him. He wanted her. Yet he resisted. All so interesting.

He was unlike any man she'd met. Maybe she was

hanging out with the wrong kind of men, men who took what they want and more and damn the consequences.

"What? Do you need to tie me up to get off?" She waited for his reaction. That was, if he would let her see it again.

He released her and stepped back. "You'll cooperate or you'll cause a lot of undue harm to those you care about," he said. His warning hung in the air.

"What do you mean?" She didn't like the sound of that. Only a handful of people had any claim to her affections and no one knew who they were.

So far his threats hadn't bothered her¾well, not that much¾but the way he worded this threat told her it was different. More serious. She didn't like the way he was looking at her. Why did a chill run down her back?

"St. Vincent's Dower Orphanage," he said simply.

A wave of dizziness came over her. All of the fight drained out of her. She closed her eyes, refusing to look at the triumphant glimmering in his.

He picked up a folder sitting on a nearby chair and threw it on her lap. Inside were pictures of children and teachers walking from one building to another. Their smiling faces shining up for the photographer to take a shot.

Included was the orphanage's budget with several lines of the most sizable donations highlighted. The name Olivia Roth Foundation was quite prominent on the columns. How did he know? No way could he search her cover name in one day. They'd been working on this for months. Her stomach turned. She swallowed. She'd only used the name Roth during her off time, never tied to her work. And there were several orphanages named after Saint Vincent.

The orphanage where she'd lived the first ten years of her life after the authorities plucked her out of a trash bin averaged an infant a month without a surname. The Mother Superior believed using a saint's name helped the child to stay on the righteous path. When Olivia was brought to St. Vincent's, it had been a cold January morning, the day after the blessed saint's day. Little good her name did her.

"I don't have to tell you, if we notified the authorities about your contributions, you know what would happen. The government frowns on organizations that receive money from known illegal activities. They'll shut the place down. Many of the children would be placed in less desirable facilities," he warned in a cold, hard voice.

She covered her eyes. Her body felt as if she was on a runaway roller coaster. They had her. She'd never jeopardize the orphanage. Because of her money, they could afford food, clothing, and a good education for the children, and just as important, the proper staff to search backgrounds on the couples coming to adopt or willing to foster.

She dropped her hand. "Okay." She didn't give a damn if he saw the tears pooling in her eyes. "Just remember, if anything happens to the orphanage or anyone involved with it, all deals are off and I'll kill your ass. I'll not rest until your whole organization is destroyed, person by person. So what do you want?"

Her stomach rolled again with the thought of what would happen to the orphanage for sure if she refused. She tried to ignore the throbbing above her right temple.

He eyed her for a few seconds. "First, you'll follow orders without question. Second, you'll fill us in with all the work you've done since being recruited by The Circle eight years ago. Third ..." His voice changed to a buzzing in her head. Frustrated with his long list as she wanted him to go away, she resisted the temptation to close her eyes and sleep. "... sixth, you¾"

Holding up her hand, she interrupted him just as a pinprick of pain shot into her skull. "Wait! You're giving me a fucking headache." She'd never been good at taking orders.

He stared at her, probably trying to figure out her angle. Only this time, she was telling the truth. A massive headache had hit about the time he'd finished saying "fifth."

Maybe it was the drug he'd used or the hit she'd took, but the bright sharp pain nagged at her to throw up and she wasn't sure how much he would like his shiny black loafers after she finished with them. Maybe the green tint of her face gave it away, but he handed her a gray plastic pan just in time.

Talk about embarrassing. How could she be sexy and dangerous and threatening when he'd seen her throw up her guts? Vomiting like a little wimpy girl.

She closed her eyes and leaned back against the pillows. In seconds a cool cloth landed on her forehead. Cracking one eye open, she found him watching her with consternation. He handed her a small paper cup filled with a blue mouthwash. After a quick swirl in her mouth she spit it out into a new clean pan. Who would ever guess the head of the OS made a decent nurse?

When would the embarrassment ever end? She hated being weak in front of the enemy. What had he expected after all he'd put her through?

"Hey, quit looking at me like that. I'm human. Anyone would be sick after ... ah, hell, leave me alone."

Unable to take any more of his dark eyes measuring her, and her coming up short, she turned her back to him, hugging herself and bringing her knees up, squeezing her eyes shut.

"Sleep and we'll talk later," he said as she heard his footsteps move away.

She hoped sleep would come and give her a break from the pain. Between her head and bruised and aching body, it was no wonder she was sick. Maybe the drug still in her system would keep the night-terrors away. It had before. Then again, she never gambled for a reason. She always lost.

<<<>>>

The nightmare started as it always did. She was playing on the floor with her one and only baby doll in the middle of a large room. Sunshine streaming through a tall window warmed her cheeks.

A shadowy figure walked into the room, towering over her, blocking the sun. In a booming voice, he said, "You're too old to play with dolls. Come with me, child. I got a more interesting toy for you to play with."

He grabbed her arm and lifted her until only her toes reached the floor as he marched toward a door with bluish light emitting around the edges. She knew if she let him take her into the room, he would hurt her. But no matter how much she screamed, scratched, or kicked, he still opened the door and threw her inside. His high-pitched laughter bounced against the walls. She could beg him not to hurt her again but she knew he would.

Please don't. Please. Please stop.

"Olivia, wake up."

Her eyes popped open at the same time her right hand shot out, lower palm forward, stopping an inch from shoving Collin's nose into his skull. He'd grabbed her wrist.

"Careful. You were asking someone to stop." The concern in his voice she didn't need or want.

"You know, you're no prince charming, but I would hate to accidentally kill you. I have a feeling Big Foot would object and then I would have to kick his fat ass."

One eyebrow lifted. "Fat ass, uh?"

She wiggled to a sitting position after he released his hold. When a little sting on her arm caught her attention, she looked down. A new red dot on her skin explained why her headache had faded away. They'd shot her up with something. She hoped that was all they'd done while she'd been out. "By the way, you've got a bad habit of waking me up."

Though he didn't smile, a little crinkle at the corners of his eyes told her he liked her spunk. That was interesting. No concern about her almost killing him or threatening his buddy. Was he already so sure of her? Maybe she could use that to her advantage.

"What do you want?" she asked. Had he stayed with her the whole time she slept? "How long was I out?"

She stretched, lifting her arms above her head and pressing her toes against the covers.

His eyes flared amber. She liked that. Responding to her was good. Hell, it was only fair. He was quite aware of her response to him.

"You've been asleep for a couple hours." He folded his arms. "And not a restful sleep at all." One dark eyebrow lifted.

So he wanted to know what she'd dreamed. No way. How often had she tried to forget after waking? She wasn't like most people, forgetting as soon as she opened her eyes. Boy, that would be nice. Considering she'd actually lived the nightmare that made it harder to forget.

Finally coming to the conclusion she wasn't about to explain, he picked up a large camo bag and handed it to her.

"Get dressed. Time for you to start earning your keep."

"How about a shower? Toothbrush? Hair brush? You get the idea." Her mouth tasted like an old shoe and she bet her hair looked like a stack of straw.

"You'll find everything you need in your room. I'll take you there as soon as you get your clothes on."

Before she could say anything about privacy, he walked into the hall, closing the door behind him.

Well, that was easy. Of course, she was stuck in a room without windows, and she had a good feeling the next room he placed her in would be no different. The bag had a pair of her sweatpants she used to exercise in and a sports bra for running. No thong. His choices were rather fascinating. Or was she over-examining everything?

She glanced at the door and jumped off the bed. A wave of dizziness forced her to hold the footboard until she regained her balance. Then she slithered into the sweatpants, jerked off the hospital gown¾ugly thing¾and pulled on the bra. She wasn't surprised to see him walk in no sooner than she finished. In vain, she ran her fingers through her hair, patting down the strands.

"Lead the way, master," she quipped.

"I prefer sir." He looked serious, not a grin or flare of amber to tell her different.

Sir, huh? Yeah, right, like that would ever happen.

She watched his tight ass move down the hallway. Tight and uptight. Did the guy ever let loose? He stopped in front of elevator doors and pressed the down button.

As she stepped into the car, the red numbers overhead dropped quickly until they passed G and started with B numbers. It finally rested at B10. Where were they? Hell?

She'd already been there once and had plenty of souvenirs etched onto her body to prove it.

Of course, he already knew that.

Whatever he dished out, she would protect the orphanage. She'd endured before, and compared to Theo, Mr. Uptight was a walk in the park.

Chapter Four

The elevator paused and a red light bathed the small enclosure before the doors opened.

Grinning at the thought, Olivia stepped out. Ten? She still couldn't believe the size of the building hidden beneath the street level.

Within feet from the metal doors, a large open area revealed soft natural-colored walls with plants and a waterfall tinkling into a small pool focused in the center. Each step as she followed Collin revealed overstuffed chairs in little nooks, perfect for small-group meetings, and two exercise rooms with what looked like a cafeteria in between.

"What is this? A spa?"

As she expected, he ignored her question and turned into a short hallway. Beautiful, expensive looking artwork hung at the end of the hall. They stopped in front of a steel door that wouldn't look out of place in a prison. He punched a long list of numbers into the stainless steel keypad and a series of clicks emitted from the lock. The door swung open. He stepped to the side and waited for her to enter first.

"It's your new home," he said.

Go figure.

She walked into a spacious living room. The flashing red lights in each corner warned her of cameras watching her every move. She wondered how many more were hidden. An apartment tastefully furnished with 24/7 surveillance.

Collin stood back as she examined the kitchen and the archway leading to a bath and bedroom. With each step, her blood pressure rose. Flushed and sick to her stomach, she hoped she was wrong until she noticed the small chip on a corner of the coffee table. It was her furniture. The entire apartment was filled with her personal effects. Sure he'd told her they had gotten her things. But she'd thought clothes, makeup, maybe even her deodorant but not everything.

"My clothes *and* my furniture?" She paused in her examination. "Why?"

"We want you to be comfortable."

"More like that you hoped I would stay, refusing to leave my possessions behind." She suspected material things would never stop him from escaping.

"Maybe."

Furious and trapped, she stood in the middle of the room with her hands on hips. How had he known the odds and ends she'd collected over the years represented her home? Her first home.

She threw back her head and blinked several times. Dammit. A red glow caught her attention. She hated the beady little lights taunting her from every angle.

"How did you get through my security system?" Her gaze narrowed onto him.

"Nic had a hell of a time. Who set up the security at

your house?" Collin sat in the middle of her couch, placing an ankle on one knee and stretching his arms along the back.

"I did." She'd worked months getting the traps set. Anyone who broke in would regret it pretty quick.

He cocked his head. "You keep surprising me."

"What did you think I was? All brawn and no brain?" She wasn't some killing machine. It took organization and intellect to set up the hits and get away unseen. Her handler told her who to hit but never the details to accomplish it. "I'm astonished they didn't blow it up."

"Four are in the hospital." Though he said it with an even voice, she detected worry in his eyes.

Uncomfortable with the thought, she wandered through the room, picking up a knick-knack she'd purchased in Singapore and rearranged it on the end table. Then she wiped off dust from a candy dish she'd picked up in Chicago and straightened a figurine from London, all mementos from her work. She felt his gaze following her the whole time.

Unable to resist, she looked toward the sofa. He watched her with cold eyes, assessing and finding her wanting.

She crossed her arms and rested a hip on the edge of her Carpathian wood desk. "What now?"

His jaw shifted as he stared at her. Only the tick-tock of her grandfather clock broke the silence.

Well, hell. What was he mad about now? She replayed their conversation and sighed. Why should she be concerned about his people? Their success with breaking into her home meant she had to live in the OS building for now. If ... no ... *when* she escaped, she would find a way to retrieve her things with or without his cooperation. Besides, she hadn't asked to be taken and sure as hell hadn't asked for them to invade her house. From what she'd seen, no children worked for the OS, so they were all adults and well aware of what they were getting into.

"Okay." She rolled her eyes. "Were they damaged badly?" She had difficulties in being compassionate.

"Damaged," he muttered beneath his breath in disbelief and then said clearly, "They'll live."

She shifted to another hip on the desk edge. Why should she care that he looked disappointed with her? She cared about the orphans at St. Vincent and he was using them against her.

"Listen, I don't know what you expect. You've got me where you want me figuratively and literally. By controlling me through your threat about the orphanage, you've proved attachments of any kind are dangerous in our line of work." She mentally shook her head. He'd shown her how she'd grown attached to more than she realized.

Hell, she was now explaining herself to him. Why did she care so much what he thought of her? She stood and paced across her antique rug from Turkey. She refused to explain anything she did to anyone. One of the best ways to live a long life as an eliminator for The Circle was to keep her mouth shut. This time her life depended on her talking.

She wiped her hands down the sides of her sweats. Tall, dark, and handsome hadn't commented on her ramblings. The only emotion she caught on his face besides disappointment was interest. At least she had that, his interest in her body, though he fought it by snapping at her. It was obvious each time his gaze followed her around the room. His attraction toward her might help in her escape.

"Excuse me while I shower." She turned and pulled off

her sports bra and looked over her shoulder at Collin. "Want to join me?"

When he remained on the couch, his eyes half-closed in contemplation, she shrugged. "Well, come in if you change your mind. If you don't, your loss."

<<<>>>

What was she up to? The look she gave him before announcing her shower warned she was planning to use him somehow.

Collin stared at the hallway long after he heard the water running. The tightness in his groin frustrated him. He needed his mind clear while dealing with her.

From their research, he learned that Olivia had lived at the same orphanage until age ten when a woman fostered her. None of the papers explained why the orphanage waited so late. Even after papers were filed for the woman to adopt her at age twelve, they never followed through. Olivia's foster mother died and no explanation provided why the woman's brother was given permission to take Olivia. By the time the orphanage reported the woman's death and the sequential questionable guardianship to social services, Olivia was fourteen and a runaway.

The last bit of information they scraped together pointed to The Circle recruiting her at eighteen. What she did to survive for four years, he could only imagine. The woman was a survivor.

He dug into his pocket as his phone vibrated, irritating the hell out of him because he didn't need another problem. Maybe he should be thankful the reminder of his duty to the OS eased his hard-on. At the same time, a knock brought his attention to the view panel next to the door.

Rex grinned into the camera and raised his middle finger.

Phone to his ear, Collin strode over to the door and keyed in the code. His second in command eyed the living room with unease and slid into a chair across from Collin. He jerked to look behind him as if Olivia planned to jump out and attack.

Collin nodded toward the hallway, letting Rex know where Olivia was as he resumed listening to one of his handlers describe a clash between OS and Circle operatives.

Rex lifted his chin in understanding and continued checking out the room while seated. He wrinkled his nose in distaste, waiting for Collin to finish his conversation. With a snap, Collin closed his cell phone and looked questioningly at Rex. The man hated Olivia and would never come into her apartment willingly.

"What's going on?"

"Word has reached The Circle that you're responsible for Olivia's disappearance. They're beginning to doubt you killed her."

Collin glanced at the hallway and back to his friend. "You know what that means."

"Yeah. We've got an infiltrator." Rex stretched his long legs out and crossed them at the ankles. "I've got Nic checking to see if they're sending messages out through the Internet or freestanding micros."

"Good. I'd hoped we would have a little more time." He needed her fully encamped and questioned about every tidbit of information she possessed of The Circle.

"Collin ..." Rex's hesitation pissed Collin off. When did his second in command hold back? Was everyone so certain he couldn't handle the woman?

"Spit it out." He gritted his teeth to keep from saying more.

"I know you examined her but could she be sending messages?"

Collin stood and walked over to the hallway. The humming of a blow-dryer assured him Olivia wouldn't hear.

"I examined her thoroughly twice and Dr. Shelton once. She's clean. We've checked under her skin and in all of her possessions for GPS micros or anything used for communications." His body tightened with the memories of touching her body, all in the name of security.

"I know you thought of everything, but I've never seen you so wrapped up with taking on a Circle operative like her. There are several operatives capable of handling her. She's deadly and we need you elsewhere." Rex inhaled deep as if he expected to be roundly reamed.

"What happened to Jack won't happen to me." Collin hated to bring it up especially when his words drained the color from Rex's face. "Maybe one day we'll get all the specifics from her about Jack and Abby. Until that time, she's needed. She's the key to bringing down The Circle."

Rex jumped to his feet. "Don't you think I don't know that?" He stomped to the door and placed his palm against the steel, bowing his head. "You're like a brother to me. I hate to see her sinking her claws into you too. She fooled Jack. Few were better than him. We all know she set up Abby."

No one deserved to live in the pain Rex did every day. For a man to lose his fiancée, the woman he planned to love and cherish forever, mere months before their wedding had redefined his thoughts of a happy ever after. Collin stopped behind him and placed a hand on his shoulder. The big man's body shook.

"I'll be careful." Collin leaned to the side and punched in the door code. "Go and get things ready. Three months and then we'll activate the plan."

When the door clicked closed behind Rex, Collin turned to see Olivia reclining on the couch with a white robe wrapped around her. Her bare toes painted a pink. They'd been red before.

"Why three months? And what's the plan?" she asked.

Absent of makeup, her face looked younger. Then he remembered her file had said she was twenty-eight. Considering the difficult life she'd led, it stood to reason why she acted older, more cynical than most people her age.

"You need to be briefed on our policies. Then we'll test you to see what skills you possess and the best way to utilize them." He watched one corner of her mouth quirk up as she tried to hold back the smile. "What's so funny?"

"You." She gave up the struggle and grinned big. "All your policies, testing, and utilizing. Why don't you talk like a regular person? And tell me in plain English what you want?" She raised one knee and the robe parted, exposing a long, smooth length of gentle muscled thigh to trim ankle. His hands itched to clasp her legs around his neck again and rejoice in the taste and heat of her body.

Relaxed and smiling up at him, she revealed her true danger. Her sex appeal. Deep inside he'd realized he held an intense attraction to her. But for now, at the beginning of her training, he needed to keep her at arm's length to a certain degree, holding himself away from her like a carrot in front of a donkey. He studied her face. If she could read his thoughts, he would be dead for comparing her to a donkey.

She turned on her stomach, arms folded across the armrest, chin on top, looking at him with a poignant softness. Though she appeared all sweetness and femininity, he knew she was lethal. What method would she use to kill him? Her hand slammed into his nose, shoving bone and cartilage through his skull, killing him instantly? Or debilitating him with a hand to his crotch and then a twist of his neck? The latter took strength or skill. While she'd been handcuffed to the bed, he'd experienced firsthand the well-trained muscles defined beneath her silky skin. She had many deadly skills.

In the business of training some of the most dangerous people in the world, he'd used every method possible to bond the individual to the organization. Over the years, he'd trained only two top operatives personally, leaving the others to the normal process, and neither had been as dangerous as Olivia. Plus the intimate bonding with the earlier operatives had never lasted longer than the six-month training, even though they remained friends.

With his gaze lingering on her, she stood and shrugged, dropping the robe to the floor.

"You were staring at me so intently that I figured you wanted to see me naked again." She bent a knee, placing her bare foot against the other ankle and lifting her breasts like an offering.

His cock sprang to attention. He wanted to take her on the floor, thrust into the hot depths of her body he'd tasted and remembered so well. One step, then another brought him close enough to smell her. The ordinary light flowery scents of soap and shampoo all women indulged in contradicted what he knew about her. No ordinary woman could hold an eighteen-pound sniper rifle, much less shoot one. Perversely the thought had his cock weeping for her touch.

He leaned over; his shoulder skimmed her hip. His mouth mere inches from the place he wanted to return to, he inhaled the faint musk of her arousal. Her sharp intake of breath satisfied his inner demon. Always good to know she wanted him as badly. He picked up the robe and placed it on her shoulders. He swept her hair from beneath the robe and brushed his fingers across a high cheekbone.

"Go to bed and sleep. I'll wake you at five. We'll start with exercise and go from there," he said a mere breath from her lips. That his voice or fingers didn't tremble proved he remained in control.

"We could do some exercise tonight," her tongue glided over his lips, "in bed."

Heat shot to his groin. Damn. The woman's moves could easily bring him to his knees if he let her. His pulse sped up with the thought of tonguing her clit and tasting honey again.

Placing a finger over her mouth, he held his head away. "Go to bed. Alone."

He walked toward the door and paused to key in the code. An itchy feeling had him glancing over his shoulder and he caught her staring fixedly at the keypad.

"Don't even try. The code changes every hour and I'm the only one who knows the sequence."

As the door slowly closed, he caught sight of her standing in the middle of the room smiling, giving him a one finger salute.

He chuckled as he walked down the hall toward his office. If he'd told her how much she had in common with Rex, she'd say he was crazy.

Considering he planned to risk the future of the OS on one unpredictable woman's shoulders might prove her right.

Chapter Five

O n, off, on, off, on. The little red light blinked in the far upper corner of her bedroom. Olivia's vision blurred. Even lying in bed, they watched her. Earlier, while taking a shower, she'd seen the camera concealed in the bathroom. She couldn't hide anywhere. How was the OS any different than The Circle? The Circle had spied on her the same way for the first few years, not until she'd proven herself.

The hum of an air conditioner filled the dark room. She smoothed the chill bumps from her arms and glanced up again. The cameras probably turned to night mode when the lights were out. That meant they could keep an eye on her even as she slept.

Was Collin standing at the controls and watching her? She slept without clothes. Theo had forbidden his women from wearing pajamas or nightgowns in his bed. Going naked so much made it difficult to sleep in cloth that twisted and restricted her movement. She even slept on top of the sheets. Her hands free to reach for a weapon.

She chuckled. From what she could tell Collin and Rex had cleared out all her weapons. She could only hope he'd missed one.

Out of the corner of her eyes, she watched the blinking light. Her gut feeling warned he followed her every movement. He waited for her to make a wrong move.

Without giving her intentions away, earlier she'd searched every inch of the apartment. She pretended to examine her precious furniture for more nicks and scratches or to search for a lost earring. After a couple hours, she examined the living room between her eyelashes as she dozed on her couch. The vents weren't large enough to crawl through and the apartment possessed only one door.

If she wanted to attempt another escape, she needed out of the apartment and access to an elevator. The stairwell would take too long. When she entered the elevator, she would need a disguise or they would shut her down in five seconds flat.

Off, on, off, on.

Yeah, the sexy boss man was watching. What was a girl to do?

A small grin played across her lips as her hand slipped between her thighs. She spread her legs a little, ensuring the camera had a straight shot. Her other hand cupped and squeezed a breast. She arched her back and dipped her head. One of the benefits of being big breasted was that she could reach a nipple with her mouth. It always incited a man into acts of passion they never planned or guessed they would do.

Her tongue swirled a tip as she cut her eyes up at the camera and she grinned.

<<<>>>

Collin grasped the monitor until his knuckles lost all color. The woman taunted him.

As soon as he'd seen her crawl into bed without a stitch on and look up at the camera, he knew they were about to see a show. He'd wasted no time shutting down the connection to the main monitoring station, but he'd been unable to resist and left it on in his office.

He had no idea a woman could do that and the way his cock throbbed, he wasn't soon to forget it.

Then her hand drifted across her belly and thrust two fingers into the place he wanted to touch again. He remembered how soft her skin felt and the sweetness he tasted. He ached. How easy it would be to zip open his pants and relieve the tension her little show created.

Shit! He stood up and turned his back to the screen. He needed to regain control of his body. Thinking about this woman all the time was not being productive. His father had lectured him and his brother about the dangers of a seductive woman. For that matter, his father taught them to never trust anyone, even each other.

Heart racing, he took several deep breaths. Relieved he had the sense to lower the sound as soon as he realized what she was doing. Instead he soaked in the music of Nickelback filling his office from a stereo system built into the wall. Then he slapped a key near the monitor, shutting down the camera.

He would give his life to the OS, but he'd be damn if he'd give that woman his soul.

<<<>>>

Olivia wanted to laugh, but the thought of how she'd affected the big boss man with her finger play brought her quickly to a climax. One day she would have the pleasure of seeing his face as she gave him an encore in person.

Men were so predictable. He'd done exactly what she'd hoped. Checking the camera one more time, she smiled. Yep, the red light was off. But in case he played with her, she threw a blouse over it.

She probably had around two minutes or less to do what was needed.

Kneeling next to her bed, she felt the edge of her mattress. What a relief; they'd brought everything of hers to the apartment. Most of the weapons they'd confiscated, but she hoped they had missed one area. She pushed the mattress off the box springs, feeling along the side. A little indention gave it away. There! They'd missed the flat metal box inserted in the wooden side. From first glance it appeared to be part of the design, but it actually held the tools needed to unlock doors and a thin deadly knife. Hanging around Theo and his fetish for knives came in handy.

She wasted no time straightening the bed. Then she slipped the kit and knife into the pocket of some pants she planned to wear in the morning. Without a second to spare she pulled the blouse off the camera and dove into the bed. Making sure her hands hovered near her groin as she pretended to be dozing. Opening her eyes to slits, she watched the camera. She'd counted to sixteen Mississippi's when the light started blinking again.

For the first time since her capture she felt back in control. In the next few days, she would be free. No place was so secure she couldn't find a way out. She'd proven that to Theo many times. Even the punishments he meted out didn't deter her from doing what she wanted.

Collin couldn't be trusted in keeping his promise about the orphanage. What man could? She would find a way to protect the children. She just couldn't do it from inside the OS.

Chapter Six

Damn! The man knew his way around security.

After two weeks of searching, she'd found a vent large enough to fit into and at a blind spot from the cameras. Five feet into the vent, she came to a metal grill with no visible lock, at least from what she'd seen.

Her shuffling around had only proved that his people were safe. Goodness, on top of that, they couldn't leave without going through three different security checkpoints. Even if she could unlock a door, there were two other measures she had to get through. One required a handprint and the other was visual recognition by guards.

Now she visited the OS's cafeteria with two guards standing in the doorway watching her. They weren't the same fellows from the day she disappeared for about twenty minutes as she scrambled through the vent and came to a dead end. It appeared since they couldn't account for her time, they were pulled off babysitting duty. She'd heard later they were placed on cleanup. And that had nothing to do with trash. Their punishment had more to do with dead bodies and the waste they left behind. She had a feeling it would be best to avoid coming across them in a dark alley-way. They probably would love to show her how much they resented her disappearing act.

She blinked. Not her problem. Her main concern was finding a way out and protecting the orphanage from any damage the head of OS sent their way.

She'd gone through the cafeteria line and chosen grilled salmon and a salad. The food was surprisingly good, although she couldn't say much about the atmosphere. Too bright. No place to put her back to a wall.

Carrying a tray to her usual low traffic area away from the vending machines and buffet line, Olivia scanned the crowd. A group of operatives dressed in sweat-stained workout clothes sat slumped over tables sipping on their sports drinks. Another group sprawled on the floor wore jeans and T-shirts and played poker. And then there were the Secret Service wannabes with their white shirts and black suits and ties. They munched on candy bars, watching the group gambling as if they expected a fight to break out in any minute.

Several heads turned, their gazes following her path to her empty table. From some of the looks she received, she might need to keep an eye over her shoulder. She doubted her new guards would protect her, at least not until others got a punch or two in. She ignored the cold stares and pretended to take her time eating as she checked out the open kitchen.

Over a period of several mornings and afternoons, while she worked out on the treadmill in the exercise room, she'd noticed that, of all the freight that came into the OS by the elevator where Collin had brought her in, no food products were included. No fresh fruit or vegetables. No sodas or meats. So that meant the kitchen had its own elevator. And probably one that wasn't watched as carefully.

"You're a brave soul."

Olivia turned to face Doctor Blondie. "Pardon?"

The woman laughed and placed her tray on the table across from her.

"After Jake and Ed were placed on cleanup, Collin had a hard time finding volunteers to guard you." The doctor sprinkled dressing on her salad as she nodded toward the two men. "Your new guards are hoping you'll try to escape during their shift."

No surprise they wanted a good excuse to cause her pain.

"Volunteers?" Olivia wished she knew what the doctor was wanting, sitting here chatting like they were friends. She gave the woman a questioning look. Who wanted to be friends with a killer?

"Yeah. Collin has a second sense on who can or will do a job. He asks and we say yes. We trust him to make the right decisions to bring us back home." The doctor dug into her salad as if she hadn't said the craziest thing Olivia had ever heard.

Forehead wrinkled, Olivia picked at the slab of fish in front of her. In The Circle, Theo had ruled like some king from ancient times. And he felt casualties were the price of war against terrorism. He would never worry about such trivial numbers. It dawned on her; no one spoke of Theo with such a tone of respect. Fear, yes. But never admiration.

Chapter Seven

Two more days of training and eating the food in the cafeteria brought pay dirt. She'd found if she ordered the sandwich special, she could wait near the end of the line and look into the back kitchen. That was where she spotted the other elevator.

Using the excuse of wanting a sandwich special to go, she watched two workers exit and return using nothing more than a key card. About the time they handed her a wrapped sandwich, a guy exited the back kitchen pushing a hand-truck filled with sodas.

She strolled over to the sliding glass refrigerators lined along the wall as if she wanted a Coke and crowded the man until he stumbled against her. Presto! She had a card and now needed the right time to escape.

With no time to waste, she strode over to the elevator in the back kitchen and slipped in the key card. Within seconds, the steel door closed seconds behind her and she released a little shout of triumph.

There were two buttons on the panel: one and two. That was simple.

A ding warned her that the doors were about to open. She leaned against the side wall so anyone standing outside the elevator wouldn't see her at first. No one walked in.

She peeked out. It was a T-shaped corridor. Straight ahead she could see metal double doors with wire mesh glass panes, while the horizontal corridor was pitch black on both ends. She shivered.

Through the glass panes as she was about to push on the handles, she spotted Rex and another man standing in what looked like a parking garage. They were talking and laughing. Then Rex slapped the man on the shoulder and turned in her direction.

She backed up, not wanting to take her eyes off the big man. But when her butt met the closed elevator doors, she darted down the dark corridor.

The clanging of the metal doors opening pushed her further into the darkness than she felt comfortable. Musty and too dark for comfort, the hallway felt endless. She pressed her shoulders to the wall and hoped Rex didn't turn on a light or look her way. She watched as he slipped his card key into the slot and tapped the button to call for the elevator car. He folded his arms and sighed. A ding announced it had arrived. He started to enter, but quickly stopped and moved to the side.

Her heart jumped. Had she made a sound? Could he see her?

Then she heard a voice and the rattling of glass. The soda man pushed his hand-truck as he shook his head, asking Rex to keep an eye out for a dropped key card. The big man shook his head and disappeared into the elevator.

She was unsure how long the soda man would take to clear out of the way, and she didn't want to take any chances of being spotted.

Inhale. Exhale. Inhale. By concentrating on breathing, she felt her heart rate slow down. She turned toward the elevator when a big shadow shoved her against the wall. Heat and unyielding muscle pressed her face to the cement blocks.

"What the¾"

She grabbed the knife hidden in the waistband of her jeans. Before she could use it, a large hand gripped her wrist and squeezed. Pain shot up her arm, numbing it momentarily. The clang echoed in the dark, magnifying the danger. She realized once again she'd screwed up.

Hand-to-hand combat was not her forte.

The big body crushing hers against the wall didn't let up. She struggled to breathe. The pressure on her chest left little room for her lungs to expand until he shifted and pushed his erection to the small of her back.

She gasped. That special scent of male and spice mixed together engulfed her senses, causing her heart to pound so hard she felt faint.

Collin Ryker.

The man had a reputation for being cold and ruthless with his enemies. With her latest escape, she hadn't endeared herself to him at all. What did he plan to do to her for punishment?

Shaking her head, she said, "I had to try one more time." No way would she ask for leniency.

He released her arm. Before she had time to react, his hands clasped her waist and with a firm touch slid up her rib cage and until he cupped her breasts and squeezed. She moaned. His hips rubbed against her. He was so hard and thick. Her cheek rested on the rough texture of the wall.

The sounds of heavy breathing and cloth rubbing together filled the darkness. A dance as primal and old as time controlled them. Olivia loved how his big body wrapped around her, rocking into the crease of her buttocks.

He unsnapped her jeans and slipped a hand down the front. Another moan escaped her as a broad finger dipped into her moisture. Her head dropped back onto his chest as she pressed herself to his thumb. She whimpered.

Why did this man have such control over her body?

"Olivia," he whispered. "If you try to escape again, I can promise you'll not live to regret it."

A simple flick of his finger and waves of pleasure shook her.

What have I gotten myself into?

Collin wanted to sink into her. He never imagined a woman could make him forget where he was and what he should be doing, and it wasn't to spend time playing patty-fingers in OS's basement. Even though she was The Circle's most successful assassin, he found her every move challenged and intrigued him.

"Do you understand?" He pulled his hand out of her pants and twirled her to face him. His grip tightened on her upper arms.

Chin down, she looked at him from beneath her eyelashes.

"Yes," she bit off.

He didn't move away. His gaze remained on hers. What was it about her? Thoughts of chaining her to him excited him more than he deemed acceptable.

"I thought you had understood before." He lifted her until they were nose-to-nose. "Do you really care about what would happen to the children? I've investigated several other facilities, and from what I can tell your money has made a big difference. Do you want it on your conscience that you let pride get in the way of a hundred-plus children's well-being?"

"I said I understood."

"But you didn't."

"What do you want? Me to beg you for forgiveness?"

"That would be a start."

"Sarcasm. You don't get it, do you?"

Her eyes sparkled with more life than he'd ever seen in another person. He wanted to bind her to him and immerse himself in what made her so alive, so vital. Most days he felt like he was a zombie, the walking dead, but not around her. He felt more alive.

"I want your loyalty." By the look on her face, she was as surprised by his demand as he was. He had a gut feeling she considered agreeing if for no other reason than to find out what he expected from her.

"No one's ever asked for that," her voice cracked.

"I'm not asking," he said with his usual bluntness.

"Ha! I have to say, you don't mince words." She wiggled out of his clutch and headed toward the elevator.

"Where do you think you're going?" he asked.

"Upstairs. I guess I need to build some upper body strength. I don't like how you can throw me around." She stopped and pressed the button as she threw an anxious look over her shoulder. The only light in the corridor shone on her and highlighted the pink coloring in her cheeks.

He liked flustering her.

When the doors slid open, he stepped in behind her. With her back to the wall, she waited for him to push the next floor button. He pressed his hands on the wall to each side of her and leaned over, caging her with his body. His mouth stopped a mere inch from hers.

"Do not try to escape again," he threatened.

"I won't." Her lips parted on a sigh.

His gaze shifted to her mouth. Damn, he wanted another taste. Just as he was about to give in, the elevator began to move.

He shoved off the wall, placing some distance between them.

"Good," he said with a measure of satisfaction and doubt.

Chapter Eight

Stupid man.

Olivia tossed the fellow over her shoulder and then rolled across the floor. In an upward twist, she jumped to her feet, prepared for another attack. Sweat poured down her face and her muscles ached, but she ignored all that as she waited for the next challenge.

"Enough."

She turned to the man controlling the exercise. Arms crossed, Collin stood on the sidelines wearing loose sweat-pants and a sleeveless sweatshirt. Nice muscles to show he worked out but not obsessively as to be bulky. What a shame she still hadn't gotten him out of his clothes.

And goodness knows she wanted to. But ever since their time in the dark, he never gave her a chance to be alone with him. Someone was always around. If not Rex or another operative, then he made sure the guards stood nearby. So much for his believing her promise not to escape.

Today, she'd thought of a way he would have to touch her.

"Over three months ago you'd said *we* would exercise." She grinned. "So far, it has been *me* exercising."

With hands on her hips, she waited to see if he would accept her challenge. He'd gone missing the last two weeks and no one would say if he would return or when. She hated to admit she'd gotten used to having him around, teasing her with his presence, mocking her when she tried to encourage his advances. Crap! She was a glutton for punishment.

Speaking of gluttons, her exercise partner chuckled and slapped a towel around his neck as he glanced at Collin. "I can understand you're nervous. She moves like she's done this all her life."

She found it fascinating how the OS people treated Collin as if he was one of them. At The Circle, no one would be brave enough to even hint at Theo for being nervous about anything. For that matter, she doubted Theo had ever taken personal interest in an operative's training. He'd never been concerned about her even when she shared his bed.

"Come on. Exercise with me." She crooked her finger.

Collin looked away as if he needed time to think. Then he moved into his stance, ready for their sparring. The next ten minutes produced a blur of kicks and throws she was sure she would regret tomorrow. When she landed chest first onto the mat and all her breath swooshed out, she stayed down.

Give her a gun. She'd show him her special skills.

"Olivia?" He stooped next to her, pressing fingers against the side of her throat while brushing her hair out of her face. "Are you all right?"

"Just ... trying ... to get ... my breath back."

After a few seconds, she was able to take a complete

lung full of air and felt better even though she was embarrassed by her performance. Had the other operative been playing with her or was Collin that much better?

"Hey, Collin, can I talk with you a moment?" a harsh voice said off to the side.

As Olivia sat up with Collin's help, Rex hovered near the mat looking antsy.

"Sure." Collin nodded and turned his attention back to her. "Stay here. Dr. Shelton will be here in a minute to look you over."

"Oh, hell, no." She wasn't about to let that woman touch her again. "Nothing's wrong. Just had the breath knocked out of me. I'll go back to my apartment."

"She can come too. We can use her," Rex said without hesitation.

She? She had a name and didn't like the thought of anyone using her. But what the hey? Maybe an opportunity would come up and she could use it against Big Foot.

Conscious of her sweaty body, she hung back, feeling like a midget following two giants. Instead of riding the elevator to what she guessed would be Rex's office, the pair led her down a couple hallways and then into what looked like a study. Books lined the walls and a massive desk reigned in the far corner. The plush carpet screamed expensive and the room smelled of Collin, that special masculine scent.

"We¾"

"Wait," Collin interrupted Rex and turned to Olivia. "You do understand if you betray us in any way, I'll have no option but to terminate our understanding in every aspect." He took the chair behind the desk.

"Like you had to spell it out to me again." She rolled her eyes. "If The Circle even suspects I'm still alive, I'm a marked woman. They would issue a termination decree. So you can only hope I live long enough to be useful."

No matter the years of service or how loyal she'd proven herself over and over again, she was as good as dead once The Circle learned she'd been captured alive by the OS. Collin's threat didn't disturb her at all. It had been expected. She'd lived with the knowledge she could die at any minute.

How different was it to serve one organization over another? Irony continued to screw with her life. The only difference between the organizations was that one was apparently more relaxed than the other, though both were deadly. And there was no doubt of why she enjoyed life like she did¾taking strange men to bed for a one-night stand and leaving them wondering what in the hell happened.

With that thought, she eased into a leather chair situated before the desk. She examined the profile of the one man she wanted and never had. The firm jaw with a five o'clock shadow. His brow furrowed in concentration. His hair was a little longer but still thick, and the cocoa color tempted her fingers to play in it. Wherever he'd gone, the temperature must've been warm as he sported a nice even tan.

"We've tracked down Mason Redmond," Rex announced as he remained standing, arms akimbo.

That got her attention. If it was the same Mason she'd heard of, he was a nasty piece of work affiliated with not one of the largest but certainly one of the deadliest terrorist groups, Inferno. They believed the only way to bring in a new world order was to see the world burn. The Circle had been looking for the leader for around two years.

"What do you know about Mason?" Collin handed her a small file. Inside showed a lanky man with bright red hair and freckles across his nose. He looked like the good neighbor who grew up on a farm and attended church on Sundays.

"He's a crazy son of bitch who wants to be king of the world." She handed the file back to him. Collin and Rex stared at her, waiting for her to add more information. She shifted in her seat and crossed her arms. "I really don't know a lot about him as I pretty much stayed out of his way. Until I'm instructed to take a target out, I never investigate. I did hear he liked to watch."

"People burning?" Rex asked.

She shook her head. "No. Fucking. He likes watching people screw each other." Why did they have such surprised expressions on their faces? Were they expecting her to blush? Maybe if they'd grown up like she had, they would see the act as a way to control the people around them and nothing more. "Oh, he especially likes married women. He gets a kick out of doing the wife. Then later he'll get the husband to fuck his wife in front of him so he can compare techniques. It's amazing what money can buy. As far as I know, he doesn't do the husband."

The big guy blushed. How funny was that? Obviously he'd never been made to strip and fellatio someone on command.

"Have you alerted the team?" Collin asked, looking at Rex. She grinned. He probably asked mainly to help Rex get his mind off what she'd said.

"Yeah. We leave at zero eight hundred hours for Phoenix." Rex's glance chilled her to the bone. "Is she going with us?"

"She's got the right equipment to grab his attention. You have a problem with that?" Collin leaned forward. By his stance alone she could tell he dared his friend to protest.

How sweet, he was taking up for her. She knew there was something she liked about him besides his body.

"She's your problem." Rex shrugged. "You know she'd fuck you over good if you let her."

"You both do know I'm here and hearing this, right?" she pointed out. Rex actually growled. Well, wasn't he pleasant? What had she done to him?

Collin shifted his attention to her. "Olivia, in operations like this one, most of us partner up with another operative. This way, we look after each other. As a couple we're actually less noticeable. You and I'll go as a married couple. We'll fly into Phoenix. If anyone asks, we're traveling up to the Grand Canyon. There's a resort we have reservations at near Camelback where sponsors of several NASCAR drivers celebrate after the big race. Mason has been known to crash the party."

"Goody. One hotel room and marital duties." She grinned big. Part of it was an act to aggravate Rex; the other part was pure anticipation. Yeah. She needed other things occupying her mind as she worked her wiles on getting Collin into bed. Her obsession with the man on the other side of the desk was getting out of hand. Once they did what came natural, her obsession would be over.

Rex muttered a stream of filthy expletives.

Eyes wide, she hooted. "You do know most of those are impossible. Goodness knows I tried a couple."

The big man's face pinked. "If she doesn't have any more information on Mason, I believe she can go." Rex's pleading look toward Collin was pitiful. The way the big guy opened and closed his fists, she should probably count herself lucky to get out of the meeting alive.

Frowning at her, Collin nodded toward the door. "I'll

fill you in later. Go ahead and get lunch. Pack what you usually take on a four-day operation."

She should be pissed by their little jock attitude, but considering she was looking forward to her one-on-one time with Collin, nothing really bothered her. Now she needed to plan how she could make him let go of his morals with her. Strange to think of the head of OS as having morals. One of the many things she'd learned during her months with them. Besides, that had to be the reason why he hadn't taken her up on her offers. Her heart thumped at a double rate. It wouldn't do for them to see how excited she was at the prospect.

"Well, okay. Don't you two guys talk about me much." When she glanced over to Rex to say something snarky, she caught Collin's expression from the corner of her eye. He shook his head, letting her know she was pushing it. "Okay, okay. I'm going."

After closing the door behind her, she leaned against it. Whoa. She hadn't realized how intense the atmosphere had gotten. Looking down the hallway, she smelled garlic bread. Oh, she would love to indulge but after the beating she'd gotten this morning, she needed to work on her technique. Something told her she would have another opportunity to best Collin. Tracking and planning eliminations rarely required the skills she'd used during her first few years with The Circle.

Heading toward the exercise area, she ignored the two guards following a few feet behind. In her short time with the OS, she never learned their names as they said it wasn't important for her to know. When they did talk to her, they mostly told her no. So she called them Beavis and Butt-head.

She passed the first room and continued toward the

second exercise room. Two women stood to the side, talking and glancing her way. One was Dr. Shelton and the other woman she didn't recognize.

"Hey, Olivia." The doctor smiled and waved her over. "Have you seen Collin and Rex lately?"

"They're having a man-to-man talk. I wanted to get away from all the testosterone for a little while." Crap, what was this? Every time she turned around she was explaining herself to people. So not her.

The doctor nodded. "Have you met Nic Savage?"

Olivia's eyes widened in surprise. "You're a girl." This was OS's head of security? How politically forward. Tickled to know the organization that had extorted her into working for them were equal opportunity employers, she stuck her hand out to the tiny black-haired woman.

When the security officer sneered at her offered hand, Olivia straightened her spine. So she was going to be like that. How disappointing. One of Olivia's interests included computers and she'd spent many an off-duty hour talking to the information services experts at The Circle. Though she would never call them friends, she knew they'd respected her interest and skills in that area. By picking their brains, she was able to set up a state-of-the-art security system.

"Actually I'm a grown *woman* and oversee a department that has four personnel in the hospital because of you and the primitive precautions you used to protect your poorly decorated fortress." The woman might be small, but she had a sharp tongue.

With one eyebrow lifted, Olivia crossed her arms and shifted to her left hip. "You and I both know there wasn't anything primitive nor was it personal about what I'd set up. If you don't have your computers rigged here with the same type of explosives, it only proves how delusional you are."

Nic moved toward Olivia, but the doctor jumped in front of her. "No, Nic. She'll wipe the floor with you and not blink an eye."

Olivia's opinion of the good doctor spiked. The two moved toward the elevator with the doctor clasping Nic's arm and whispering to her the whole way. Over her shoulder, Nic glared at Olivia.

Of course, the only response perfect for the moment was to blow her a kiss. Olivia couldn't help but smirk when the woman gasped and struggled as the doctor forced her out the door.

When she looked back at her guards, they merely shrugged their shoulders. She had no illusions of who the guards would protect. She could only hope to get in a hit or two before they stopped her.

Later in the day with no sign of Collin, she headed back to her apartment. Was he hiding from her? She laughed, thinking of the dangerous man lurking around corners to avoid her. For whatever reason, he'd told the guards she could come and go as she pleased from her apartment as long as she didn't ditch them. The two big fellows hovered about eight feet away when she spotted a familiar face sitting on an overstuffed chair in one of the alcoves divided by potted plants. Eyes half-closed like a wild beast in captivity, he studied each person who walked by.

Lucian Reilly hadn't changed one bit. He still exuded coldness and mystery some women found attractive. The same ones who read vampire novels and thought they were hot. She never understood it or why The Circle used him as a lady killer, literally. His specialty involved getting up close and personal with a woman and using her, and if the need arose, to not be squeamish about using force or killing the woman. The last she'd heard was that OS had killed him during an operation in San Francisco. Apparently that wasn't true.

"Hello, Lucian." With one eyebrow raised, she stopped in front of him.

"I heard they had brought you in. I'm astonished they didn't slice and dice you considering Collin's second in command hates you." Lucian's British accent made it sound like he was discussing tea instead of her expected death. Did everyone know about Rex's feelings toward her?

"What can I say? I'm like a cat and land on my feet. Speaking of cats, is this your sixth or seventh life?" She sat across from him with one elbow on a knee and her chin in hand, staring at him with open amazement. Theo had said Lucian was one of the best in the business, never hesitated in killing a woman. The OS was smart to turn him. He glanced at her guards leaning against the wall across from the cubbyhole. The distance was enough to allow Olivia and Lucian time to talk without interference. She hadn't expected a response but that didn't stop her from teasing him further. "So, kitty cat, we were told OS had murdered you and dumped your body into the Pacific two years ago."

"Humph." His cold eyes narrowed. "The Circle's days are numbered. If you look around, you'll see several of their *dead* operatives walking around here." He lifted his chin. "I'm really surprised they kept you alive considering you're Theo's pet."

She stiffened and straightened in her chair, forcing herself not to turn to see if the guards had heard. "You're hung up on my death, aren't you? I might've been his pet at one time, but he lost interest in me when I turned eighteen."

"If you think he didn't treat you differently than the other operatives, you're sadly mistaken." The man's eyes narrowed.

"Maybe. Maybe not. Luckily, he found another use for me or I would've been dead for sure." She never pretended otherwise.

"Luckily? If you want to call it that. More like smart."

What? Was that sympathy from him? He actually complimented her? He stood, yanked at the ends of his sports jacket. "Be careful. If The Circle captures you, you'll be begging them to finish you off."

"I know." She wanted to ask him more questions but the way he refused to look her in the eyes, she could tell he wanted to get as far from her as possible.

"You do? Of course." He smirked and then walked away.

Happy to have seen a familiar face, she'd forgotten how much others had hated her in The Circle. Partly because of her personal time with Theo, but later for her part in punishing those who screwed up. Being an enforcer, the one who carried out Theo's commands, never endeared a person to those punished. It had been six years since she controlled that type of power, but they'd never forgotten it.

Nor had she. She had frequent nightmares about it.

Collin strode by with Nic almost skipping to catch up. Olivia's gaze followed the man down the hallway. Her chest tightened with a new thought. Her nightmares might take a new turn.

Chapter Nine

Olivia's first time to Phoenix had been with Theo and all she remembered was desert and everything brown and dirty. A few years later, alone, she'd tracked down an assignment to Phoenix and found the place colorful, filled with people wanting to enjoy life to the fullest. Mind-set had a lot to do with it, and this time she couldn't wait to experience a town she'd grown to love with a man who challenged her at every turn. She was ready for whatever he threw at her.

She turned from watching the golden sun setting over the raised interstate and buildings. Not the best view, but considering the area was packed with stock car fans, they were fortunate to find a room. Of course, she wasn't complaining. She eyed the man sitting at the desk with his back to her, checking the times of the different events on his laptop.

Before they'd left on their flight, Collin had filled her in on why they wanted Mason so bad. OS needed some information about a valuable missing artifact Mason may or may not have. If the Inferno had it and sold it, they would have enough funds to purchase the plutonium they needed off the black market to complete a bomb large enough to blow up several blocks in Washington, D.C., if not the whole city. By the OS stealing the artifact, they could block the sale and destroy any chance of Inferno from existing. No funds. No operation. Then they hoped the fanatics, defeated, would think twice about crawling out the swamps they came from.

An itch on the back of her neck warned of being more involved.

"We have pit passes. That'll make it easier to scout out the area near his favorite driver." He jotted down a few notes on the pad next to him.

After receiving intel about Mason's planned excursion to the NASCAR cup race the next day in Phoenix, Collin was able to pull a few strings and score some tickets. So it appeared she'd be going to her first stock car race. Actually, she was rather excited about it.

"You think Mason will be hanging with the other groupies in the pit?" she asked.

"He's convinced several of the drivers he's a representative for Champion Oil. With the way he flashes money and talks big, anyone would believe it." Collin clicked on a couple pages, showing the layout of the racetrack.

"So what's our story?" On the way there, including on the plane, they'd played husband and wife, Joe and Lisa Murphy, on vacation.

"We stick with our story as a newly married couple out having fun and visiting our favorite sport, looking for a good time. We decided the race sounded as interesting as the canyon." He continued to click on the computer keys.

That was bothering the hell out of her. After he'd been the attentive husband all day, she wanted him to finish it.

What had he expected? She'd had so much fun rubbing against him every chance she got on the trip, maybe even becoming a little too amorous on a plane with a large group of people. Not until they reached the hotel room had his jaw unclenched enough for him to speak normally. So what was stopping him? What was so interesting about the fucking computer that made him ignore her?

"There were a couple times on our little trip I had to make up some history. So what's our story? Met in college, work? Been married three, six months, or a year?" she asked, hoping to irritate him as much as he irritated her.

He stopped clicking, stared at the wall for a moment, and then closed the laptop.

With a shake of his head, he looked over his shoulder at her. "What's the matter? I gave you the file before we left. It's not like you're an amateur." He pushed back the chair and stood.

Well, wasn't he snippy? Although he was still sexy.

"For your information, I never had a chance before you swept me out of my apartment. You do know you're my first partner." She stepped closer to him and smelled the hotel's milled soap on his heated skin.

No matter how low of a temperature they set the air conditioner, the room wouldn't cool off. Her fingers fiddled with the button on his shirt. She liked the feel of his firm pecs beneath the cloth.

"The reports said Theo personally trained you." His dark gaze appeared to measure her, waiting for a reaction.

Her stomach rolled. She wanted to say the sick feeling was from becoming overheated during the day, but she knew better. With every bit of willpower she worked to keep her breathing steady, her face emotionless.

"Theo taught me many things, but he doesn't train operatives in their duties." A slow curl of dread traveled down her spine when she turned away, hoping he wouldn't ask anything more about Theo tonight.

She moved away, snatching up a dress from her suitcase. The silky fabric slipped back and forth between her hands. The outfit was one of several they'd provided for the trip. The eye- catching colors and styles were the complete opposite of her usual attire: business casual with the occasional femme fatale gown. These screamed white trash a la trailer park. She tilted her head as she held up the tiny slip of shiny material. The edge of the dress would probably curve beneath her buttocks. She'd already thrown barely there shoes with four-inch heels into the closet.

"Who trained you?" Collin asked.

Not sure how to hang the tiny dress, she tossed it on the dresser and looked over at the man bothering her with questions. He was stretched out on the bed, shoes off, and hands behind his head resting against the headboard as he watched her.

"A man named Jason." She saw no harm in telling him.

"Kastler?" he asked with eyelids half-closed.

"Yeah. How did you know?" How did he know so much? Of course, the man was head of a secret organization.

"You'll be surprised by how much I do know," he boasted.

"Why don't you enlighten me? I heard snippets about the OS but nothing confirmed. Is it true the OS was like the central elite of The Circle?"

"Yes."

"Well?" she prompted. No way would she let him get away with his Clint Eastwood act.

"Tell me about your training." He crossed his arms.

"No. First, you tell me about OS breaking away." She sat on the foot of the bed.

"All right. I guess it's only fair. What exactly would you like to know?"

Fair? What a rare word to hear in her world.

"What part did you play in it?" she asked bluntly.

"It was my decision."

Well, he'd said four words that time. Either she needed better questions, or he needed to loosen up more.

"Why did you leave?" she asked.

"No. That's not how it's played." He gave her that half-lidded look again. A tingling swirled through her insides.

"Huh?" How could he burn her brain just by a look?

"You ask a question and I answer, then it's my turn."

"Okay." She pretended to see something on her shoe and turned her back to him, swiping at the imaginary dirt.

Could she tell him the truth about her first few years at The Circle if he asked? Maybe it wouldn't hurt for him to know, to understand what she'd gone through to become a total bitch. She squeezed her eyes shut for a few seconds. She wanted to escape from him and the emotions he made her feel. Going from one job to another had pushed away the desire to live a normal life, to be loved by a man, to have two point five children, and to own a minivan parked next to the white picket fence.

"How old were you the first time you walked across The Circle's vestibule?" he asked with deliberation.

Damn! He was good. She could lie or try to avoid the question but he must know something and he'd already proven he could sense a lie. She took a deep breath and straightened.

"Fourteen."

"The bastard," he murmured vehemently as he moved

away from the headboard, placing his feet on the floor, sitting on the side of the bed. Energy radiated from his body. He acted as if he needed someone or something to hit.

"Why did OS splinter off from The Circle?" she asked, hoping to avoid explaining why she'd entered The Circle's Main Sector at such a young age.

His forehead wrinkled as if he was finding it hard to shift gears from her answer to his. "Theo's decisions were becoming erratic after my family died."

Erratic? What a nice way to call someone loony, crazy, downright nuts. In fact, she could add stark raving maniac. Thus, the reason everyone at The Circle dreaded meeting with him. Then the last four words he'd said sunk in. What did his family dying have to do with Theo?

"What were your duties for The Circle?" His hands on his knees, back straight, he looked at her over his shoulder.

The high tension and see-sawing of emotions she'd endured since her capture sucker punched her at that moment. She sighed. "Listen. I'm tired of the fucking around and playing twenty questions. What do you really want to know?"

He moved off the bed, walked to the dresser in front of her and leaned broad shoulders against it. If she reached out, she could touch his legs. But she remained near the end of the bed and concentrated on the carpet's pattern.

"What is Theo to you? And why did he bring you into The Circle so young?" he asked, his low voice almost apologetic.

She didn't need his pity. Shit happened and just because it happened to her more than others was only a fact of life.

"Where do I start? Why not from the beginning, eh? That way you'll understand ..." What had she convinced herself mere seconds ago? Oh, yeah, that she was a bitch, and she never believed in whitewashing the truth. "When I turned ten, the orphanage became too crowded and they fostered me out. Carol. The woman's name was Carol Brinks. She took me in and was kind. For three years I lived in heaven. I worked hard on my lessons. I had a rough time understanding so much, but Ms. Carol was patient, kind, encouraging, loving. I was a good girl for her. Then she died." She shrugged. "It was a stroke. Her brother showed up the day of the funeral and took me home with him. I knew that first night why he kept me. I ran away eighteen months later."

Aware of how her voice sounded robotic, all emotions turned off, she still grappled with her guts twisting and churning on each word and memory.

"I'd been on the streets for little over two months, pulling tricks for Sweet Daddy near College Park when a tall handsome white-headed man saw me. Theo promised to take care of me. Sweet Daddy refused to give up a part of his lucrative income. So Theo sliced him up until he bled to death."

She'd never told anyone about Carol and especially about Theo's special talent with a knife. That last bit of information could get her killed in the most painful ways.

Wasn't baring her soul, so to speak, supposed to make her shoulders to feel lighter? Or was that her chest? Didn't books and movies all claim instant relief, like an antacid?

Well, she didn't feel better. She lifted her head. He looked as if he was listening to a weather report. Why had she really told him so much? Maybe she wanted him to understand what made her what she was.

"Finish," he commanded and glanced away.

The son of a bitch was judging her. Let him. She didn't

care. If she allowed what others thought of her to drag her down, she would've committed suicide years ago.

"For four years I warmed his bed and was grateful each day I lived." Never had a more bitter truth been told and she wished everyday she could forget. "Each day with him, I made sure to learn a new weapon or tactic in surviving inside The Circle." Her chest tightened. Well, there went the feeling of relief. "I wanted to ensure, when he finally tired of me, he would have a reason to let me live." A clammy chill coated her skin as she began to tremble.

At the time he'd brought her into The Circle, she'd met her predecessor, a pretty little blonde with sad blue eyes. One day she'd been there and then the next she was gone.

Two years later, Theo had threatened sixteen-year-old Olivia by telling her how he'd fucked the girl and then twisted her neck when he climaxed. It had been the blonde's eighteenth birthday. Theo claimed when a woman reached that age she became boring, useless, like so many other women. So she made sure not to be boring or useless, in or out of the bedroom.

Oh, God, she'd wanted to kill Theo for years but had been too afraid to admit if he deserved to die, she did too.

Even before she entered The Circle, she'd already had her first kill. She'd stabbed Carol's brother in his fat gut and watched him bleed to death as she grabbed her stuff to leave that last night. Her body shook as it had so long ago. Memories of the terror and the loneliness crashed in on top of her, bringing back those feelings best locked away but never forgotten.

Chapter Ten

Despite Collin's warm hands on her shoulders, Olivia couldn't stop shaking. She hated feeling weak. Smothering underneath his kindness, she pushed him, blindly slapped her hands against his chest and then her fingernails reached for his eyes. He clasped her hands for a second to give himself time to move back. With a twist of her body, she was off the bed, crouched in a fighting stance, ready to take him on for real.

She struck out with her left foot, hitting him square in the stomach. He grunted, staggered back, giving her a ferocious look, and then blocked her next two kicks. Her arm hit the television and her hip slammed into the desk chair with each swing or kick she used. The room was too small for them to truly fight without alarming the other guests with the crashing of lamps and furniture. She quickly realized he remained on the defensive, only blocking her moves.

She took a couple steps back from him, panting like an overheated dog. Her gaze drifted down his body to see a bulge beneath his zipper. The thought of him being turned on by her story pissed her off.

"You sick bastard!" She stared pointedly at his crotch.

His upper lip curled. "Fighting with you makes me horny."

"Oh." She exhaled and all the air left the room.

"Are you okay?"

"I'm fine," she bit off.

He tilted his head as his eyes narrowed.

Of course, she didn't mean it, but she was unsure how to handle her feelings on hearing him say the word *horny*. She'd instantly wanted to spread her legs for him.

She turned her back, afraid of what she would do. Beg him to fuck her? Her weak knees and the moisture soaking her thong told her she was lying by denying him and herself. But, oh mercy, that reasonable little voice in her head reminded her that no matter how bad she wanted him, she needed to take a cold shower and rein in her lust for a man who had control of life and death over her. He'd made it plain he didn't want her body no matter how his cock hardened in her presence.

An arm came around her waist and lifted her off the floor while a big hand covered her mouth. She kicked back and heard a grunt. Good. Probably only his shin but it should leave a bruise. She landed face first on the bed and Collin's weight kept her down. He jerked her arms back, tying her up with what felt like a silk tie. At the rate he was going, he would have to replace his whole wardrobe of ties.

"What the hell are you doing?" she asked, her voice sounding airy. He continued to press so hard on her back she struggled to breathe.

"I've let you work off some steam, now it's only fair you let me have my turn," he said in a guttural tone.

His hand slipped into the front of her jeans and yanked the snap and zipper open, shoving them below her hips. He didn't do anything more for several seconds. Then she felt a light flutter on her buttocks. Had he pressed his lips to her?

Then she heard another zipper. He was going to fuck her like this? To wait all this time and have her looking away? No way! She'd wanted to see his face when he came into her the first time. She wiggled, trying to turn over but he held her down, controlling her. In her struggles the bedspread rubbed her cloth-covered breasts and they hardened, aching for his touch.

He slapped a bare buttock. The sting promptly halted her movements.

"Be still," he ordered and smacked the other one. His fingers brushed across the sensitive skin, likely tracing the outline of a red handprint.

The spot burned as hot as she felt between her legs. She imagined he enjoyed marking her like that. Never a lover of pain, nevertheless her body tingled in all the places she wanted him to suck, lick, and fuck.

Then his heavy body rested along her back. His cock found a cradle between her butt cheeks but nowhere near an opening for them to enjoy. He kissed her neck and tugged at her earlobe with his teeth. She groaned. When he began to rock, pressing her hips into the mattress, she pushed back and his breath heated her neck. His cock slid up and down the crevice perfect for the motion. She continued to apply friction to her breasts and against his groin. He thrust harder, rubbing an absurdly long and thick cock against her, but not into her.

"Please," she begged. "Fuck. Me. Please."

His hand slid beneath her and a broad finger slipped between the moist folds. As soon as he touched the stiff little clit, it was over for her. He rammed her smarting cheeks twice more and then he released a soft groan and warmth filled the small of her back.

A flutter near her shoulder felt like another kiss and he lifted off her. With a tug, her hands were free, but he held her down for second.

"Wait a minute, don't move. I'll get you a towel," he said.

She couldn't move anyway. Every bone in her body had melted from the most intense ... what would she call that? A brawl? Sex? She wasn't sure, but she had a feeling he hadn't intended for it to happen. He'd been so cool until she began fighting him. He'd been telling the truth. He hadn't wanted her until she tried to kick his butt. The only man she'd never been able to defeat. Maybe that was why she wanted him so bad too.

A warm wet cloth wiped at her back. Then he gently dried her skin. His attentions were so soothing she didn't dare move a muscle for fear of him stopping.

"Are you okay?" he asked, his hand caressed her waist.

She closed her eyes. Couldn't he just leave her alone?

"Olivia?"

With a deep breath she turned over. Those beautiful dark eyes of his were filled with concern. She liked that. She also liked how he looked with mussed hair and his shirt wrinkled. Dark blue splatters decorating the front shook her up. He'd lost control. She was used to losing control around him, but this was the most he'd allowed his desire full rein. It had to be disturbing for him. Poor baby.

She looked at the alarm clock. "No worries. If you don't mind, I'll take a shower in the morning. I'm beat."

Giving him her back, she shoved her pants the rest of the way down her legs, and then crawled under the sheets. Like a virginal bride, she unclasped her bra beneath the covers and tossed it toward her suitcase on the other side of the bed, not caring if it hit its mark or not.

He still stood beside her bed watching her with dark brooding eyes.

Then she faced the wall, ignoring whatever was bothering him. He got what he wanted. Didn't most men? Sure, he brought her off but the relief was fleeting. That she knew better than anyone and it didn't really matter.

So why was her chest tight and tears in her eyes?

<<<>>>

Collin sat in the chair farthest from the bed. In the two hours since she'd fallen asleep, he'd hoped, if he remained quiet and watched her, he could understand what in the hell he was thinking when he ... hell, what had they done?

He'd nearly raped her. She'd been fighting him and then, before he realized what he'd done, he'd been pumping against her creamy peach buttocks. Somehow he'd remained in control enough to refrained from sticking his cock into her and fucking her senseless.

Sure she begged him to fuck her. It would've still been rape. She hadn't wanted him at first. Only later had she changed her mind. His need was there, barely restrained below the surface. He'd wanted to pound into her. He knew how close he came to hurting her by taking her the way he really wanted to. He wiped his face and shook his head.

Her soft skin rubbing against him, smelling the delicate perfume she used, knowing she could kill him any moment if he released her, all added up to a lethal woman he wanted more than breathing. But he couldn't take her. He needed her on the edge, wondering when he would give her what she wanted. Acting as the carrot was becoming difficult. How much longer could he last?

His cell phone vibrated. He checked the screen and then answered, "Yeah." He kept his gaze on Olivia during Rex's quick explanation. "Are you sure?" After a couple more questions, he hung up.

She hadn't moved. He would let her sleep through the night undisturbed. They had a long day ahead of them tomorrow. Mason had disappeared and they could only hope he wouldn't miss the big after-race party at The Phoenician in Scottsdale.

He stripped completely and slid into bed next to her. The smell of sex and Olivia surrounded him. She moaned and her butt squirmed against his hard cock. A smile flitted across his lips. Unsure if she sensed his presence and wanted space, or she hungered for his touch as much as he craved her taste, he refused to think anymore about it. Instead he snuggled a little closer. He was sleeping with her whether she liked it or not.

She whimpered and grabbed his hand, pressing it to a firm full breast. Her nipple pebbled as he cupped her but he held back from doing more. He almost whimpered too.

Another smile lifted the corners of his lips. He couldn't wait until morning to see her reaction to his invasion of her bed and person. There was no doubt her irritation would keep him on his toes.

He pressed his lips to a bare shoulder and closed his eyes.

Yep, seeing Olivia in action tomorrow was going to be a treat.

Chapter Eleven

"I'm going to kill the son of a bitch," Olivia muttered as she sauntered back to the couch with an apple martini in her hand held high.

Maneuvering in the crush of people while trying not to spill her drink or fall on her ass and show off the aforementioned body part was difficult. Collin had been no help by insisting that she wear the strip of shiny material she'd scorned the night before. She made sure to use her stilettos on tennis shoe–covered feet, maybe more out of spite since she wished she was wearing a pair at that very moment.

"What did you say, doll?" Mason asked over the pounding music.

He scooted over and patted the seat next to him. His gaze skimmed over the roomy hotel suite slammed with NASCAR drivers and their wives or girlfriends, race team owners, and all the people who supported or sucked them dry. Those beady pale blue eyes returned to her but as always landed on the dark depths of her cleavage and didn't move no matter what she said or did in an attempt to bring his attention to her face.

"Nothing much, sugar." With a slight wiggle, she scooted into the spot the tall, rawboned redhead indicated. With any luck her thong wasn't showing to the rest of the room. "Mostly about how crowded it is. I really wish we could go somewhere private and have some fun."

She hated this part of Collin's asinine plan. Her abhorrence of parties, especially crowded ones where bodies rubbed against strange ones wasn't helping her attitude. Just as her stomach rolled whenever Mason caressed her arm or leaned on her.

She understood Collin's plan but that didn't mean she had to like any of it. So far the entire day had been a slice of hell.

Waking up with Collin's hand playing with her clit almost guaranteed her being in a good mood until she caught the look in his eyes. He'd only amused himself, to see her reaction. She'd rather he'd done it to start a mutually satisfying moment, yet again, he held back.

What was the man? A sadist? No. Wrong one, but probably that too. A masochist. Yeah. He must get off abusing himself. She'd never known a man to hold off his satisfaction for so long and he was showing his expertise at it. Well, except for his release on her back. Later he'd pay for teasing her and then placing her in the present position of dodging this slime ball's octopus hands.

Then he informed her, Mason had disappeared, and they would prepare for the party that night by skipping the race. Mason never missed the party.

Skip the race? Well, hell. Collin refused to have sex with her and continued to tease her, and he stuck her in a stuffy hotel room. And then to take away the opportunity to experience powerful motors revving in testosterone-laden air, well, that was cruel. A sadist, masochist, and an asshole.

For now, the plan was to find a way to separate Mason from his bodyguards. As she'd told Collin and Rex, the man loved to fuck married women while the husband hung out nearby and clueless, and then later, convince the husband to fuck the wife in front of him. Collin instructed her to encourage Mason's interest and not kill him.

She wanted to kill both of them. Men!

Instead she'd found out more. Yes, Mason loved screwing married women, but not while the husband was in the other room or stood by and watched. Turned out their psycho was bisexual and loved for the other half of a relationship to join in. Talk about an interesting turn she looked forward to telling Collin. Would he go through with a three-way? He always acted like he had a stick up his ass, maybe there was a reason. Then again, Collin might kill Mason if he tried. So here she sat, trying to find ways to keep his hands off her goods and still keep him happy. And figure out a way to get back at Collin.

"Where's that good-looking husband of yours?"

"Why, sweet pea, don't you worry a bit. My little ol' husband will be back any moment now." She was laying on the southern accent thick, but from the way Mason, a city boy from Chicago, was drooling from the corner of his mouth, he loved every minute of it.

"You're sure he would like to play with us?" he asked as he placed an arm around her shoulders and leered at her breasts. She grabbed his dangling hand and threaded her fingers between his, more to keep him from grabbing than anything to do with closeness. He licked her ear¾yuck! Collin owed her big time¾and whispered, "Wouldn't you like me to have one of the drivers join us?"

She really wanted to teach the creep a thing or two

about manners, but Collin needed time to find an empty suite at The Phoenician. Many of the fans had left after the race and the rumor ran through the crowd a big dog who had reserved one had left an hour ago. The suite played a part in the plan of setting the stage for the creep's expected seduction of Olivia. Only Collin didn't know Mason expected a ménage à trois.

"Oh, no. True, I love a man in a jumpsuit, but I'm not a helmet licker by any means. It's the man out of the uniform who counts." She patted his bony knee. "My hubby likes men as aggressive as he's shy." She had to bite the inside of her mouth to keep from laughing. Wait until Mason and Collin were alone together. He deserved everything Mason dealt out for leaving her to be ogled and pawed.

"Is that right?" he asked as he leered down her blouse. She caught his other hand before he slipped it between her legs. His head jerked up. "There's your handsome husband now." Mason nodded toward the entrance.

Dressed in black jeans and a white shirt unbuttoned far enough to see a little chest hair and plenty of tanned skin, Collin craned his neck looking for them in the crushing crowd.

She waved her hand. "Yoo-hoo!"

Collin strode across the room as the partygoers moved out of the way. His eyes appeared to be on her and Mason, but she could tell he was aware of all the people surrounding them. Did they sense the danger walking near them?

"Who's your new friend, sweetheart?" Collin asked as he leaned down and kissed her.

She grabbed the back of his neck and took advantage of his mouth. He'd probably planned for the kiss to be perfunctory, but no way could she pass up the opportunity to aggravate him. Instead she found heat racing through her body with his answering thrust of tongue.

"Hey, you two, get a room." Mason cackled.

Collin pulled away and used his thumb to wipe off her Luscious Pink lipstick from his bottom lip. The man had a gorgeous mouth even if he was wearing a smirk. His eyes met hers. Did she see a flare of anger? Or had he gotten carried away with the moment too?

"Speaking of rooms, darling, I just got us the Presidential Suite. Let's check it out."Collin's smirk changed to the breathtaking smile she'd seen him give Doctor Blondie her first day in the OS.

She had to keep reminding herself he was acting, playing a part for Mason's benefit. Her confusion confirmed she was not good at working with a partner. His eyebrows rose, waiting for her to continue the act.

"Then let's go and check it out." Pretending she'd forgotten the man soaking in Collin's presence, eyes wide she looked over at Mason. "Oh, honey, would you like to see the suite too? I've heard it's gorgeous though not as big as the one in the main building." A part of her wished he would say no. Sure, it would hamper their plan, but she might wangle a couple interesting minutes with Collin.

Mason grinned big. "I'd be honored."

Disappointed but hiding it, she moved toward the door with the men close behind as two mammoth-sized shadows came out of nowhere and followed them into the hallway. She could think of several ways to get rid of the bodyguards but every method was loud and messy. So she tried a different tactic.

She turned to Mason. "Sugar, don't you think your boys

are really unnecessary. They would cramp our style, you could say. You know two's company, three's a ménage à trois, but four or more is a messy orgy, and we don't want that. This time." She raised her eyebrows in promise for the future.

Mason stopped and narrowed his eyes at her. Had she gone too far and was he on to her? When those pale eyes centered on Collin, she knew they had him.

"Boys, you can go back to the party and have the night off," Mason ordered.

The one with the shaved head raised a hand to plead. "But, Boss, you don't¾"

Mason interrupted. "Did I ask your opinion?"

They shook their heads and turned back to the party.

"Fuck. They have a room full of horny pit lizards and they want to argue." Mason leered at her breasts. "How much further?"

"We're on the floor above this one." Collin held the elevator door open as they entered. In seconds after they stepped off, he unlocked one of the double doors. The suite was immaculately decorated and opened onto a large terrace, giving the main room an airy feeling.

"Oh, honey, it's beautiful." Her hand glided over the back of a puffy sectional couch. "Would you gentlemen like a drink?" She headed for the bar.

"Wait!" She stopped in her tracks with Mason's bark. "Let's skip the unnecessary pleasantries. I want to see you kiss her again and make it hot." His demand was directed toward Collin.

Oh, ho, her boss man didn't like that but what reason could he make up to say no? To save the situation, she stepped between Mason and Collin.

111

"Show Mason how good of a kisser you are, sweetheart." She skimmed her hands over his chest and then around his neck. At first, his lips were unyielding as she savored the opportunity to kiss him again without fear of rejection.

"If that's the way you kiss your wife, no wonder she's looking at other men like they're all-day suckers. And I have a man-sized sucker here for her," Mason said as he rubbed his quite noticeable erection.

Crude as it was, Mason's derision was the kick Collin needed. He turned her head back to him and his mouth sunk onto hers as he thrust his tongue, taking her breath away by the forcefulness.

"Yeah, man, fuck her mouth good with your tongue. Give it to her." Mason moved in closer and Olivia really wished he would disappear. She needed more from the man kissing her and without an audience. Who knew how long Collin would play along with Mason?

Hands came up and cupped her breasts, but she knew Collin's hands were on her waist. Mason was getting impatient and Olivia wanted to throw up.

Collin released her and pushed her away. She stumbled back and laughed, wiping her mouth, pleased that the move caused Mason to drop his hands. Collin turned from her as if the kiss meant nothing. Maybe it hadn't. So much emotion, anger was behind the kiss and she liked it. A lot.

It was time for the boss man to be brought down a peg or two. "Which way to the ladies' room?" she asked with as much casualness she could muster.

Collin gave her a questioning look but pointed down a dark small hallway on the right.

"I'll be back," she said and then added, "You and Mason have a good time and I'll be back before you know it." She blew him a kiss and quickly stepped into the shadows. Not wanting to miss a thing, she peeked around the corner into the living room she'd just left.

Mason didn't waste any time. He grabbed Collin's crotch, massaging the shaft she loved feeling against her body and said something Olivia bet was even cruder than before. Instead of cussing and jerking away from Mason, Collin grinned in a way that sent cold chills down her spine and then his hand chopped the side of the man's neck. Mason dropped like a piano from a high-rise.

"Olivia, you can come out now." His voice sounded calm, even like he was unperturbed by her trick.

Not until she stood in front of him did she see his cold, furious look. Oh, damn, had she pushed him a tad too far? Then Mason groaned and a flash of embarrassment crossed Collin's face. Priceless. She burst out laughing.

Collin did what he'd become good at, he ignored her and bent over the man, rolling him onto his stomach. With a knee on Mason's back, he grasped his wrists. "Get the satchel behind the bar and hand me the handcuffs and rope."

Less than five minutes later, Mason was tied up. After a quick call by Collin, Rex and several other operatives entered from the terrace, wearing uniforms that proclaimed the best rug cleaners in Scottsdale. They rolled the man in one of the rugs and simply walked out of the hotel.

"Kind of like Cleopatra. Hey, why didn't you do that to me instead of that crappy drug and stupid stretcher?" Olivia poured herself a snifter of fine brandy from the bar and raised it to her lips as her gaze followed his movement across the room. Watching him had become her latest hobby.

"You were unplanned and there wasn't a rug in the

hotel room." He stopped in front of her and glowered. "Your little fun and games could've ruined the operation."

She tossed back the drink. The smooth liquor burned in a good way down her throat. "I knew you could handle it." Then she realized what she said and giggled. "Handle it! I guess Mason handled it too."

His impassive look bothered her more than she liked. She'd rather he stayed mad at her.

"Olivia." He lifted the glass out of her hand and sat it on the bar. "Your life depends on your following my direction."

Heat from his body drew her one step closer. "You're fond of threatening me." Her breasts flattened against his chest. "I think I intrigue you, make you want to find out what makes me tick." The last few words she said in a whisper near his ear. Her tongue gilded across the pulse at his neck and along his jaw line.

He smelled and tasted so good. Her heartbeat felt like it had stopped.

Then his fingers clutched her shoulders and held her away as he glared at her. He was always glaring at her. She tried her best to hold back the grin but one corner tilted up. The flare she loved seeing in his sinfully dark eyes burned with emotions he kept tightly in control. Then his mouth covered hers, tongue dipping and exploring. Her belly flipped and a tremor shot between her thighs, moistening their depths.

He released her so fast, she stumbled.

"Fuck you," he spit out. His chest heaved as he backed away.

Using one hand on the bar beside her, she regained her balance. "That's what I've been trying for days to get you to do." She couldn't manage a grin this time. She was dead serious. Never had she wanted a man so bad.

He didn't say a word, his gaze said it all. Though he'd teased her for months, for some crazy reason, she was unfuckable in his eyes. A ball of hurt congealed in her stomach. Motionless, she watched as he turned his back to her and strode out of the suite.

Chapter Twelve

Olivia stared at the stars as she floated in the water. The twinkling above was like white Christmas lights decorating the sky. A constant celebration of life. She wished she could fly up and touch them and escape this stupid world. She grinned at the whimsical thought so unlike her. Taking a deep breath, the heaviness in her chest lightened. All her cares disappeared as she drifted in the cool liquid. She loved the smell of chlorine and how it reminded her of the time before her foster mother had died and their days at the community pool.

At the edge of her memories, she fought back the dark ones and dunked her head in the water and quickly resurfaced. Floating at the outermost boundary she concentrated again on the sky above her.

She liked how the hotel's larger pool was far enough from the brightest lights, letting her enjoy the sky's natural light show. Several shooting stars burned short paths to earth. Music and people's conversations echoed across the large expanse. She leaned further back, letting the water fill her ears for a moment, muting all sound. That wasn't very smart considering she possibly had people hunting for her, wanting her dead. She didn't fool herself in believing The Circle wouldn't find out she was still alive. True, she needed to be alert at all times, but everyone needed a break from the world.

After she realized Collin didn't want her help in searching Mason's suite, she decided to put on the swimsuit OS had supplied her for the trip. The turquoise one-piece clung to her body in ways that made it almost more indecent to wear than any of the itty-bitty two pieces she owned.

Looking down at her nipples thrusting against the clingy material as water poured out of her ears, she wondered what Collin would think of the suit? Would he like to run his hands over the silky cloth and thumb the hard nubs begging for his touch? He probably would and then get mad when she wanted more from him.

Releasing a sigh, she shook her head. His hot-cold routine was wearing thin. She had no idea what his problem was, but she did know she would have to find a way to quench her hunger. So far, self-gratification wasn't getting it. She really wanted Collin and no one else. Anyway, if she'd been inclined to go elsewhere, none of his people were brave enough to fuck her.

A burst of laughter drew her attention to the other end of the pool. The party had spilled out onto the patio. From the corner of her eye, she caught movement near a palm tree. She swam silently to the shadows and watched a couple stroll toward a cabana a good distance from the party, mere feet from her. She heard the woman giggle as the man reassured her they were alone. Before Olivia knew it, she was front and center to the couple stripping. The man pressed the woman face first over a chair and then he mounted her. Their grunts and moans, groin slapping buttocks, had her breasts aching and her hand covering the clenching need between her thighs.

Damn, she really didn't need this. Diving into the warm water, she remained close to the bottom until she reached the ladder on the other side. She grabbed the white towel she'd left on a nearby lounge chair and wrapped it around her. Chill bumps covered every inch of her body. Arizona temperatures at night dipped quick and low. She slung her hair over one shoulder and twisted as she walked toward the suite. Mason's bodyguards wouldn't look for their boss until daylight and they would be long gone by then.

She skirted around several couples, admiring one man's muscular frame. He was as tall as Jason Kastler and had sun-kissed blond hair like his too.

"Christ," she bit off as she stepped behind a pillar, her gaze darting around the patio, looking to see who was working with him. Surely everyone could see her heart knocking against her chest. She peeked at Jason again. Who was he decoying for?

He laughed and leaned over a brunette, his back to Olivia. Without risking a moment more, she darted into the nearest doorway. Taking long strides, she worked at looking like a person set on a certain path but not truly running. And goodness she wanted to run. Though she'd teased Jason while reporting to him, he could be deadly when provoked and he would be none too happy with her defection.

The cool air in the suite brought out more chill bumps as she stepped into the foyer and leaned against the wall. Strips of light shining through the vertical blinds broke up the floor and gave the room a closed in feeling. One step forward moved her from the cold slate floor to the carpet.

Her bare feet sank into the thickness and she curled her toes.

Her attention caught the darker shadow in the chair. "I saw Jason Kastler," she said, proud her voice stayed even and low.

Collin stood. "Where were you?" His deep voice was steady with a thread of menace twined in.

She dropped the towel. "Enjoying the pool."

Though she couldn't see his eyes, her body sensed them drift down to her breasts and hard nipples.

"You were taking a chance on Mason's people seeing you." He stopped so close she felt the heat blasting from his body.

She pressed her chest to his. "They never looked at my face and their eyes never stray from what's cold and warming against your delicious body as I speak." A little shimmy of her shoulders emphasized what she meant.

His big hands clasped both sides of her head, holding her still as his lips came to hers. "You keep pushing and you'll regret what you start." He slammed his mouth over hers, thrusting his tongue deep and she answered with her own. His earlier refusal forgotten in the heat of their kiss.

Moaning when his hot hands cupped her cool breasts, she bowed her back, hoping he wouldn't push her away as he had so many times. His fingers bunched up the material and jerked, the top section fell to her waist. Hard hands covered her naked swollen breasts and massaged them. Between her thighs a heavy throbbing sensation warned her she was about to come. How did he arouse her merely by touching her breasts? His head dipped. Using lips and teeth he tugged at the sensitive tips, then sucked hard, pushing the nubs with his tongue against the roof of his mouth. One hand clasped her mons and pressed. That was all it took. She whimpered, trying to hold it back but unable to resist. The man's hands were deadly and gifted.

With one hand she pushed her swimsuit to her ankles and kicked it off. She shifted one leg between his and rubbed her groin on his thigh. He inhaled and stood straight.

<<<>>>

Collin struggled to regain control of the situation. Damn! The naked woman rubbed against him like a cat in heat and he liked the hell out of it—wanted to throw her on the floor and fuck her like the animal she brought out of him.

Steeling himself, he took a deep breath and shoved her shoulders to the wall, keeping his pulsating cock away from her.

"I've been waiting for you. Don't leave like that again. It'll be daylight in less than an hour. His guards will be looking for him not long after sunrise. If we don't move now, we'll be fighting our way out," he warned. Remembering what she'd told him, he added, "Jason Kastler and The Circle are the last of my worries."

She leaned toward him. "Then a quickie it is."

He jerked away from her touch. "Enough. Get your clothes on." Instead of protesting as he expected, she shrugged and sauntered into one of the bedrooms.

Bending over, hands on knees, he sucked in the cool air. He needed his cock to soften enough to walk without hurting. The woman was remarkable. She possessed more guts than ten men and she turned him on faster than a light switch. His plan to keep her interested in him to control her was backfiring. He chuckled. He had a hell of a time keeping his mind on business whenever she drew near.

Standing straight, his body eased enough for him to move, he pulled out his cell and keyed in a number. As soon as the person answered, he demanded, "What in the hell are you doing here?"

"Hey, man, I've got to go where my master sends me," Jason said in his good-old-boy voice. The line was quiet for a few seconds and then he added, "Meet me in the seventh cabana near the Canyon pool. I've got some news for you."

Collin pressed a key to cut the connection. He glanced toward the bathroom. The sound of water hitting tile tipped him off that he had fifteen minutes tops.

Less than five minutes later he stood in the shadows of one of the many bright yellow and orange tents lining the edge of the pool. The sharp smell of chlorine tickled his nose. One second he was alone and the next a dark shape walked up.

"How's it going, old friend?" Jason held his hand out.

Collin shook his hand briefly. "As well as can be expected." He eyed the tall man. "How are you feeling?"

"Another day closer to death." Jason looked away for a second.

Nodding, Collin understood he'd rather not talk about the cancer eating at his body. "I need to get back. What do you have for me?" The tall man standing in front of him had been a mole for the OS from the beginning of the split. For Jason to want to meet face to face, it had to be something important.

"The news at The Circle is that Olivia isn't dead." Jason crossed his arms and pursed his lips as he looked down at the cement beneath his feet.

"What details do they know?" Collin watched the door

to the hotel, hoping not to see Olivia or any early risers exit. The place was nearly deserted with parties over and everyone passed out in their beds.

"Someone said her favorite orphanage had a healthy influx of funds. They had already suspected the OS had something to do with her disappearance." Olivia's ex-handler stuck his hands into his front pockets.

Normally such a move would make Collin nervous, but he trusted Jason with his life. They'd grown up together and always had a connection like brothers.

"Fuck. Does everyone know about the orphanage?" Collin asked. He shook his head. Olivia would be horrified if she knew her secret hadn't been much of one.

"No. Just me and Theo. Theo is a little paranoid about his women and especially one as deadly as Olivia." Jason checked the clock on his cell phone. "For now, he's searching for Joe Murphy. Did you know there's at least ten thousand Joe Murphys in the U.S. alone?" Not expecting an answer, he added, "I've got to go. Be aware, someone in your organization is giving out tidbits of information. I haven't had any luck finding the person's name. The info is being channeled directly to the top. It's only a matter of time before Theo believes his informant and then who knows what he'll do? If it had been anyone else, he'd send out a contract for a hit, but in this case it will be more personal and he'll want her to have a slow and lingering death. That's the kind of man he is."

"Yeah. I know." Damn, he really thought they would have more time. "Take care of yourself."

"You watch your back. And remember your promise. When it's time, you'll do it quick. Maybe you can use it to your advantage." The operative stared hard at his old friend.

Collin nodded his confirmation without saying another

word. Then Jason slipped out and headed around to the front of the hotel, jumping over a short fence along the way.

Collin waited a moment longer and then entered the hotel through the entrance near the pool. He needed a few minutes to come to terms with his friend's imminent death from such a cruel disease. As soon as he walked into the suite, he knew something was wrong. The whirl of an electronic device starting up filled the room and a small green light bounced off the wall and then disappeared. He guessed it was now dancing on his back.

"Olivia, what the hell do you think you're doing?" He raised his hands and slowly turned around.

Feet spread apart, dressed in black with a sporty red trim jacket, she held the sniper rifle they'd recently returned to her and forwarded to the hotel in several containers. He'd been impressed by its microcomputer, perfect for shooting in any kind of weather. Presently she had one eye to the night sight. Damn, the woman was stronger than he gave her credit for as she was holding, elbows out, an eighteen-pound rifle and it barely moved. "You do know from this close of a range my torso would disintegrate into a hundred thousand tiny pieces, spreading blood and me everywhere in the room."

"Like I care," she spit with menace. Her hand trembled and the barrel wobbled.

"Can we talk about whatever has set you off?" He hadn't expected her to become so angry about his turning her down.

She shifted the rifle against her cheek, probably easing up a tight muscle. "I thought this job was too easy. What was the real reason I'm here? Have you worked out some type of trade with Jason?"

Damn! He didn't need this now. The sun was peeking

around Camelback Mountain. They needed to get out of there.

"No. You'll have to trust me." He was a crazy fucker because all he could think about was how damn good she looked holding that rifle.

"Oh, that makes a world of difference. Not!" She made another adjustment of the pad next to her cheek. "You get me all hot and bothered and then ignore me. You never finish what you start and I can't¾" As she crumbled to the ground, Rex caught the rifle.

"Motherfucker! What were you thinking? You're going to fuck around until she kills you? Bloody hell! There wouldn't be anything left for me to pick up." Rex started breaking down the rifle, slapping each part into the shaking hands of one of his men.

Collin knelt next to Olivia, pressing two fingers to the artery in her neck. His heartbeat matched hers as it continued to speed up.

"What did you shoot her with?" Collin asked as he smoothed her hair out of her face.

"The same as you did before. Twilight." Rex sneered.

"Damn, she's going to be pissed again. We can't keep knocking her out." Collin scooped her into his arms. "Let's go. Thank goodness we've got a private plane back."

"I'm all for dumping her out over Texas." Rex followed, leaving the cleanup for his crew.

"Now what has Texas ever done to you?"

Rex's laughter bounced off the high ceiling and turned the head of the clerk behind the desk as they walked through the lobby.

Shifting her weight one more time in his arms, Collin nonchalantly headed toward the waiting limo. No one stopped or questioned him about carrying an unconscious woman. Handing out a few grand to a couple of employees helped. Anyway, what was one more passed-out partyer to the hotel?

Collin settled Olivia in the backseat with her head in his lap. Her face relaxed and pale, she looked younger. He lifted her hand and kissed a finger, the same one that had been on the trigger. Thank goodness, she was a pro. Otherwise, she could've accidentally killed him. No matter what she intended to tell him when she woke up. She'd been more upset about his refusal to sleep with her than she was worried about his betrayal.

He chuckled. But would she ever admit she had a soft spot for him?

Chapter Thirteen

Olivia stared at Collin as he interrogated Mason. He was driving her absolutely nuts. When she'd woken up in the hospital bed again, he'd merely said, "No. We're not trading you," and then walked away. She'd been pissed and wanted to teach him a lesson, but until she found a way, she'd wait for an opportunity.

In the meanwhile, he'd been telling the truth. She remained at the OS, watching Collin drill Mason on where the artifact was and who had it. What was so important about an old sword anyway?

The door behind her opened and in the reflection of the glass separating the two rooms, Rex hesitated, making it obvious he hadn't known she was in the observation room. Kind of sweet, the way he eyed her with distrust instead of his usual out-and-out hatred. Per the OS grapevine, Collin had given Rex a stern talking to about his attitude toward her. She wasn't sure why Collin thought it necessary, even though it did make working with Rex tolerable. Like that would actually stop Big Foot from trying to kill her. Anyway, she still owed him for knocking her out twice, once with his fist and the latest with drugs.

"Come on in and have a seat." She waved her hand to the uncomfortable metal torture devices they called chairs.

"So Mason still hasn't broke?" he asked the obvious.

In her attempt to get along with Collin's second in command, she stopped the smart-alecky comment she wanted to make and merely shook her head. "In the last three days, I've been tempted to confess to anything, even in knowing where Jimmy Hoffa's body is just to make Collin stop. I don't know how Mason's not giving it up."

Rex turned, forehead furrowed. "You know where his body is?"

Cutting her eyes over to the big man, she sighed. "No. I was making a funny."

He blushed. "There were rumors that The Circle had a hand in that. So I thought Theo may have ... never mind." He turned the chair and straddled it, placing his arms across the back. "Mason's the hardest nut for Collin to crack in a long time."

"Nut is a good word to use. The guy's crazy." Hand under chin and elbow on her knee, staring at Rex, she asked, "Why's the artifact so important?"

"Partly because it used to belong to Benjamin Ryker."

"Collin's dad?" she asked, watching Rex suck on his bottom lip in deep thought before dipping his head. "Oh. How did it leave the family?"

"Not really sure. I do know the red diamond in the pommel is worth a pretty tidy sum. But the story is, 'whoever owns the sword will control The Circle.' A bunch of shit if I've ever heard." He snorted and glared at Mason in the next room. "That idiot either found a way into The Circle's Main Sector or had inside help and took it. Thankfully we caught him before he could sell it to the highest bidder." A crooked grin lit his features. "I bet Theo's fit to be tied." Rex darted a concerned look at her.

"No. I don't care what you think. I don't have a direct line to Theo." His apprehension made sense. She'd been an eliminator for The Circle. What Rex didn't know was Theo treated her as he did any woman. Like she didn't have the sense to get out of the way of a speeding bullet, thus she was expendable. Though she had as much freedom as any male operative, she'd known at any time he could order her eliminated and not blink an eye in regret.

Eyeing the red-headed maniac, she wondered how he heard about Theo's sword. During her time as Theo's mistress, she'd seen his collection of medieval artifacts. He loved that collection more than anyone's life. But she didn't remember a sword with a red diamond or Theo mentioning one.

The door on the other side of the interrogation room opened and Dr. Shelton walked in carrying a small tray with a white cloth covering it. Collin spoke to her and exited.

Olivia stood and leaned back against the far wall with her arms crossed, not feeling comfortable being alone with a psycho. Her gaze darted to the door as she expected Collin to return any second.

The doctor took Mason's blood pressure and checked his pulse, ignoring the man's obscenities. When she pulled out a large syringe, his face turned red as he struggled with the cuffs holding him in the chair. Suddenly one of the cuffs opened and he backhanded the doc.

Slamming her body into the door, Olivia darted to the other side of the interrogation room before Mason could work free of the last handcuff. Out of the corner of her eye, she caught Rex rushing in behind her.

With a smooth, powerful kick, her foot landed square in the middle of Mason's chest, pushing him against the wall away from the doctor on the floor. "Get Shelton out of the way!" she shouted at Rex. The room was too small for all four of them to maneuver.

When Rex hesitated, she knew they would be in trouble if she couldn't convince him to leave. "I can hold this asshole off until you move her out of the way." She blocked his attempt to grab her.

"This asshole is going to have your heart for supper," Mason shouted. His spittle sprayed her and ticked her off. Who knew what type of germs the jerk had? She remembered the disgusting way he'd mauled her at the party.

"For God's sakes man, say it, don't spray it," she jeered. By the look he gave her, a person would believe she'd called his mama a whore. He yelled and leaped at her. She took a deep breath and kneed him in the balls as his hands touched her neck.

A loud "humph" and the foulest gust of air brushed passed her. Luckily she moved to the side as Mason vomited on the floor and then followed it face first, landing in his own filth.

"The bitch has sent my nuts to my spleen," Mason said in a high-pitched voice.

"What in the hell is going on in here?" Collin stood in the doorway, arms crossed, scowling at her.

"Hey, don't look at me. He started it." She pointed to Mason. The man had rolled over onto his back with his knees to his chest. His regurgitated supper smeared from face to knees.

"Rex, give Dr. Shelton over to Rick." The bald orderly

stepped around Mason and took her from the big guy. "Take Mason to the showers and clean him up. Get someone to help and keep a gun on him. Then you can do what's needed to make him talk. I'm tired of fooling with his ass." The other orderly stood nearby Mason holding a Glock two-fisted, arms straight out. Collin returned his attention to Olivia. She really wished he hadn't. The man looked as if he would love nothing better than to dump her cold, lifeless body in a ravine. "You." He jerked his head toward the door.

Did he really believe she would meekly do as he said? Hell, no! She hadn't gotten to be The Circle's lead eliminator without some guts.

"Is this how you thank the person who saved your precious doctor's life?" Hands on hips, she huffed.

That was when her stomach protested the horrible smell in the tiny space. A clammy and cold feeling washed her face. If she didn't get out of here, she wouldn't be responsible for what happened next.

"Olivia?" Collin reached for her and she stepped back not wanting to be sick on him. She clamped her mouth shut, in effort to hold her stomach back by not breathing anymore of the foul air.

When he scowled at her, she knew he misunderstood her reaction.

She closed her eyes hoping that would help, instead the earth shifted and she swallowed, instantly regretting it. Her knees buckled, but then a light-headedness engulfed her, causing her to feel like she was floating on air.

Unable to hold her breath any longer, she tentatively inhaled. It was fresh and clean. Warmth flooded one side of her body. She opened her eyes. He'd picked her up and they were in the hallway. Collin looked down at her in his arms, his dark eyes filled with worry. She liked that, him worrying about her. Had anyone ever worried about her except in how she would kill them? Why did she have to ruin her vulnerable moment with that thought?

He continued to carry her, turning several corners and causing her stomach to roil with each turn. The OS was a freaking maze. They came to a huge double door she'd never seen before. At least eight feet wide and definitely castle worthy. He stopped next to a box on the wall, shifted her until she leaned against him and the wall. He then spread his hand on the glass, a blue beam flowed down his palm, and with a two-tone beep the doors drifted open.

"I'm okay now. I can walk." She'd enjoyed being in his arms, but the feminist side of her said to protest.

The man had his ignoring routine down to an art. When he picked her up and stepped into the huge room, she gasped. It *was* a fucking castle. Or at the least, it wouldn't be out of place in any stone and mortar stronghold a person could find in freaking England. Heavy furniture and tapestries everywhere with gargoyles of all types and sizes. What was up with that? Did he have a fetish for them?

"You can put me down now. I feel better. I won't barf on your ... my God! Is that a silk Persian rug?" she asked, her eyes wide and disbelieving.

She stared at the beautiful brown and blue design as they left the room. He hadn't hesitated when they walked over it, but she recognized it. One similar to it was sold by Christie's a few years ago. She'd wanted it so much but the bidding had reached a few more million than she had.

The wide hallway was lined with shelves that lit up as they walked by. Displayed on the glass were *objets d'art* that appeared old and rare.

Using his shoulder, he opened another wooden door

about half the size of the first set. The bedroom was as large as her suite. In the center sat a huge bed covered with a royal blue comforter and several matching pillows. She'd expected the bed to be on a platform and drapery all around it, considering the tone of what she'd seen so far. Though large, the bed looked normal and almost out of place. She checked the ceiling. No mirrors but a beautiful mural of stars and a quarter moon were painted realistically.

Instead of dropping her in the middle of the bed, he continued to a small door off to the side. Inside was a well-appointed bathroom consisting of a separate shower and bath, and a double sink, mirrors everywhere, and another door that probably led to the toilet. The man didn't believe in doing anything halfway.

He released her legs, letting her body slide down his. Oh, yeah, she liked that. She was all better. Wanting to taste those stern lips again, she leaned in. He stepped back.

Her body shivered. How much more of his teasing could she take? Either she would lose her mind and kill him or maybe she would get over her obsession. With his masculine good looks, broad shoulders, and the dangerous amber glint in his dark eyes, how could she not be half way in love with him?

Oh, hell.

Chapter Fourteen

Olivia stumbled and leaned back against the countertop in the bathroom. She needed to pull herself together. Being around him all the time almost drove her crazy and just because he acted like he cared. She needed to remember who he was, the master controller of the OS. Everything he did was for the greater good of his organization. And men were assholes. She was a grown kid from a trash bin. She was a killer. Those were facts. She liked facts. She could deal with facts. Ah, hell, she was falling apart.

Collin pulled out a cloth and soaked it with cool water from the silver faucet. While one large hand cupped her cheek, he used the other to wipe her forehead with gentle strokes and then follow a trickle of water to her neck. "Does that feel better?"

Only able to manage a nod, she closed her eyes. Had anyone ever taken such tender care of her?

The cool cloth worked its way over her collarbone. He pulled down the crewneck of her T-shirt and swiped the top of her breasts. Her nipples hardened. Then the cloth swept up and over to the back of her neck as he lifted her hair.

She shivered.

"Cold?" he asked.

"No." It felt like ages since he'd last kissed her. Those lips of his were made to lick, bite, and suck on. Full but firm like the sensual man he'd proven to be to her.

Without touching him anywhere else, she tilted her head up and kissed him. Light and soft like he'd kissed her the first time. She no longer felt the cool cloth. He clasped her body to his, lifting her until her toes barely touched the floor as he took over the kiss. She loved how he invaded her mouth and wanted more. His hips ground against hers. He was hard and she loved it. On remembering what he'd done to her that first night, hell for that matter the night in Phoenix, she decided turnabout was fair play.

She wiggled until her feet were flat on the floor again. Her hands slipped down until she held shaft and balls through his slacks. Pleased by the way he hesitated in sucking on her tongue, such a turn-on, she massaged until he swelled bigger and harder beneath her hands. With an ease she hadn't expected, he allowed her to unzip and unbuckle him. When she finally had his hot flesh in her hands, she squeezed enough to make him gasp in her mouth. Oh, yeah, he liked a little roughness. She'd guessed right.

She shrugged her shoulders and pulled away enough to run her tongue along his strong jaw. Then she slid down his body to her knees.

He was beautiful, long and thick, not too much of a good thing. She loved men's cocks and understood why they loved playing with them so much. She did too. Hot and hard, she rubbed her cheek along his length.

"Dammit, woman, put me in your mouth and suck." His voice guttural, almost sounding as if he was in pain.

Grinning, she licked the tip and savored the muskiness that was uniquely his. Unhappy with her dawdling, his fingers clutched a handful of hair and pulled back until she was looking up at him.

"Just having you on your knees nearly makes me come, but I want that beautiful mouth sucking my cock hard now." His amber eyes flared so bright they almost frightened her. That just made her hotter to have him in her mouth, to show him what he had to be afraid of.

She took him as far as she could with one pull. Then using all the skills taught to her by Theo, she proceeded to give him a blow job he'd never experienced. His cock hit the back of her throat as she breathed slowly through her nose. Before she knew it, she was becoming even more excited by the moans Collin emitted. The best part was that she could tell by the foul words he used, he resented like hell his need for her touch. His fingers held her head but didn't guide her. Her fingers caressed and rubbed his balls and then slipped to a special sensitive spot between his cock and anus. When he was about to come, she pinched him.

"Fuck!" Without pulling away from her mouth, he leaned down and grabbed her arm, squeezing hard. "Don't do that again." Her mouth stretched in a way he would know she was grinning. "I mean it, Olivia."

Oh, the bigger they were, the harder they came. Still grinning around his cock, she took a long hard pull, thrust a finger into his anus and he exploded at the same time. He shouted and slammed a fist onto the countertop behind her, jabbing his cock deep into her mouth until he was limp.

Faster than she'd ever seen him move, he jerked her to

her feet. "Damn you, won't you listen? You're always pushing it."

She laughed and then he covered her mouth with his as his hand yanked her zipper down. He ate at her mouth as if he loved tasting himself on her lips and tongue. Then he plunged his hand between her legs and jammed two fingers into her wet cunt. One knuckle rubbed the small knot of nerves as he thrust another finger into her. Just having a part of him in her, even if it wasn't the part she craved, had her hips meeting his touch and when he whispered, "Come for me," she screamed against his mouth as wave after wave shook her body and she continued to tremble for several seconds more.

Before she could recover, he turned her to face the bathroom mirror. Her lips were swollen from his rough kisses. Her eyes shone with unshed tears and her hair mussed from his hands, she looked soft and feminine and well used. Never had she looked more like a woman and it all was brought about by the man studying her with his dark eyes.

Seconds ticked by and nothing was said; no movement was made. Then he shifted, sweeping her hair out of the way, and kissed her neck. She tilted her head and closed her eyes. The tenderness in his touch was more than she could handle from him. Abuse and anger she understood. She'd grown up with such attitudes, but the look in his eyes before his lips met her skin, they were filled with awe and nothing about her was worthy of such a look.

"Let's fuck," she said.

His eyes narrowed as his face flushed in anger. Oddly, even though she wanted the tender look gone, she mourned the loss. She'd only disappoint him. She leaned back into his hard body.

When her gaze met his again in the mirror, she caught the softness of pity. No way would she let him or anybody feel sorry for her. She was what she was and had come to terms with it years ago.

"Well?" she asked, expecting him to turn her down and she wasn't disappointed.

He released her and stepped away. "Get dressed. We have somewhere we need to be."

She turned facing him. "What is wrong with you? You like my body and I like yours. So why do you never want to fuck me?" From the way his lips straightened and the grooves on both sides of his mouth deepened she could tell her question bothered him. Was it really the question or that she asked it at all? Or maybe he was one of those prudes who hated to hear a woman swear.

Knowing she was about to poke an angry lion with a short stick, she smiled. "Did I find out your secret? You like boys?"

His head snapped up and his hands stopped arranging his semi-hard cock in his jeans. Then he laughed. A belly full, body-rich laugh. "You would like that. Then you'd think you're safe from me."

"There has to be a reason you haven't fucked me." She grinned back.

"Who says I haven't?" He didn't even look at her when he said that.

That wiped off her grin. She knew of men who loved screwing a limp unconscious woman. He had to be teasing her. Right?

After he zipped his pants and snapped them, he looked at her with one eyebrow raised.

She was still standing with her jeans open and riding

low on her hips. Her face warmed. He made her feel like a schoolgirl having her first tryst in the boys' locker room.

"Go. Put on a pretty dress for me. We're going out." He chuckled and walked into his bedroom leaving her to figure out what in the hell just happened.

Chapter Fifteen

Ticked didn't quite describe how she felt at the moment. After the little episode in the interrogation room and the sequential hot moment in his bathroom, he'd barely said a word to her. After thirty minutes of driving she'd insisted on knowing where they were going.

"Shut up and relax" was all he said in the most blasé way.

She sat across from him in the limo and raised her eyebrows. One red stiletto encased foot traveled up his leg and then toed him between his thighs until her heel rested against his crotch.

"Excuse me?" she asked, her tone threatening and reminding him of his manners.

His hand circled her ankle and lifted, taking her shoe off. He kissed the bottom of her foot and blew on the instep before he played Prince Charming and slipped her shoe back where it belonged. Then he placed her foot beside him, his hand still around her ankle. Smart man. Otherwise, her heel would find itself in his groin.

"Please be patient," he said, his voice husky and low.

Though she wanted to move a few inches away from his warm touch, she remained still. She'd already tested his temper by wearing black pants with a beautiful frilly white blouse instead of the requested dress. She hated wearing dresses. They made her feel helpless. She despised that feeling and he knew it. If not for his sexy grin, she'd have slapped him.

His amber eyes glittered with humor as if he knew what she was thinking. Unable to move her gaze from his, he lifted one dark eyebrow. His look turned her common sense into ash. Nothing else could explain how she'd fallen, even partially, in love with him. The possibility scared her. She might as well stab herself in the heart and be done with it. Frustrated with her unwanted feelings, she stared off at the passing streetlights, determined to appear unaffected by his machinations.

A couple times she tried to ease from his grip but his long fingers held on. She'd almost reached the limit of her temper and told him to go to hell when the limo pulled up to her favorite restaurant. How could she not forgive him? When it came to dining, the man knew how to treat a lady.

Well, that was what she thought until after they'd eaten and he decided to take a little walk in the park. She'd sensed he was up to no good at the restaurant. He'd acted as if they were a normal couple. Who in their right mind would believe that?

"Tell me again why we're out here?" Olivia swiped at a bug trying to nest in her hair as they waited near the reflecting pool in the Centennial Olympic Park. She squirmed on the metal bench. The thing was hard and colder than a dead frog.

Collin reached over and flicked another bug off her

blouse. "We're meeting my contact out here. He claims to have more information about the sword."

She crossed her arms and watched the water bubbling up next to the pool.

The wind had picked up, mussing Collin's hair. He looked younger with it falling in his eyes. She fisted her hands. The urge to touch his silky, thick hair ate at her.

"When is your freaking contact going to show up?" She swatted at a mosquito.

<<<>>>

Collin's gaze moved to the woman standing nearby. Though she tried to hide her excitement in being with him, her flushed cheeks and shining eyes gave her away. She was unlike any woman he'd ever met. No way could he say his life was boring, especially the past month. Nothing about Olivia was dull. She fascinated him. Like a snake charmer fascinated a cobra. Now the question was, was he the snake charmer or the cobra?

"As always trouble follows you wherever you go." Jason stepped out of the shadows, nodded at Collin and took a furtive look at Olivia.

Collin found Olivia's reaction to Jason's presence and her realization he was their contact most interesting. Eyebrows raised, she crossed her arms, bending a knee and resting on one hip as her mouth stretched in a bitter line.

"It's good to see Collin didn't kill you." Jason stepped a little nearer.

"Jason, you might want to refrain from getting any closer." Collin rubbed his chin, trying not to grin when Olivia dropped her arms and straightened.

"Olivia understands. Don't you, sweetheart." The tall man moved within a yard of her.

"I wondered how they could've known where to find me in Seattle and how they knew about the orphanage. I told you about the orphanage in a moment of weakness. You used me. You betrayed me, you lying filthy cock-sucking asshole!" Her kick shot out and barely missed as he leaned back, his long hair almost touching the ground. Collin was happy to see the man's illness hadn't hampered his ability to defend himself. In an unexpected move, she twisted and her fist came down on his hip. Jason was faster, luckily for him; otherwise, he'd be on the ground in a fetal position, crying.

"Damn it, Olivia! That wasn't fair. It could've killed me." Jason limped a few feet from her, eyeing her with hurt. "I take back that I was happy to see you alive."

"Reunions are such magical times," Collin murmured. "Olivia, sit over there and wait if you cannot play nice."

His stomach and groin tightened. He liked the look she gave him. For the next day or two he'd better watch his back. In fact, for the last three days he'd expected her to find a way to make him pay for not fucking her in Phoenix and now he added the more recent rendezvous in his bedroom. The woman's hormones were her weakness. For now he was a challenge to her.

Though he'd noticed her watching him with a look of puzzlement, as if he didn't fall in a mold she was familiar with, other times her gaze would soften and a dreamy look would come to her face. Those times bothered him. He didn't need her in love with him. From what he'd heard and learned of her, he'd never guessed she would be susceptible to such a useless emotion. Surprisingly, she followed his orders and gracefully sat on the bench, turning her back to them.

"You asked for this meeting. We need to leave before someone wonders what we're doing out here." When he noticed Jason staring at Olivia, Collin gritted his teeth. His jaw popped as he brought his need to hit his old friend under control. "Jason," he bit off.

"She's never minded anyone like that. Everyone's scared of Theo's temper, but that had never stopped her from smarting off to him. How did you do it? I thought no one could tame her." His blond head shook in disbelief as he waited for Collin's answer.

His friend truly didn't mean anything by his comments but the thought of anyone trying to tame Olivia was laughable. That wildness and her constant unpredictability was what he loved about her. Love? Maybe too strong of a word. He shut away that crazy thought and pointed a finger at Jason. "You're stalling."

"Sorry, man. I hate to tell you but the sword is back in Theo's possession." His tone said it all. No way would they reach it now.

"We have Mason. So how did he find out where it was?"

"It appears two of his cohorts decided they wanted the money for themselves and not the cause. They sold it back to Theo. Their bodies washed up on the beach in Pensacola this morning."

"Theo doesn't play around." Collin clenched his fists. "Did he take it back to the Main Sector?"

His friend nodded.

"Do you know if he put it in the safe in his rooms or the main vault?" Collin asked.

"I'm not sure about his personal safe, but it's not in the organization's vault. It would be recorded if he'd locked it up there. Probably his rooms then." Jason pursed his lips and looked down. "I'm not sure if I can help you. The vault,

I might have, but his rooms are too secure. He won't allow anyone but his current mistress in there, and she's too scared of him to try anything. Only Olivia's been in his bedroom and come out alive."

"Yeah." He hated to imagine Olivia catering to that psycho.

Collin had heard Theo bought his latest mistress when she turned nine from her drug-addicted parents. The man didn't deserve to live.

Theo had been unstable for years and continued to grow more so each day, so his fixation on the sword would be useful. Certainly the weapon was old and priceless, but Theo was convinced that if he lost possession of the sword The Circle would be destroyed. He considered himself to be a modern-day King Arthur and the sword his Excalibur. The sword was the thread in releasing Theo from his uncertain grip of reality. His weakness would provide the perfect opportunity for Collin to take over The Circle.

The sword might be the final thread, but Olivia was the scissors.

He glanced her way. Would she be willing to break into the Main Sector and steal the sword from underneath Theo's nose for the OS?

Chapter Sixteen

Olivia hit the bag with her foot again but harder. Imagining Collin's face on it helped tremendously with her focus. She'd been with the OS for five months and gone on one and a half missions. The walk in the park to meet Jason couldn't be counted as a full mission. What was the purpose for the OS to bring her in if they didn't need her? The role of arm-candy for Collin could be filled by any number of OS operatives she'd seen. Her talents were being wasted. For that matter, he'd been scarce and she hated how she missed his company.

She slammed her foot into the dangling bag one more time before switching to the other.

"How about a partner?"

Well, if it wasn't the man himself. She leaned over and pulled a towel from the handlebars of a nearby stationary bike. Wiping at the sweat on her forehead and neck, she eyed the head of OS.

Collin wore sweatpants as he had the last time he'd practiced with her, but these clung a little tighter, possibly an older pair. Instead of a sleeveless sweatshirt, he wore a black T-shirt. The cotton material stretched across his pecs in a way that made her mouth water. She could imagine running her hands over the broad cliff of his chest to the rippled abs she knew were below.

"Sure, if you think you're up to it." She tossed the towel back onto the handlebars.

"If I remember from last time, you were the one having trouble keeping face-first off the floor." He lifted one eyebrow as his lips fought a grin.

"Oh, it's going to be like that. Talking all that smack. Let's see if you like the smell of mat sweat." Her heartbeat picked up speed. Having him touch her even in mock fighting was better than the nothing she'd gotten for so long.

They moved into their fighting stances and Collin struck first. Hands and feet shot out in quick succession as grunts marked each hit. Minutes passed and she held her own as determination guided every movement until he pushed her to retaliate in the same fury. She wanted to show him a little of why she'd been so valuable to The Circle.

"Collin, I need to talk you now," Rex's deep voice came from the side.

Just as Collin turned his head to look at his second in command, Olivia, already in the midst of a punch, thrust the heel of her palm into the middle of his sternum.

Collin staggered back, wheezing from the unexpected hit.

"Bitch!" Rex bellowed and lunged for her.

With a twirl and side kick, she swiped his hands away before he could touch her. She stepped off the mat. Hands on hips, chest heaving, she grimaced.

"You know, you've got a nasty habit of interrupting us

whenever we're practicing!" She sneered, making it obvious she wanted him to try something.

Hand held out, Collin moved between them, his face pale and drawn tight. "No! I knew better than to let myself get distracted."

With concern, she watched Collin rub his chest. "Are you okay?"

"I'm good." He took a deep breath and flinched.

"Get Dr. Shelton!" she said to a nearby attendant.

"No! I'm okay." Collin shook his head. "What's up, Rex?"

Knowing she probably should leave them alone but worried about his condition, she stayed and offered him a bottle of water. He unconsciously grinned and thanked her for it as he listened to Rex.

"Let's go in your office." Rex gave Olivia an angry look. "She'd better come too. She's part of it."

Unsure what set off Big Foot again, she waited to see if Collin agreed. This was too much like the last time they had exercised and Rex had interrupted. Was it finally a new mission? She could use a break in the monotony of her new life at the OS.

He stared at Rex for a few seconds. "Okay. Let's go." Then they headed down the hallway to his office. Collin hadn't looked her way. Her gut said it wasn't a mission. To think of it, Rex appeared too satisfied about something.

Olivia didn't move. She hated the thought of just following them without protest. Nothing in Collin's attitude encouraged her to believe he would protect her from Rex and whatever the man had on his mind. But if she didn't follow, he could accuse her of anything and she would never have a chance to take up for herself. Rex had said it concerned her.

She jogged to catch up with them.

No sooner than they walked into Collin's office, Collin faced Rex, eyes narrowed. "What have you heard?"

Olivia remained standing, forcing her fingers to relax their grip on the sides of her sweatpants.

"We've gotten news that The Circle will hand over two of our operatives if we release her." Rex jerked his head toward Olivia.

She cut her eyes over to Big Foot and sighed. "The Circle doesn't take operatives captive." There had to be a misunderstanding. The Circle always released the operatives after taking their weapons. Then again, her former organization had told her the OS murdered many of the operatives she'd seen walking around breathing and living in the OS headquarters, like Lucian. The look she received from the men warned her she was in for a long night. She flopped into a chair and her muscles eased up, thanking her for the relief.

"Yeah. I know. They usually kill them." Rex stood, arms crossed, next to the desk as Collin sat in the large black leather chair behind it.

"We don't take them captive or kill them. We let them go." We? Old habits were hard to break. Anyway, what were they trying to pull? Collin's grave face showed he didn't believe what she was saying. While Rex's became redder with each word as she defended her former employer, "I've never killed an OS operative."

Before all the words were out of her mouth, Rex roared and lunged for her. Collin dived over the desk, paper and file folders flew everywhere, knocking them all onto the floor before Rex's hands grabbed her. She scuttled out of the way until her back hit the wall. Deep inside she knew she'd just missed dying.

<<<>>>

"Stop it, Rex." Collin straddled the big man, holding him down by his arms.

"What the hell is wrong with him?" she asked.

Collin wasn't sure how long he could hold Rex back. Seeing so much white of his friend's eyes demonstrated how crazed he was to wrap his hands around Olivia's pretty neck and twist.

Centering his attention on the man beneath him, he leaned in close to Rex's ear. "This is not the way to question her about Abby's death or your brother's betrayal." He didn't want to hurt Rex unless he was pushed. Collin had been aware of the man's pain in losing two people he loved, but he'd never realized how it had eaten away at his sanity. Though it had happened five years ago, Rex still refused to come to terms with it.

"She's lying," Rex said between gritted teeth.

"We don't know that. It's all speculation." Collin sensed Olivia's impatience behind him. If she heard what they were saying, she was keeping quiet. "You'd promised to keep your cool around her."

"It's true. Fuck it! Another operative died bringing the information to us." Tears filled the big man's gray eyes.

"We'll find out the truth. Give me time." He wished he could wipe away Rex's pain, but the man would have to work it out on his own. The decision was made. He would send Rex on a mission, while Olivia remained at head-quarters.

"But will you be able to follow through with the decree? Will you kill her?" Rex grabbed the front of Collin's shirt with trembling fingers.

He wanted to mash Rex's face in and tell him no, but

his friend was right. As head of OS, following through with decrees of termination were his responsibility and the only way to control many of the more dangerous operatives working for his organization. No matter how much he hated it all. Only how could he tell his friend he hadn't decided to kill Olivia? She was the key to reaching Theo, to pushing the crazy man over the edge.

Clasping his friend's fingers, he pried them from their grip. "I'll do what's needed." He stood and held his hand out to Rex. "Now tell us what you found out." He moved behind his desk and watched Olivia's face as he ordered Rex, "Tell her everything; include what we believe The Circle's new objective has been for the past five years." He wanted to see if any emotions were revealed on that serene countenance of hers.

Rex's face turned red. "The bitch knows¾"

Holding his hand up, Collin said in a level, firm voice, "Humor me. Tell her. No accusations. Just facts."

Like a soldier recounting a battle lost, Rex pulled his shoulders back. "Five years ago, Abigail Rodriguez and Jack Drago¾"

"Drago? Boy, I've heard of that name. He's absolutely insane," Olivia interrupted. She stood but quickly placed a chair between her and Rex.

"Olivia." Collin shook his head, frowning. He noticed she kept wiping her hands on her sweats as if she was trying to clean them without success. "Jack's Rex's brother."

"Rex Drago?" Her face paled. "I never put ... I remember hearing about you. I don't know why I didn't put two and two together. Rex. OS. Not many people have your name and size and the scar ... you wiped out an entire Circle team singlehandedly."

Collin raised his hand to stop her babbling. It disturbed

him more than he imagined; Olivia never babbled. From Rex's stance, he guessed he needed to help his friend continue the account or Rex might lunge for her again. Before he could say anything, Rex started talking.

"She'd gone to New York City to shop. She'd been so excited." Rex's deep voice brought their attention back to him, his gaze staring off in the distance as if he could see the past.

"Abby was captured by The Circle," Collin said as sadness pulled at his face.

"I wasn't there for her. I was on assignment in the mountains of Peru and couldn't get back in time. Jack¾" He swallowed deep; his eyes searched the ceiling as he regained his composure. "Jack went after her." His horror was reflected in his eyes. "He disappeared. Not too long after that we received her burnt corpse with a note. Jack had been too late to save her. Instead we received a note saying he wasn't coming back but staying with the OS. He'd fallen in love with one of Theo's whores." The big man shot a murderous look at Olivia, making it clear he referred to her.

By the way Olivia inhaled and her expression cleared of emotion, he believed she remembered. When her gaze jumped to his and stayed, she confirmed it.

"Rex," Collin warned. He waited until pain-ridden gray eyes turned to him. "Stick to the facts we know." He picked up the report off the floor, thumbing through it as he waited for Rex to continue.

"It's a fact. She fucks everything that moves if it will benefit The Circle and¾"

"Enough!" Collin pointed to the door. "Leave. I'll tell her the rest."

He was surprised by Rex's outbursts. Until Olivia came

on the scene, Collin would swear his second in command had nerves of steel and nothing fazed him.

Even days after returning from Peru¾a mere week following the news of Abby's death¾and later when his brother disappeared, Rex had handled his work professionally and his temper stayed steady. He guessed Olivia's presence brought it all back to his friend.

Of course, there was the one blip on the screen¾The Circle team Rex came across on the way back to finish his assignment in Peru. Although Rex hadn't killed the team as Olivia had accused, he did cause a lot of damage, sending two of them to the hospital in critical condition.

Yeah, obviously, having Olivia under their roof was becoming too much, especially after they received the newest report.

Not until the door slammed shut behind Rex's back did Collin return to his seat and relax. He looked at the woman who remained quiet during most of Rex's tirade as she brought her chair upright and eased into it.

She leaned an elbow against the armrest as if she needed support and placed a fist beneath her chin. "The woman, Abby? How special was she to him? Or is all his angst about his brother?"

Again, she wasn't acting like herself. Why was she trying so hard to be casual about the requested information? Or was he reading too much into her body language?

"They were lovers."

Her forehead wrinkled. "And?"

She wasn't kidding. She really thought there had to be more. Wasn't being lovers enough? Why was he surprised? During the years when most children learned compassion and love, she'd spent them in an overcrowded orphanage, later in an abusive home, and then who really knew how long on the streets? When she was still vulnerable, The Circle had picked her up. They probably appeared to be her salvation.

"They were getting married. She was shopping for her wedding dress." Collin's eyes felt gritty. Rubbing them, he almost missed her flinch. So she finally understood what was eating at Rex.

"As I've been trying to tell your friend, I never met his brother and I haven't killed a woman. I wasn't much for socializing with the other operatives, and they always sent me after men." She crossed her arms, rubbing her upper biceps as if she was chilled. "So. Are you sending me back?"

Chapter Seventeen

Olivia told herself she didn't care what he decided. But that was a lie. She wanted to live a little longer. She wanted to know what was between her and the man looking so intensely at her. He watched her every move, examining her every expression. Probably only fair since she couldn't take her eyes off him.

"Why only men?" he asked.

"What? Isn't it obvious?" She wished he would just tell her if he was sending her back.

For the last five months she'd been treated better than she'd ever remembered. She even felt safe for the first time in her life. But she knew deep inside he was sending her back.

Cold eyes betraying nothing, he looked at her as he would at any murderer. So what did it really matter what he thought of her? Maybe it was time for her to go back. At least her life was worth two of his operatives. That was a step up in her opinion.

She leaned back in the chair, looking at him with half-closed eyes. "Listen, I hate men. No, I'm not sexually interested in women. I already have a pussy. Why would I want another one? I put up with men for one reason only. Their cocks. Big throbbing ones. A real live hot, hard cock is ten times better than any synthetic one at satisfying my needs. I like playing with them and then leaving before they want more. Was that what you wanted to hear?"

The burning sensation in her stomach said it all. She hated this discussion. She hated that he couldn't bring himself to care enough to protect her. Why she expected any man to protect her when she'd done it for herself all this time, she didn't know. She just did.

"I think you're telling me you hate men, hoping I'll send you back. Then I would prove you're right about your assessment." He walked around the desk and stood in front of her. "But you also told me what you liked about men."

The soft material of his sweats hid nothing. Her talk about hard cocks had excited him and she liked the view.

She pulled her gaze away from the impressive sight. "You have a bad habit of not answering my questions," she said as she sat up straight, threw her shoulders back and chest out. Let him see the hard tips of her nipples through her shirt. Only fair.

"And your question was?" He leaned over her, clasped her upper arms, lifting her out of the chair. His strength excited her. Knowing he was one of the few men who could wrestle her to ground kicked up her heartbeat. She took a deep breath and inhaled his special aroma.

"Are you sending me back?" Deep inside, she guessed she wanted a no, needed him to tell her no, put her needs in front of others. Just once she wanted someone to care enough to protect her. Harping on it wouldn't make it so, but she was tired of being alone and defending herself against all odds.

"Yes," he said as he stared into her eyes.

She hit him. His head snapped back, rolling with the punch. He'd expected it. Clenching her other fist, she struck him again, sending his head into the other direction as she jerked up her knee. With a small sidestep, he ensured the most painful hit missed its mark. Her knuckles pounded with pain from connecting with his rock hard jaw. She grabbed his arm to throw him but he countered and they both landed on the floor. His body pressed on top of hers.

What had she truly expected? She'd just wanted him to be different. Just once she wanted someone to give a damn about her, to fight for her, not against her.

"Don't cry," he said as his thumb wiped a tear from her cheek.

The warmth running down her face felt so strange. She blinked.

Crying? She never cried.

Angry and hopeless. Feeling sorry for herself wouldn't solve a damn thing. She hated feeling this way. This craziness running though her brain and making her so malleable around him drove her to believing in a future with him. What a crock.

It was just lust. He'd been playing with her for months. He never intended for her to stay. She was only a means to an end, insurance to regain what was taken from him. He offered himself like cheese to a rat and she'd never seen the trap. Lust had blinded her and the only way to see clearly was to take from him what she deserved. If she fucked him, she would be back to her old self: cold, unfeeling, methodical, and especially sane. As sane as a killer could be in this psycho world.

Clasping his head, her mouth covered his. She savored his heat, taste, all that made him Collin. His mouth softened as his tongue thrust inside hers. Electrifying darts of pleasure shot to her groin causing her to arch her back and press her hips to his hardness.

With one hand she pulled up his shirt, moving apart far enough to toss it to the side. Taking a deep breath, she yanked her shirt off to rub her breasts against his bare chest, loving the rough hair tickling her nipples. He hunched against her groin, stroking his cloth-covered hard penis into her soft folds.

Every inch of his body she touched was so lovely and hard. She wiggled her pants and thong down to her knees as they continued to kiss and then she kicked them off.

He hesitated.

"Please," she begged.

She shoved at his sweatpants. Then she pulled them down with her toes until they reached his ankles. His mouth dropped to her breasts to suck at the tender nipples, she arched into his pull. Then he started to sink further down her body. She grabbed his shoulders and with surprising ease, urged him onto his back.

"I need to feel you inside me." She worked to regain a speck of control. "If I've never told you, I can't get pregnant. I had problems when I was younger ... uh ... never mind the details, the doctor said I was clean." Not the most romantic words to tell a man, but she didn't have time to waste. Maybe that was why he played with her and never followed through on their lovemaking. Condoms by no means played a part in their foreplay and none appeared to be sitting around now.

"Shut up," he snapped.

Words after her own heart.

He pushed her back, hovering, with dark eyes flashing the amber she recognized as desire. Broad hands squeezed her thighs as his long fingers dug in, surely leaving bruises. She loved the idea of him marking her. Thoughts of his powerful body covering her, filling her, brought a frenzy feeling of need crashing around her.

His first thrust was so hard her back slid on the rug. She moaned as her eyes soaked up the emotions flickering across his face. Immense pleasure and yearning.

He pulled back and plunged again. He was big, solid, and filled her like she'd always imagined. She reached for a small male nipple and twisted.

"Damn! What was that for?" he asked next to her ear in his usual low voice. The pain didn't slow him down. Actually, she believed he grew larger as his cock continued to drive into her, beating his groin against hers as if he couldn't get deep enough. She liked it. Her fingernails gripped his buttocks, encouraging him to keep up the pace.

"I owed you," she said, reminding him of his treatment of her during that first night.

He grunted with each downward slide. She was going to be sore in the morning. And she would savor every ache and pain. He felt so good, so much a man.

His thrusts became faster. He wouldn't last much longer. To make sure she met his climax with one of her own, she rotated her hips, rubbing that certain spot of hers along his cock. She bit the side of her mouth, holding back her vocal release as Collin's guttural moan echoed in the room.

The weight of his big body resting on hers was almost as satisfying as the sex. He shifted as if he wanted to move off her but she held on, squeezing him to her.

"Wait a minute." She closed her eyes in pleasure, inhaling the scent of their lovemaking. Contentment weakened her muscles as she soaked in his heat. When he rolled over, he stayed inside her and kept her tight to his body.

A couple minutes or maybe a couple hours had passed when he rotated his hips. She'd been savoring the feel of his hot body and hadn't wanted to move. He was as hard and big as before. She sighed and then grinned.

After taking a nibble of his shoulder, she whispered against his damp skin, "So you're trying to impress me." She kissed the side of his neck. His heartbeat picked up speed.

So he liked her tasting him.

"Try?" His hands cupped her buttocks and he sat up and then stood, holding her to his body.

Talk about impressed. She was no lightweight and he'd lifted her as if she weighed no more than her favorite sniper rifle. Not only impressed, but so turned on she whimpered. The muscles bulging across his chest and around his upper arms were a sight to behold. She wouldn't be surprised if she flooded him with moisture along his groin and thighs. One thing was for certain, she wanted him moving inside her again.

He swiped papers, folders, and a lamp off his desk.

"Shh! Someone will interrupt our play." She didn't want Big Foot coming to his friend's rescue.

"Soundproof" was all Collin had to say.

Good. Next time she climaxed, she could let go without worry.

When her bottom met the cool wood, he shoved her back until her shoulder blades warmed the surface. With her legs spread wide and Collin towering over her and filling her, she felt like a sacrifice waiting to be serviced by the pagan priest. Oh, she liked it. The man knew his business. She also liked how he stood above her all threatening with a hungry look on his handsome face.

His amber eyes remained on hers as he lifted her legs beneath his arms and pulled back until only the tip touched her, then he plunged in. Each thrust shook her body, her breasts quivered and ached, she wanted more, wanted him to slam harder into her. His gaze moved to her breasts. She cupped them, offering them as enticement for him to lose control.

He threw his head back, hammering into her as he gritted his teeth.

Her back bowed and she screamed as intense ripples flickered from her groin and outward. In turn, he released a long groan and gathered her into his arms, falling back into one of the overstuffed chairs in front of his desk. Her knees rested next to his hips. His heartbeat pumped so hard she felt it against her chest. His cock slid out with a rush of warmth. Weak and uncaring, she rested her cheek beneath his chin.

Was this what heaven was like?

What a crazy thought. She never equated sex and happiness together. Sex had been a way to satisfy an urge or calm her nerves after a job. With her ear pressed to his chest, she heard his heartbeat slow from the frantic pace to a steady thump.

How beautiful. She wanted to remember this moment forever.

She wished ... oh, screw it! She knew better than to wish for anything. It would be better to wish for her mind to clear and not think of tomorrow or the next day, or whenever Collin planned to hand her over to The Circle and the man who controlled the organization with fear.

Only thing she knew for certain was that day she would most likely die.

Chapter Eighteen

The week passed by with the quickness of a lifetime.

Olivia waited each day for Collin to come and tell her he'd found a way to save the operatives without sacrificing her. Each day slipped away without her hearing a word.

With the news of how valuable she'd become to the OS and the possibility she could make a run for it, Collin changed the code on her door.

That hurt, but the icing on that crappy cake was when he sent four guards instead of her usual two each day to her apartment to escort her through her normal routine. They hated guarding her as much as she hated being guarded. Only this morning did she spot him at the end of the hallway speaking with Dr. Shelton and Nic Savage. He'd turned away without looking her way.

Bastard.

What did he think? That she would expect special treatment after he fucked her? Hell, yes. That was how it worked. She experienced the best sex she'd ever had and she wanted him to admit the same.

With a lift of her chin, she turned away and followed the wonderful scent of food down the hallway. For some wild-hair reason she'd decided to eat in the OS cafeteria this morning. Maybe she was hungry for more than the chef's cooking and her own company. Maybe being in a room full of people and the guards sitting at another table, she could pretend she was waiting for a friend to show up. She looked around and noticed how everyone avoided her eyes.

What could they say to a dead woman? That was right. She was one of the walking dead. Time was short and death was a certainty when Collin sent her back to The Circle.

She was pitiful, sitting here pretending like she didn't care. Isolation had never bothered her before, but during her months with the OS she'd felt like just another operative and not a creature to be feared. Christ! She'd become not only pitiful but maudlin too.

"Olivia." The voice she'd wanted to hear again came from behind her. She turned and Collin held out a coat. "Time to leave."

So that was it. No goodbye sex or long chat, not even a last meal.

She looked down at her clothes: jeans, sneakers, and long-sleeved green pullover shirt. The color brought out the green of her eyes. She shrugged on the wool coat as he helped her. His hands rested on her shoulders for a fraction of a second.

The desire to scream and kick while accusing him of misusing her almost reached the surface. Instead she swallowed the urge. The guards eyed her as if they expected her to explode any minute. The distaste on their faces pinpointed how they felt about her. Well, today she would act like a lady and ignore their sour looks. She breathed deep and followed Collin with her guards behind her.

An hour later, the limo bounced into a large field on the outskirts of Atlanta. A standard-issue white van used by The Circle waited, vapor pouring from the tailpipes.

During the ride, she'd watched the scenery pass without saying a word. What was there to say? *We had the best sex ever and I might love you?* No. It was only lust talking. There wasn't enough time left to explore either possibility.

Four men stepped out of the side of the van. Two of the men in the middle supported each other, bruises colored their faces and blood stained their clothing.

Maybe if she lived long enough, she could find a way out of The Circle. There was a slight possibility Theo wasn't aware of her complacency. Once he dropped his guard, she could escape and return to the OS. She blinked a few times to clear her vision. Collin had made her soft, dreaming of a normal life even within another killer organization. After taking a deep breath, she turned to the man across from her.

"Olivia¾" Collin started.

"Don't¾" They spoke at the same time. Unlike others who would sheepishly laugh, they stared at each other until she spoke first. "Don't let them see you. Theo's people may try something. Killing you would be a big coup."

"I'm surprised you haven't tried it. It would get you in Theo's good graces."

Surprised? Her cheeks heated from the insult he'd dealt her. Had he really expected her to try to kill him after the time they shared? She would love to know what Collin really was thinking.

Nothing showed on his face. Lust and anger were the only emotions she'd seen anyway. The only problem with lust was its usefulness in trapping someone. Maybe he planned it to work like that. He'd trapped her and made her want to stay. Maybe her attempts to escape failed for that reason. He fascinated her in ways she couldn't understand herself. Hell, she already planned to find a way to escape The Circle and return to him. If he would have her. If she lived long enough.

"I'd best warn you, if you betray Jason to The Circle, he'll kill you before they can kill him." Dark eyes stared steadily into hers. Who would've ever guessed amber eyes could be so cold?

Silence held reign until she lifted the handle, and the click of the door opening broke the spell.

"Well. Goodbye." She waited for him to tell her he'd changed his mind.

Instead he looked at her without blinking an eye and said nothing.

Her short burst of laugher sounded cynical even to her. She had to hand it to him; he was consistent. "Well, okay then," she said and pushed the limo door open.

"You'll survive," he said barely above a whisper.

She looked over her shoulder; her brows pulled together. When he didn't say anything more, she stepped out and carefully closed the door. Survive? She'd been doing that most of her life, hoping she could make it from one day to the next without being killed. Only thing, hope was no longer in her vocabulary. What a horrible thing for him to say to her.

The cold swept over her. All the normal feelings she'd regained during her time with OS were gone. She was frozen solid like the unfeeling creature she'd been before but even more so. Now as the walking dead, she wondered, why would Collin ever deem her worth saving?

Her love had never been wanted by anyone, especially him.

That last thought shook her. She really had become pitiful. Was this what love did to a person? Made her weak? She straightened her shoulders, preparing herself for the hell ahead.

As she walked by the men, they glared at her. Eyes and noses swollen, they were beaten and bloody, while she looked healthy and not a hair out of place. Oh, appearances could be so deceiving. Her soul had been stripped bare, leaving nothing inside. She lifted her chin and stepped into the van.

She gasped.

"Welcome back, Olivia."

Theo sat in the cargo area of the van. The flat screen in front of him showed the limo. His face cast blue by light, showed no emotion. With his arms crossed, he appeared stern but not angry. Did that mean he wouldn't kill her for now?

"Master." She dipped her head toward him. Old habits were hard to shed. He required his women and a few of the men to call him master. Why only a few of the men? Olivia never asked and preferred not to know why. She was certain it would make her sick. She took a seat, facing the back of the van.

"Who brought you back? Collin? His side kick, Rex? It would give me great pleasure to kill them both." He eyed her casual clothes. "I'm pleased to see they were smart enough not to mistreat you."

Back straight, sitting tall in the seat, Theo could've been a king from olden times with his booming voice, proud bearing, and thick snow-white hair. His most outstanding feature was his piercing blue eyes. He'd made many operatives pee in their pants from fear by the power of those eyes alone.

"Some trusted lieutenant. I didn't get his name. He's not important." She hoped he believed her.

Collin needed a little extra time to load up the wounded operatives and leave. She stuck her trembling hands into her pockets and stamped down the yearning to look one last time. Taking her eyes off Theo wouldn't be healthy. Any interest she showed in the limo could easily mean their deaths and only an idiot would trust Theo.

"I'm surprised. Collin had always been an intelligent boy," he said as doubt stretched out each word.

Without flinching or dropping his gaze, she silently waited for his assessment.

"You've changed in the months of your captivity. You're not being impertinent. No snappy comebacks."

Relieved but making sure not to show it, she took a calming breath. For some reason, Theo believed the OS's story of her being held against her will. Of course, the truth would eventually catch up with her and then Theo would do what she expected. Kill her.

"I'm tired and just want to go home." Then she remembered her home had been compromised by the OS. Face flushed by her unusual lapse of memory, she sighed. "Maybe I can stay at the Main Sector?"

"You're always welcome to enjoy my hospitality." His cold blue eyes narrowed. Had he misunderstood her request? His scouts had probably told him about her home being stripped by the OS.

Hunched over, he moved to sit with her and snapped his fingers at the driver. The van rattled and swayed as it returned to the asphalt and traveled down the interstate. Each second that passed, the tension in Olivia's chest eased.

"I'll have Marie prepare your old room," he said.

Oh, God, that was the last thing she needed to contend with. Her stomach boiled with the thought of Theo touching her again. Think! How could she say no without pissing him off?

"You're kind and so considerate to invite me to stay with you. But surely Marie would be hurt to see an old rival so near your private rooms." Before he could deny any inconvenience, she added, "A. J. probably will need to debrief me and it'll take some time. I'm sure she could find me a place to crash."

Theo's current enforcer, A. J., had been Olivia's second in command until she'd given up the position to work in the field. They'd always gotten along, though never friends or confidants. Hopefully, the woman would be willing to help.

"You're right. Marie can be rather possessive. I'll make sure A. J. brings you back to me. Then we'll have dinner together like old times." He patted her knee, letting his hand stay.

Her stomach clenched, trying to keep down her breakfast. She blamed Collin for this. He had the power to save her and refused to help. Hell, he seduced her into staying.

Unable to withstand the two-hour drive to the Main Sector with Theo's hand on her, she crossed her legs, forcing his hand off her knee. She held her breath, waiting for his explosion of temper.

He chuckled and crossed his arms. His uncharacteristic reaction scared her more than the yelling she'd expected. He'd said she acted unlike herself. It wasn't anything compared to him. What game was he playing with her?

<<<>>>

"Collin, you haven't listened to a word I said."

He looked over to Nic sitting in front of his desk with papers piled in her lap. They were going over the extra security measures put in place since Olivia left that morning and their continued efforts to find the sectors housing The Circle's facilities.

"Yes. You were talking about how prudent I was in blindfolding Olivia whenever we approached or left the building. So our location should be safe for now," he said in a monotone voice.

He stood and walked to the bookshelves and pressed a small lever beneath the center shelf. A section opened and inside the niche a large range of wine, whiskey, and tequila bottles and various shapes of glasses lined the shelves above a small sink.

"Want a whiskey? I know you like this one." Holding the bottle of Jack Daniel's by the neck, he poured a good-sized tumbler.

"I'll pass. It's barely past noon." Nic came up beside him and placed her hand on his arm. "She got to you, didn't she? Besides the body to die for, what do you see in a bitch like her?"

He shook his head. "I understand her. She's a survivor." In a well-practiced move, he tossed back the drink and exhaled before pouring another one. When Nic remained quiet, he added, "She's the way she is because of how she was brought up and the things she'd gone through. Her life hasn't been easy. We're a lot alike."

"I don't know why you would say that. After your family was murdered, you had to start over from scratch while protecting over a hundred people from the crazy machinations of a mad man. But you still have a heart and soul. That woman has neither." Brushing hair out of her eyes, she flushed and ruffled the short strands on the back of her head. "What do you plan to do about her?"

"That's my business." He nodded toward the stack of papers in her hand. "Did you find anything on the Main Sector?"

"We've narrowed it down to three places." Pointing to the largest red mark on a satellite map, she cleared her throat. "Every location that woman gave us was deserted and dismantled. They didn't even leave a paperclip. No evidence left to pinpoint where they went. She must've tipped them off."

"Let's stick to the facts." There was no way for Olivia to warn Theo. He'd made sure of that. He thought she might have refused to give them the location of the Main Sector if any of the operatives' children were housed there. Olivia would never endanger them.

"We should hear from our scouts by tomorrow morning. Once they locate the buildings, they'll see if they can infiltrate and confirm." Flipping through her pages, Nic jumped when Rex knocked before walking in and she promptly scattered sheets on the floor.

"Sorry. I didn't mean to scare you." He bent down to help pick them up.

"No ... no ... I'm just a little nervous about this mission." Red faced, she snatched the papers from him, never looking into his eyes, and said to Collin, "I'll check on the scouts and let you know what they've found so far."

Collin nodded and sipped on the whiskey in his tumbler as he returned to his desk. Nic's temper was well known and he found it interesting how she never raised her voice to Rex. It was obvious to everyone but Rex that Nic had a crush on him. But his friend still mourned Abby and no other woman existed for him. Collin understood.

Though he didn't love Olivia, he already missed her. She made him feel more alive than he had in years.

He halfway listened to Rex's report on their attempt to follow the van. The look on Olivia's face when he told her she would survive made his insides squirm. He'd struggled with finding the right words to erase the hopeless look on her face. Instead the training he'd received from his father had kicked in and those cold words escaped his lips. Certainly something his father would've said.

As a child, he'd admired his father. Later as an adult, Collin had realized the cold distance his father maintained with the people around him including his family and friends had become dangerous and destructive. So much distrust and anger. There was no wonder someone had massacred him and most of his family.

His father trained him and his brother to be replicas, but Collin had wanted more. When it came to those he had a personal connection with, he'd wanted to be softer, kinder. Yes. He had a soft spot for Olivia.

Raising the glass to his lips, he took a long swallow. Though Theo was unlike his father in some ways, he was more treacherous with his fascination with the sword and his warped sense of honor. Collin was well aware of what Theo did to traitors.

So how long would Theo allow her to live?

"Collin? Dammit, listen to me." The big guy eased into one of the chairs facing the desk.

He blinked and focused on Rex's furrowed brow.

"Are you in love with her?"

Collin wanted to laugh in Rex's face, but the thought of saying no felt wrong. He didn't have time to contemplate the ramifications if he admitted that. Did he?

Even when she wasn't around, she confused the hell out

of him. He carefully placed the empty glass on the desk and pushed it away with one finger. Elbows on the smooth top, he rubbed his eyes and sighed.

"How I feel about her has nothing to do with tracking down Theo before he orders another hit on our people."

Rex stared for a moment and then looked away. "I saw her getting all chummy with Lucian the other day." His gaze returned to Collin.

He lifted his head and eyed Rex. "Were you able to hear what was being said?"

"No. But I stopped Lucian and asked." The big man chewed the side of his mouth as if he wasn't sure what to say. "He claimed she had no idea The Circle lied about their operatives' deaths at the OS's hands. He also said not to trust her. She'll betray us in a heartbeat." He leaned forward. "You have to see she's dangerous. We should've made an example of her when we had her. We could've shown Theo what would happen to him."

"Rex," Collin warned.

"As far as we know, she has told Theo everything. They probably had a good laugh over our gullibility, and in any minute, Theo will attack and kill us all. Is her pussy that good?"

Collin slammed a hand on his desk and stood. "Fuck you! I'll keep you and our people safe. I'll stake my life on it!" He took a deep breath. "All I need from you at this moment is to find where the Main Sector is. Then we can steal the sword and see if the theory of pushing him over the edge will weaken him. We need him vulnerable. At that time, we can eliminate him."

Chapter Nineteen

"Come in, Olivia." Theo wore chain mail and an ankle-length surcoat with a huge red cross on his chest. On his head, he wore one of the smaller crowns he loved, more of a coronet. The man did love the medieval period. During the time she'd lived with him, it wasn't unusual to walk in and see him wearing full-plate armor.

If not for the queasy feeling in her stomach, she'd laughed at the ridiculous image he portrayed as he tried to act debonair with a sherry glass in one hand and a cigar in the other near the head of a preposterously long dining table. She had to admit, even with his strange getup, no one could say Theodore Owen Palmer wasn't a distinguished-looking man.

"Sit here."

Since all of her clothes were still at the OS, if Nic Savage hadn't burned them by now, Theo had his current mistress, seventeen-year-old Marie, provide her with one of the dresses he insisted women wear whenever they entered his inner sanctum. He actually kept a large closet filled with all sizes and colors.

Tight beneath the breasts and free flowing to the floor, the dress would be considered modest except for two things. One, the bust was cut low, showing plenty of cleavage to the point she was certain her nipples would show if she breathed too deep. The other was the soft blue cotton, so thin it was see-through and revealed her lack of underwear, another crazy rule of his. He claimed he wanted women to feel like women. Strange how having no bra and panties could make a woman feel vulnerable. She hated wearing the gown and resented his male chauvinistic rules. Hell, she was no longer his woman.

And thank goodness she had enough wit to pull off that feat. Smartest move she'd ever made was squirming her way out of his bed and into a productive position with The Circle. But considering he welcomed her back without any suspicions about her time away, she had to play along and hope he wasn't setting a trap.

"Where's Marie? I would like to thank her for picking out this gown for me." Olivia smoothed the material beneath her rump as she slid into the seat on his right, remembering to keep her shoulders back so not to spill out.

His mistress was pencil thin and timid to the point Olivia worried about Marie's health.

"I didn't want interference. You and I have a lot to discuss." He handed his cigar and empty glass to a female servant wearing in a transparent yellow gown. She'd discreetly entered the room and immediately left.

Olivia's fingernails dug into her thighs and her stomach clenched. She hoped Marie was okay. Just as Olivia had quickly and painfully learned when she belonged to Theo, Marie would know better than speak without being first spoken to by her master, and never argue. Olivia had thought she could handle dinner alone with him, but memories of the humiliations inflected by the man sitting nearby ate at her sanity. She wanted to shout at him, inflict the pain he'd inflicted on her. Only it would serve no purpose but ensure her death at his hand. Her plans didn't include death. So she gave a brief expected grin and remained quiet.

The servant served each course with efficient ease. Theo spoke only of general current events and some of the small changes he'd made in The Circle's security. By the time coffee and another cigar for Theo and a tea with lemon for her were served, the muscles around Olivia's mouth felt strained from smiling at the appropriate comments. Theo believed in waiting until a person had a full stomach before talking business.

"After A. J. debriefed you, she sent me the report. They appeared to treat you well."

"They kept me locked up most of the time." Had he heard different?

"Uh-hm." He sat staring at her.

She worked at keeping her face clear. Last thing she needed was for Theo to believe she had feelings for the OS's chief.

"So what do you think of Collin Ryker?" he asked, pushing back his chair to lean over the offered light from an accommodating servant.

Had she betrayed her feelings? "I think he's a dangerous man." That was true. Every time she'd been near him, she'd felt like a zookeeper with steak smeared over her body in a tiger's cage.

He smiled, nodding. "That he is. No mistake about that." Theo said it as if he was proud of Collin. "When he was growing up, I was certain he would be a momma's boy. After his parents died, I took him in, gave him guidance and loving discipline. Then what does he do? After all that I did for him? He takes the heart of my organization from me. I'll never understand his cruelty. He continues to kill my people without rhyme or reason, interferes with my objectives." Theo stared at the smoke twisting its way to the ceiling. Then he looked at her with an almost reproachful cold blue stare. "You've seen it from the inside. Are his operatives close to rebelling? They must be tired of his unreasonable demands and egoistic ways."

She fought the urge to laugh. His descriptions of Collin reflected those of himself.

"No. What little I saw, they appeared satisfied and respectful." Walking the verbal tightrope wasn't exactly her forte, but for her to tell Theo the operatives loved Collin would be suicidal.

"Hmm." His eyes narrowed.

Time to change the subject, and thankfully he loved talking about his collections. She looked around the dining room, seeing the John William Waterhouse's *Lamia on Her Knees* he often admitted was his favorite, along with several new pieces of art set in the medieval period. Though she loved the paintings he chose with their vivid colors and romanticized scenes, she never understood Theo's interest in them. She never made the mistake of believing him to be a sentimental man. When her gaze landed on the usual swords and pikes over the fireplace mantel, they reminded her of Collin's search for his father's sword.

"I see you've acquired a couple of new paintings," she nodded to what looked like a Lord Leighton she'd never seen before.

"Ah, yes. I was fortunate to come across a few that came

up for sale during these unfortunate times." Theo tilted his head. "So he told you about the sword."

A chilled wind blew across her back, taking all the blood from her face. Pulling herself back together, she said, "Actually someone else did. So you have it?"

She didn't expect him to admit to it, but figured what the heck? He was going to figure out, even though not at the beginning, she did stay with the OS of her own free will toward the end. He then would kill her sooner or later.

"Would you like to see it?" he asked, pushing his chair back and standing up, his body leaning toward hers.

She wanted to step back, to pull away from his suffocating heat. Her vision darkened around the outer perimeter. It wasn't a good time to faint. What had happened to her during those few months with the OS? Never before had she been such a wimp. Of course, she'd never cared about living and now she did. Collin had shown her what living was really about.

"Sure." She stood when he pulled her chair back and fought the revulsion of touching his arm. Even with cloth and mail separating her from his skin, she could feel the ropy muscles others were unaware of.

"This way." He led her down a familiar hallway. Each step brought her closer to one of her nightmares.

She repeated in her head, *He's only showing you the sword; you're too old for him; he's only showing you the sword; you're too old for him ...*

"I've redecorated my bedroom since you were last there." He made it sound as if she cared and would be heartbroken by the change.

"Oh, did my blood ruin your carpet?" She bit the side of her mouth. What had gotten into her?

"Ah, there's my wild girl. I hate to think Collin stole all

your spirit during your time at the OS." He pushed the large cedar door out of the way and inside appeared to be a crazy man's idea of a harem. Diaphanous curtains of all colors covered nearly every inch of the walls, blocking off several sections of the massive room she remembered. An open window somewhere allowed breezes to ruffle the material, giving the occupants a feeling of being in a dream. A suffocating nightmare was more like it.

"Very diaphanous." There she went again. She bit her bottom lip in the hope she'd keep her mouth shut.

"It suits my taste for now." He pointed to a small sitting area with dozens of pillows surrounding one large chair, obviously the master's. "Have a seat there and it'll only take me a moment to retrieve it."

She made herself as comfortable as a fly could be in a web. *Inhale through the nose; exhale through the mouth.* She hated this feeling, this room. All the flowing gauzy material felt stifling.

In less than five minutes he returned. "Here we go." He had a long stiff strip of black velvet in his outstretched hands. "Come and look. I want to see your expression when you unwrap it."

She rose in front of him and lightly touched the soft cloth. A hardness warned her of what was beneath it. With careful movements she pushed back the velvet. Inside nestled the most beautiful sword she'd ever seen. Latin script covered most of it, along with roses and vines etched into the shiny steel. But the pommel held the largest red diamond she'd ever imagined. She'd seen them on the Internet but never one for real.

"Go ahead. I know how you appreciate weapons. This is one of the finest." Theo's eyes gleamed with lust. The thought of willingly being near him should have terrified her, but she knew it wasn't lust for sex but power. He believed the fable about whoever owned the sword would be in control of The Circle. And like most powerful men, he wanted to ensure no one took what he already possessed.

She reached out and grasped the pommel. With little effort she lifted it from Theo's hands. Her eyes widened. The balance between the pommel and the blade was so perfect. It gave the sword a feeling of weightlessness. If she believed in magic, she could easily imagine the sword possessing powers.

"Careful. Wouldn't want you to cut yourself." Theo stood back with a wary eye.

Only for a moment did she think of using the sword on him. The blade appeared to be sharp enough to slice through flesh and bone without slowing. From her many lessons in self-defense, she knew her upper body strength was not enough to make the downward slice fast enough or the thrust hard enough to kill. She would only make it easier for Theo to exterminate her.

She carefully ran her finger down the flat surface of the blade, enjoying the cold heat of the steel beneath her touch. Yes, the sword could inspire anyone in trying for more if they possessed it.

"I love its deadly beauty," she muttered. The sword belonged to Collin's father. Collin and the sword belonged together. With a tinge of reluctance, she returned the sword to the velvet sheath and Theo's hands.

"You see why so many have died to own such a sword. The diamond is said to be from King Arthur's crown and brings the owner power and strength and wisdom." Theo lovingly caressed the pommel. "The gold wire on the grip woven with Guinevere's hair brings wealth and compassion. She was fourteen years old to Arthur's thirty when they married." He wrapped the sword with a reverence she'd never seen Theo treat anything or anyone.

Considering Theo had one foot in the psycho pool, she held back any thoughts on the validity of his claims. No matter what he believed, he was not thirty years old and certainly no King Arthur.

After he returned the sword to its hiding place within what she remembered was his dressing room, she asked, "How did you get the sword back from the Inferno?" Since the news had spread throughout the Main Sector about it being restored to The Circle's safety and A. J. had mentioned it to her, she figured asking was okay. Theo rarely tolerated questions of any kind.

"There are those who owe me their loyalty." His gaze traveled over her body and his nose wrinkled in distaste. Luckily for her she had a grown woman's body, well curved and full breasted.

"I'm as loyal as long I'm not lied to." She bit the inside of her mouth. Oh, shit. Where in the hell did that come from? Her old self had returned with a vengeance. Before her time with Collin, she taunted Theo because she didn't care if she lived or not. Now she wanted to live and needed to be more wary of the crazy man's temper. He'd ignored most of her smart-ass comments in the past but never had she come so close to calling him a liar.

White eyebrows scrunched together, he snapped his fingers and several of his guards entered the room.

"As I've said before, you've changed and not for the better. This little visit has been most informative. I've decided Collin has influenced you in ways I hadn't antici- pated. Maybe he's even turned you against me. Until I check a little further, A. J. will keep you under surveillance."

For a moment there, she'd been worried he would order her death. Light-headed from relief, she walked over to the guards without complaint. One guard reached for her but jerked his hand back when she glared at him. They wouldn't touch her. They remembered how deadly she could be when touched without permission.

Ironically, she had to fight the urge to kiss each of them. Just knowing she could walk away from Theo's creepy room was plenty to celebrate without adding he'd given her enough time and information to steal the sword.

Chapter Twenty

Olivia took a couple quick steps when one of the guards pushed her into A. J.'s quarters. The click of a lock being turned confirmed they still didn't trust her. When she walked out of the foyer into the living room, The Circle's enforcer was piled up on the couch crying.

"Why are you back so soon?" Wiping her wet cheeks with a sleeve, the dark-headed woman scooted to a sitting position and looked away, her face flushed and swollen. Then she moved toward the large open kitchen, not waiting for Olivia's answer.

A. J. loved to cook and some of the most-expensive–looking pots and pans hung over a granite countertop. The single empty bottle of beer sitting on the counter told part of the story. Being The Circle's enforcer was a lonely business and no one better than Olivia could sympathize.

Giving the woman a few moments to pull herself together, Olivia looked away and cleared her throat as she chafed her arms. She needed to get rid of this ridiculous dress and pull on some jeans and a warm top. That was if A.

J. had anything she could borrow. Otherwise, the clothes she'd arrived in would have to do.

Never one to share confidences, but considering A. J.'s earlier help in getting ready for Theo and their past association, she decided confiding a little in her wouldn't hurt. She'd liked the woman's attitude about life back in the days she'd trained her. But Olivia had been wrapped up with getting away and never tried to get close. And besides, she sure couldn't get more dead than dead if A. J. decided to turn her in. She had a feeling they may have more in common than she first realized.

"As usual I ticked off Theo but this time I went too far. I called him a liar. Well, not straight out, although he understood what I meant. I knew my mouth would get me in trouble, but I had hoped to last through a fun day." She watched for A. J.'s reaction and was beginning to doubt her intuition until the brunette burst out laughing.

"I'd given anything to be a fly on that wall. Of course, then those tacky wall coverings would knock me off." A. J. grinned, her brown eyes blinking innocently.

"Tell me about it. Have you seen his newest surcoat? Who wears surcoats, for that matter?" Olivia had never had a girlfriend but could easily see how she and A. J. could become close friends.

They then flopped on the couch and talked about their jobs, Theo, and men in general. "When I walked in earlier, you were crying. Was it about a man?" Olivia asked.

A. J. rubbed her eyes as a heartrending looked pulled at her face. "Today is the anniversary ... he died." On a deep breath she shook her head. "I was feeling sorry for myself. You know how hard it is in our job ... other male operatives are so self-centered, wanting a quick lay and nothing else. Then, if you try to date outside the sectors, the rules are so strenuous and the guys never understand why you can't talk about your job." She shook her head.

"Yeah, I know what you mean." Olivia then told A. J. about sleeping with an OS operative but not that he'd been the head honcho himself.

The woman stared at her hard. "Yeah. I think you do understand. You love that guy."

Hell, even A. J. saw the symptoms. No matter how many times Theo had said she'd changed and she wanted to argue, she had, and it was all Collin's fault. Never had she been so obsessed with a man. All she could think about was stealing the sword and taking it to him. Perhaps she could convince him to let her stay with the OS. Damn it! There she went again, acting pitiful.

After a swallow of the sixth cold beer A. J. had handed her, she asked, "Do you want to help me break into Theo's bedroom? Actually his dressing room."

"His secret safe?" A. J. waved her beer in the air.

"Some secret, huh?" Olivia giggled and then covered her mouth. She never giggled.

Rolling off the chair onto the floor laughing, A. J. held up her beer, miraculously not spilling a drop. She held her ribs with her free hand. "Okay. No more beer. We need to sober up if you want in the safe."

Olivia groaned.

A. J. burped.

Her new friend's surprised expression had Olivia doubling up. After a few moments, she tried her best to regain control, but as soon as she looked at A. J. again, she burst out laughing. "Sure. Sober."

Chuckling, A. J. then released a snort.

By the time they regained control and took turns in the

bathroom, they began planning their assault on Theo's dressing room safe.

<<<>>>

Crap! Crap! Crap!

How did she get herself into these situations? Hanging upside down outside Theo's bedroom window at two in the morning wasn't necessarily a safe or smart activity.

It had all started with trying to find a way to contact Collin but as expected, all transmissions in and out of the Main Sector were tracked. And of course, her leaving for a short trip was out of the question.

When she was about to give up all hope she found an ally in The Circle and it wasn't her ex-handler, Jason. That traitor treated her as persona non grata and had warned her that she would be suspected of lying if she told Theo about his involvement with the OS. He'd even added, "Only liars fuck the enemy." He'd only confirmed what she'd always known, he was a prick.

Her new ally was A. J., Theo's enforcer.

Five hours later, she was hanging upside down while A. J. fed the line from the roof until she could peer through the open window into Theo's bedroom. With all of her blood rushing to her face, she had to fight the need to throw up the six-pack and two pots of coffee she'd downed earlier.

She signaled to lower her a little further. With one hand on the sash, she pulled herself head first into the window, keeping an ear out for anyone moving inside. She shoved the curtain to the side and looked around, and then wiggled onto the window frame. Her hand shook a little as she worked at unclipping herself from the feed line. She dropped the rope outside the window, making sure it hung from the roof in easy reach for her escape.

As she'd thought, the open window was in Marie's dressing room. Theo would never be so careless. His was next door without windows. The man thought no one would dare infiltrate the sector, much less his private domain.

A small hallway separated the rooms from the rest of his private suite. She eased into the hallway, guided by memory and the small night-lights mounted near the floor, and stepped softly toward the other door while listening for any sign of movement from the bedroom. If Theo kept the same routine, he'd been in bed hours ago and wouldn't be waking for a few more.

She finally reached the other dressing room and stepped inside, closing the door behind her. First, Theo's favorite cologne engulfed her. Taking a couple deep swallows, she dared her stomach to rebel at such a critical time. Second, she hated the feeling of pitch black emptiness surrounding her. Not waiting a moment more, she unhooked the flashlight from her harness, flipped it on, and took a step forward. She jumped when lights flashed on the floor and traveled toward the far wall and continued along the molding until she could see.

"Shit!" She hadn't expected Theo to go so modern as to install motion-activated lights. That was new. She hoped like hell he hadn't changed his safe and added an alarm too.

After turning off and hooking the flashlight back, she pushed several tunics to the side, uncaring if she wrinkled them, and eyed the large safe. He still used the old-fashioned dial combination. Nothing looked different, but was it a trap?

A cool breeze tickled her neck alerting her a second

before a hand covered her mouth. Then a strong arm hooked her around the throat, lifting her off the floor. She was dead meat now.

"What in the hell are you doing in here?" The soft voice was so not Theo's.

Olivia stood motionless.

Collin grumbled, "I can't believe you've gone back to him. What price did you demand? A bigger rifle? Money?"

She dropped her hand and triggered a release with a finger. Cold steel slid carefully out of her sleeve into her palm. Reaching behind her with the knife, she pricked a space between two of his ribs where the blade would do the most damage if she pushed.

"I was getting you a present, and if you don't let me go, I'll do more than draw blood," she warned in a whisper. With relief, he let her go, but then his arm slid down her chest, allowing his broad hand to skim over her bound breasts. She'd found years ago, it was best to wear a sports bra to rappel down the side of a building.

She turned to face Collin. It took all her concentration to keep the excitement off her face and out of her voice. Desire to hug him with all her might was tempered by the knowledge he hadn't come to take her back. Considering he wore all black while standing in the middle of Theo's dressing room made it obvious his plans had more to do with Theo and the sword.

"A present, huh?" he asked with a hint of amusement.

"You're such an ass. Yes. Before you escorted me out of the OS, that was all I heard, that you wanted the sword." She kept the thought of how stupid it sounded to herself. Though she knew what people believed could make the difference in succeeding or not. Theo believed the sword could protect him in his position. Collin believed he could take over The Circle with it. What did she believe? That she could win a man's cold heart with a piece of steel.

"Then let's get to work." He pulled a small glass bottle out of his pants pocket.

"Is that acid?" she asked, not even wanting to think about the possibility of him breaking the bottle while he'd carried it so close. She had a few vials of the stuff in a special case at home. Then she remembered, Collin's people had wiped out her place, who knew where they were now?

"Yeah. The fastest way to open a safe." He leaned over and peered at the seam of the metal door.

"There's one other faster way." She elbowed him out of the way and began turning the dial.

"How did you get the combination?" His question hung in the air between them with the silent accusation of *from Theo.*

In a whisper, she answered, "He's the least imaginative man I've ever known. Even if he changed it, it will be similar." Theo had used his birth date. When it didn't open, she tried changing the order of the numbers.

"Try zero-four, zero-three, seventy-six," Collin whispered in her ear and placed a hand on her waist. Did he think he had to remind her he was still nearby? Heat from his body scorched her side and perversely she wanted to move closer to him. Oh, yeah, she hadn't forgotten he was there.

"The date when The Circle was created?" She dialed the numbers and released her breath when the clicks signaled their success. The three-by-five door swung open and inside documents and long boxes perfect for jewelry filled the array of pigeon holes. On the bottom shelf rested a long silver box. Engraved on the top was the word, *Excalibur*. "You've got to be kidding."

"That's what Dad and Theo called it." His eyes had a faraway look to them.

She remembered he grew up in The Circle, living in the treacherous atmosphere but with the support of a strict father and a loving mother. When she came into the organization, he was away at college and just as well since Theo had her sequestered in his suite, seeing to all his perverted needs.

He pulled out the box and popped open the clips. Inside was the black velvet–covered sword. "Check the hallway. We need to get going. It's taken us too long as it is." With efficient movements, he closed up the safe.

Desire to argue was quickly forgotten when she heard a thump and muffled scream on the roof.

"Shit!" She reached for the door. "Let's get moving." Checking one way and then the other, she waved him to follow. Instead of the window, she turned toward the front door. With what she heard from above, her planned escape had been compromised. Hopefully A. J. was okay.

At the last corner before reaching the door, she heard whispering. Pressing her back to the wall, she glanced at Collin. He did the same with the velvet-wrapped sword held to his chest like a knight standing at attention.

Then Olivia heard a door open, followed by a girl's voice. "No. I didn't hear anything, master, probably one of your bad dreams. Let me warm you some milk and you'll feel better." A young girl came around the corner and gasped, covering her mouth, eyeing Collin with a mixture of fear and appreciation. It was Marie. Before Olivia could make a move to silence her, Marie placed a finger to her lips.

"Go. I've stopped him from investigating the noise for

now, but the guards are most likely on their way to tell him what they found on the roof." The blonde clutched her robe tight. "Leave now."

Well, wasn't that a surprise? The girl had a head on her shoulders and didn't appear timid at all. Olivia had a feeling she was an excellent actress and Theo deserved everything she dished out. With a nod toward Marie, Olivia stepped toward the hallway door when the girl stopped her.

"Wait." Marie placed her hand on Olivia's arm.

Cringing from the unexpected touch, Olivia moved a step closer to Collin. "What? We need to go." Was the girl changing her mind and playing a trick?

"I overheard Theo talking on the phone about some secret weapon he's bringing in to annihilate the leader of the OS. Sorry, that's all I know but I wanted to pass it on," Marie whispered into her ear.

"Okay. Thanks." Olivia wasn't sure what to make of Marie's help and information, but she knew they didn't have a minute more to waste and within seconds she'd led Collin to an unpretentious door down the hallway from Theo's suite.

"A closet?" Collin asked with concern for her sanity clearly written on his face.

"Yes and no." She stepped inside and shut the door behind him. The room had what she knew Collin expected: boxes of toilet tissue, rags, furniture polish, brooms, and mops. Reaching beneath the bottom shelf, she pressed a button and the far wall slid open. She caught a couple brooms and a mop from falling inside the dark cobweb-filled tunnel. "I made this discovery a few years after coming here. I was hiding from Theo and found it by mistake. Maybe it was a maintenance hallway or something your dad designed and Theo had forgotten." Slapping at a cobweb, she ducked inside. Once she turned eighteen and Theo had replaced her, there hadn't been a need to use it again.

"Why didn't you use this way to get in?" Collin asked as he followed her down the slight incline.

"Though I know the way in from the closet, I haven't found a button or lever on the outside." They emerged from a small alcove outside the Main Sector. Security lights lit the ground in spots, while the full moon brightened the sky to an eerie gray.

"I bet you drove Theo nuts disappearing whenever you wanted." He placed his arm across her waist and held her back as he looked around. The woods surrounding the Main Sector were about twenty yards away, giving the cameras on the walls a clear view. "Wait."

Even having Collin touching her through layers of clothes had her heart racing more than their near capture. Eyes narrow and cold, he still held the sword in his other hand. The velvet had fallen from the blade and the sight gave him a medieval appearance, especially with his black clothes and ferocious look.

"Unless they caught it in the last eight years, there's a small three-foot wide area the cameras don't cover." Regretfully she moved along the wall. Touching him would have to wait. "There. See the two sweet gum trees twined together like lovers?"

"Yeah."

She imagined he didn't miss anything. "From the wall to the area around the tree is the cameras' blind spot."

"Good. I left a car on the road east of here." He charged into the woods.

As she followed him, the moonlight flickered in and out of the trees. Everything felt weird, surreal. She'd sealed her fate. If Theo had any doubts the OS had taken her by force before, no matter how true it had been, he would certainly know she betrayed him this time. No turning back. She looked at the man leading the way. His broad shoulders moved with each slice, the thick humidity not slowing him down.

She grinned. Feeling light and carefree, her smile widened. She enjoyed working alongside Collin. The sensation was weird and wonderful. Would it last? If Theo had anything to do with it, no.

Then Olivia remembered Marie had said something about a secret weapon. What was Theo up to?

Chapter Twenty-One

Collin pulled up in front of the small cabin he'd rented under a false name in the Smoky Mountains. The woman next to him examined the surrounding area with a suspicious eye, probably expecting him to give her back to The Circle.

"I still say we would be safer at the OS headquarters." She stepped out of the midsized car and headed toward the front door.

"Headquarters is in lockdown. No one can get in or out during the next forty-eight hours."

He had many reasons and one was to make sure that Theo didn't try anything crazier than he already had. Rex would take care of their people in Atlanta, while Collin made his next move from Tennessee. That was the agreement he and Rex had made when they met at a rest stop near the Tennessee state line. Plus knowing that the sword was with Rex and in a safe place, Collin could plan his next step to take over The Circle.

"Do you plan to hide out in the mountains and let Rex do your dirty work?" she asked, arms crossed as she glared at him. "I hate wildlife. I want the city where I can take a decent bubble bath and a decent meal."

Who yanked her britches and tied them in a knot?

He shook his head as he lifted a box and duffle bag from the trunk. One glance at her and he concentrated on navigating the steps to the front porch. The pink in her cheeks and her eyes shiny with anger only made her more beautiful.

His body tightened and ached to find relief in that hot body of hers. Hard to believe it had been less than two weeks since they had made love. Hell, he had a hard time believing she'd only come into his life less than six months ago. She'd become an important part.

As she stood next to him, he inhaled the scent that was all Olivia—sweetness and tart rolled together. It was time for him to pull back and chill. The thought of letting her get too close scared the shit out of him. She would know he wanted her and how she affected him. And she was trained to use every advantage.

After unlocking the door, they walked into the living room and paused to take in the sight through the wide glass panes. The dusky mountains in the distance and the tree-filled valley below them were breathtaking. They could pretend they were alone in the world with such a view.

"There's only one bedroom. I'll take the couch." He nodded to the brown leather sofa sitting in front of the large flat-screen television and fireplace.

"Fine!" She slammed the bedroom door behind her.

What was that about?

He shrugged and dropped the box on the kitchen countertop, then the duffle bag behind the couch before returning to the car for more supplies. He wasn't sure what her problem was but he knew the next week was going to be interesting. He needed to keep his mind on preparing his final plan of attack against Theo, but there was no way he could keep his hands off Theo's ex-mistress.

<<<>>>

Unsure of why she let the man get to her, she pulled out the snub-nose revolver she'd stolen out of his supplies. He was crazy if he thought she would go weaponless for long. Then again, she hadn't been completely unarmed. She lifted her shirt and pulled out the wicked-looking knife from its scabbard attached and tucked into her pants. A. J. had provided the weapon. Knives were silent killers if used correctly.

She hoped A. J. survived whatever Theo planned for her. But maybe her new friend had talked her way out of the situation. Although unpredictable, Theo's ego got in his way and he often thought his people too afraid to betray him. Besides, just like Olivia, A. J. understood the risks.

She hid the knife and scabbard under the mattress. Then she checked the gun. Yep, fully loaded. What was the use of having a gun if it wasn't loaded?

Looking around, she decided staying in the mountains might be rather nice after all. The large bathroom had a shower and a Jacuzzi wide enough for two. Thoughts of making love with Collin in the midst of mounds and mounds of bubbles flushed her face.

She turned away and was happy to see another door leading to a wraparound porch. Good. What a relief to see another way out of the cabin besides the front door.

A knock on her bedroom door had her reaching for the gun where she'd left it on the nightstand. She shook her head. Like Theo and his cronies would knock before breaking down the door. Time to get a grip on her nerves. After she checked the safety, she slipped the gun beneath a pillow.

"Do you want a sandwich?" Collin asked through the door.

"I'll be right out." She stared at herself in the mirror. When she'd broken into Theo's dressing room at two this morning, she'd never expected to find herself two hundred plus miles away and in need of a brush. Her hair stuck out of her ponytail and framed her face like a frizzy cap. What little makeup she'd worn—hard to believe it was less than twelve hours ago—to the meeting with Theo had sweated off during their run through the wilderness. "Go ahead and eat without me. I'm going to clean up first."

There was silence and then she heard, "Okay," and footsteps moved away from the door.

A strange feeling of loneliness came over her. She wanted to open the door and ask him to join her, to touch the hard warm surfaces of his body, to taste the musky favor of his skin again. What was it about this man that made her want more than she ever wanted? More than she deserved?

An ache poured over her body. Every scratch and bruise shouted its mistreatment. Time in the Jacuzzi would do the trick.

She cranked up the flow of water and stripped. As soon as water reached a reasonable level, she climbed in and added bubbles. Once the bubbles reached her chin as she leaned back, she shut it off and turned on the jets, closing her eyes and enjoying the massage.

"Shit, this is almost as good as a man," she said to herself. Bending a knee, one jet hit the spot on her hip where she'd slammed into the wall trying to reach Theo's window.

"I hope to God not."

"Christ!" The water sloshed over the side and a slow spread of dark blue ran along his pant leg. He lifted the material a little to see the damage, wiping at the wetness. She leaned back again. "You deserve it for scaring me like that," she teased.

Resting one hand on the tub near her head, he leaned in almost nose to nose. "Do I really scare you?" His dark eyes flared as he looked down.

She was sure he received a nice how-do-you-do from her taut nipples peeking out of the bubbles and she couldn't resist inhaling deep to see how he would react. When his gaze lifted, her breath left her. The heavy lidded look he gave her would've brought a moistness between her legs if she hadn't already been sitting in water.

"Oh, hell, yeah." She tilted her head up and met his lips. No tenderness wanted or given as she immersed herself in the kiss. Just pure carnal pleasure as she took his tongue into her mouth.

His hand covered one breast, squeezing and releasing the fullness as a callused thumb rubbed the nipple. Their lips separated, giving each other time to breathe. His forehead rested against hers as they watched his hand massage her breast.

Unable to hold back any more, she rose to her knees, water pouring off her. Taking her time, she pressed a few quick kisses to his neck and unbuttoned his shirt with a slow pull and tuck, working her way down. Before she reached the last button he stood and jerked it off. In seconds, he was naked and climbing into the water with her.

His hands clasped her rib cage and lifted her, placing her on her knees above his lap. Considering she was no featherweight, his actions revved her engines into high gear. The play of muscles across his upper arms and chest stretching and bunching sent shivers of delight straight to the area where his cock sought entrance. With a shift of her hips, he slid in, long and hard. She sighed. He chuckled and thrust. He felt so wonderful, filling her with pure heat.

The slow, easy pace building with each rise and fall of her hips gave her time to examine his handsome face. In fact, they watched each other as she rode him, immersed in each other's pleasure. His eyes glittered with an emotion she didn't recognize but quickly found herself in his arms and out of the water.

"Damn! We'll do slow and gentle later," he groaned in her ear as he slapped her back to the wall and thrust faster.

Around his back she crossed her ankles and twined her arms around his neck, holding on with all her might. Her breath came in pants with each thrust. The cords along his neck stood out as he strained to bring her to a climax with him. His big hands hooked under her arms and lifted until her breasts were even with his mouth. He sucked a nipple into his mouth and bit.

That was the final push she needed. "Aww! Collin!"

Her fingers clasped his head to her as her body bowed. She went limp and he shoved into her for the last time. His long groan brought a smile to her face.

Her arms tightened on his neck when he moved back with her still in his arms and walked into the bedroom. He leaned over and yanked off the bedspread and dropped her on the mattress. Before she could complain of the cool sheets, his heated body was on top of her and he plunged into her again.

"Oh, my." Wide-eyed, she stared up into those amber eyes she found so fascinating. "You're still hard."

"A little trick I learned in Bangkok." He kissed her and then pulled back a little. "Now we do gentle."

She gasped when he sucked in a nipple and tugged at the tender flesh. His big masculine hands skimmed over her sides to the flare of her hips as he spread kisses down her torso until he reached the place she wanted his expertise again. When his mouth covered what actually throbbed for his touch, she opened her mouth and sighed. He licked and nipped at the hard knot. She groaned. The man was an expert.

He shifted his shoulders until her legs dangled over them. Every swirl of his tongue brought an answering thrust of her groin. He acted as if he planned to feast on her all day. When he thrust two fingers into her, she bowed her back and shouted his name. As she climaxed, he moved over her and eased into her warmth. His thrusts were slow and measured as if they had all the time in the world. Before she realized it, her body responded with another intense climax.

By the time he'd finished with her, she was so weak she couldn't protest when he moved away.

He walked into the bathroom. The jets stopped and then she heard the gurgling of water draining from the tub. A moment later he returned, strutting to the bed, heavy cock swaying, and pulled a sheet over her before he slipped in beside her. With one arm, he drew her body into his, arranging her head on his arm. She smiled.

"What's so funny?" he asked.

"Nothing. I've never felt so weak afterwards." With her eyes closed, she inhaled the scent of sex and Collin and smiled again.

"Good" was all he said before she fell asleep.

<<<>>>

Collin brushed the back of his finger down her soft cheek. Though sound asleep, she puffed out sighs each time he touched her. It was charming.

Instead of the dangerously beautiful femme fatale he'd met on an airplane in Seattle, she looked like a pretty twenty-something woman sleeping in his arms. So much more treacherous and lethal to his plans and heart.

Olivia whimpered.

He kissed her forehead. "Shh, I'll take care of you. You have nothing to worry about."

She sighed.

Yeah, completely dangerous. He leaned over and checked under the mattress for his gun. Earlier, he'd found her stash of weapons and couldn't help but be proud of her initiative in protecting herself. Hugging her to his body, he fell asleep too.

Chapter Twenty-Two

"Rex, I don't give a flying fuck what you think about the plan. Tell me what you heard. Time is about to run out and I need to dump this phone."

Olivia stood near the corner of the cabin's wraparound porch listening to Collin's conversation on a disposable cell phone he'd obviously picked up while in Pigeon Forge. The cell would be used one time and then broken into a hundred pieces, a standard procedure for any operative. He'd snuck out to make his call and she'd guessed he was making plans without her. And she was right.

"Secret weapon? I heard something about that but nothing definite. Did they give you any details?" He stopped his pacing and stared blindly into the lightning bug–filled evening. "No? Then it's probably a bluff."

With eyebrows raised, he held the phone away for a moment. Rex's deep timbre reached her ears as he yelled. Then Collin said in an even tone, "Settle down. I'll call you tomorrow night. Make sure everyone's in place at the time we decided." He chuckled. "No. She hasn't been a problem." Another chuckle. "For God's sake, maybe your problem is you haven't gotten any in a long time. Rex?"

He glared down at the phone and then placed it to his ear again. "Rex?"

He chortled and dropped the cell phone on the porch and stepped on it. The sound of cracking plastic echoed in the quiet night. Once he picked it up, he started taking it apart, slamming it against the rail a couple times to break the more stubborn parts.

Then he glanced at the trees beyond. "Olivia, do you have any idea what Theo's secret weapon is?"

Crap! Of course, he would know she was eavesdropping. She was beginning to feel like a klutz around him. What she'd always heard was correct; love made a person an idiot. Hell, she'd even slept soundly last night. She wasn't even sure if she had any of her usual nightmares.

The last six nights had been magical with Collin. He'd been a giving lover and careful to make sure she climaxed twice as many times as he did. She wished ... no, wishes never came true for people like her.

She tightened the cloth tie on his robe. The few times they went into town, they'd picked up a few items of clothing, underwear, and other essentials for her, but she preferred to wear his robe in the evenings after they made love. Inside she cringed with that thought. It was just sex, really good sex with Collin; she couldn't forget that.

Toe-to-toe, she rested her hands on his chest. Oh, my, he felt so good. That was part of her problem. She only had to be in touching range for all sense to leave her, and each time they made love she thought she would finally have enough of him, but her need only grew. Her brain had become mush. Her killer instincts nil.

She tilted her head and rubbed her cheek against his

hand as he caressed her neck. Then he slipped the robe off her shoulders and continued to caress her as the night air and his touch brought her to a fevered pitch. There was decadence to her being naked outside while he was clothed. She didn't care. She was becoming obsessed with him and she'd worry about it later.

His hands returned to her shoulders and pressed. She slowly went to her knees. During her descent she unsnapped and unzipped his jeans. His hard penis fell easily into her hands. Wrapping both hands around him, she licked the sensitive knob, causing Collin to groan with pleasure. Her mouth took him inside as she flicked the slit with her tongue. She squeezed with one hand and fondled his sac with the other. Then she lowered her mouth further and then pulled back, building the rhythm he hinted at with every groan and thrust of his hips, not sure how much longer she could wait until she had what she lovingly sucked between her legs instead of her lips.

"Fuck, Olivia," he moaned.

She moved her mouth off him but continued massaging his length. "Oh, yeah, you better," she said and grinned up at him.

When he grabbed two handfuls of her hair, she thought he would lead her mouth back to his cock. Instead, he brought her to her feet. "You're really something, you know that?" Then he took her mouth.

Knowing he tasted himself on her tongue almost sent her to her knees again. His mouth left hers to dip to one taut nipple. He sucked so hard the burn bowed her body and she rubbed herself against his rough denim clad leg. Just as he switched to her other breast, they heard the crack of a stick breaking. They froze and then dropped flat to the porch, making their bodies as small as possible, less of a target.

She pointed to the direction the sound came from and then held up the palm of her hand in question. He nodded and then tipped his head toward the door hidden in the shadows. Without wasting a second, she crawled away as he stayed close behind.

<<<>>>

Collin watched her deliciously naked peach-shaped butt wag its way toward the side door. Until his dying day, he'd never need pharmaceutical help in maintaining a hard-on. All he would need to do was remember that sight. At least he had the presence of mind to zip up his pants.

The first gunshot missed him by four inches, spraying splinters into his face and arms. Scrambling for the door, they fell inside the cabin with another round of gun fire and flying fragments.

"Get your clothes on and we'll leave through the bedroom window." He glanced to see if she was following orders, and she'd already pulled on a thong and jeans. Every move had her breasts swaying and jiggling. When his cock began to fill, he turned away. Fuck! He had to keep his mind on getting away. "Don't forget the Beretta Sub-Compact and your knife."

His grin widened when he heard her gasp behind him. So she'd thought he hadn't noticed the missing Beretta or that she possessed a wicked-looking knife. After buttoning up his shirt and snapping his pants, he turned back to her. She was dressed, hair pulled back in a ponytail.

"Here." He tossed a small backpack to her. "Throw in what you believe will be useful in the woods."

She threw it down. "No way! We need to leave in the car. I'm not a Girl Scout and I don't do the outdoors for anybody." When she turned to glare at him, her eyes widened and she grabbed his arm. "Shit! You're bleeding." She snatched a handful of tissues from the bathroom counter and dabbed at his cheek.

Pulling away from her unusual feminine hovering, he nodded to where gunshots continued to take chunks out of the outside walls.

"You know we're sitting ducks here and will certainly be in the car. Through the woods is the best way to shake them." He strapped his other Beretta to an ankle and then clipped on a sling to a lightweight MP5 submachine gun, pulling it over his head and under one arm.

She shook her head. "You do understand that's not just a couple miles of woods like behind the Main Sector? That's miles and miles of wilderness. People have been known to disappear and never be seen again. I refuse ..."

Before she could persist with her complaining a loud crack and then tinkling of broken glass warned them that someone was coming in.

Shots were fired into the bedroom and they ducked behind the bed. He heard movement a few feet behind him and he turned as a dark figure jumped. Without a second to waste, he fired and the power of the submachine gun flipped the body in the air and away from him. Then he heard another intruder and looked over to Olivia.

It looked as if she was hugging the dark dressed man, but when the other gunman slipped to the floor, Collin caught the flash of a red-coated blade. She'd stabbed the man in the back, probably straight into his kidney. The shock to the man's body would paralyze him until they could make their escape, unless she decided to slit his throat.

She never ceased to amaze him.

They turned out the lights and waited for a few minutes, listening to the continued gunfire outside while the man at Olivia's feet whimpered.

"Slit his throat," Collin commanded.

"No," she simply said and opened the window, crawling out.

If he didn't know better, he would say she looked a little pale. Was the thought of taking a man's life up close too much for the sexy assassin? Interesting. Another layer of the most fascinating and deadly woman he'd ever met.

Chapter Twenty-Three

Olivia ignored Collin as she sat shivering next to a stream. They'd stopped to quench their thirst and take a break from the relentless terrain. It didn't matter the sun was straight overhead, but for some freaking reason the warmth wouldn't reach them. Fingers spread she began counting off each one.

"What the fuck are you adding?"

His face was swollen on one side from jumping a black-clad Circle lookout, using his fists so others nearby would not be alerted. Low-hanging branches left new scratches across the other cheek as they had run from more gunfire. And all of that didn't include the cuts he'd received from the flying splinters the night before, even though they were dry and angry looking, giving him a more intimidating look than usual.

"I'm counting how many times I threatened to kill you. I've decided there has to be a limit. Then I can give up and just kill you!" She squinted. "Considering how miserable I am right now, I wouldn't have to worry about getting all mushy about you."

"Mushy, huh?" He grinned and winced when his cheeks moved up.

"I'm glad you're hurting." She leaned over and began rubbing her feet.

The tennis shoes she'd thought were so stylish had worn blisters on her heels. With all the walking up and down rough terrain that probably hadn't seen a human being since the beginning of time, she wanted to scream and throw her hands up in disgust. Sure, most likely he'd saved their lives, but if she hadn't been blinded from being so horny, she would've asked why in the hell they had gone to a cabin out in the middle of nowhere with no real protection, instead of his well-fortified building in a civilized place.

The rumble from his chest alerted her and when she looked up, he burst out laughing. So handsome and masculine, he almost hurt her eyes looking at him. He'd finally loosened up enough to let the submachine gun hang from its sling and held it to his side with one hand.

She smiled with him. Even during their days and nights of making love he'd never appeared so relaxed as he did now.

Just like a man. He enjoyed having the odds stacked against him.

He wiped at the corners of his eyes. "You're definitely a city girl."

"There's nothing wrong with that."

She shifted, bringing her other butt cheek to rest on the rock beneath her as she rummaged through the backpack looking for a way to protect her heels. All she needed was a stick-on bandage or socks. Socks would be lovely.

Facedown in the pack, she felt something soft brush her arm. She scrambled off the rock, pulling her knife and looked around. A white ball rolled to a stop a couple feet from where she'd sat seconds ago.

"Socks!" She held them up and grinned, feeling giddy.

Collin's laughter didn't bother her. She had socks! She snatched them from the ground and at the same time kicked off her shoes. The thick material felt so wonderful against her mistreated feet.

"We need to get going. It's not much further," Collin said.

"Not much further to where? Tell me again, why in the hell did we go to a cabin in the woods instead of that nice protected building you have?" she asked more to aggravate, knowing he wouldn't answer. Then she noticed the little silver box in his hand. "Why in the bloody hell didn't you tell me you had a compass?"

"You never asked." He stood and picked up his backpack and adjusted his hold on the MP5.

"I never ..." She closed her eyes and inhaled. Such a man! When she opened them, he was several feet away. "I expect an answer this time. Where are we going?"

That felt more important at this juncture. Get out of the sticky situation first and then insist on all of the answers later.

With efficient movements, she sheathed her knife as she slipped into her shoes, cringing a little from the backs touching her heels even with thick socks.

"It'll take about a half-hour hike and we should come across a relatively flat field," he said as his eyes scanned the area.

"And? What happens then? A helicopter picks us up?" Sure she sounded hopeful, but she didn't really feel that way. Hope wasn't in her vocabulary after hiking and hiding in the forest since dawn.

"Yes." He kept walking.

She glared at him as she hesitated beneath a massive hickory tree. Had he said what she thought he had? He knew that a helicopter would be picking them up? And he hadn't felt a need to tell her earlier? Several quiet strides brought her up against his back to press her knife to his kidney.

"I think you better stop and explain."

He slowed his steps. "Olivia, get that pig-sticker away from me."

His no-nonsense voice made her consider dropping the knife. Just then the whoop-whooping of a helicopter overhead changed her mind. For emphasis, she jabbed the tip, most likely breaking a little skin. Poor baby.

"If you don't want us to miss your ride, you better start talking."

"We don't have time for this," he muttered.

He turned, his foot kicking at her feet as she jumped out of the way. At the same time, his hand sliced through the air, trying to knock the knife from her hand. He miscalculated and she acted instinctively, rolling her wrist away.

Blood quickly covered his sleeve. "Fuck! You cut me!"

"You deserve it, asshole!" She glared back at him. God! She hoped she hadn't cut him too deep.

Before she could step away, he took the knife from her, throwing it into the tall grass and grabbed her shoulders as he put them nose to nose.

"I'm trying to save us."

He looked at her, eyes narrowing as his forehead creased in a frown. Then he kissed her, a tongue-possessing, soul-searching, mind-blowing kiss.

Her heart quit beating. The world stopped spinning. Falling in love with him was the most dangerous thing she'd ever done. Once they returned to civilization, she needed to escape. Better to disappoint him now instead of later.

After he released her, she didn't try to make him answer her or trip him in any way. They ran for the helicopter as its big blades continued to spin. Once on board, Collin shook his fist thumb up and the big hunk of metal took off. When she looked at the clearing below, she saw about a dozen camo-wearing men emerged from the tree line, firing at them. The pinging of metal hitting metal had her scooting to the middle.

Talk about a close call. She closed her eyes for a moment, head resting back. Numb and tired beyond reason, she turned to stare at the man sitting across from her as he chatted with the OS operatives manning their escape.

He'd never answered her question of why they had stayed in the Smoky Mountains. She'd become so involved in touching him, making love, and seeing what would come of their time together, she'd completely forgotten her doubts. So why risk their lives when the OS's building was as safe as any fortress? He was up to something and it certainly didn't have anything to do with protecting her. No matter how she would like to deny it, that hurt.

The roaring engines sputtered and then went quiet. Thankfully the whoop-whooping of the blades continued. The pilot was screaming at his copilot as they flicked switches and turned dials.

Olivia watched the ground coming closer and faster as the helicopter dipped to one side. Her heart pounded with the beat of the blades. She checked on Collin and was surprised to see him watching her. The look he gave her brought warmth to her face. She'd never had a man watch her like he did. His stares had turned from distrust to desire. He needed to know how she felt even if he didn't return the feeling. Fear seized her in its grip. She was afraid their last few seconds on this world would be over before she told him she loved him.

Oh, God, she did.

As she opened her mouth to shout the three words, she stopped. What expression would be on his face if she told him?

Now or never.

She cleared her throat and then the engines burst to life, long enough for the pilots to pull up the helicopter's nose, causing her stomach to flip, and they landed with a jarring slide.

"Olivia, are you all right?" Collin waited until she nodded before turning to the pilots to find out the damage.

Talk about glad! She was relieved not only to be alive but she hadn't made a fool of herself by shouting her feelings. Being vulnerable, especially to Collin, spelled disaster. However she felt about him had to be hidden. Men used women in the name of love. Besides with an organization to run, his position required that he not get involved with ex-Circle operatives.

How would his people trust him if they saw his tenderness toward her? His hard-nosed reputation was important to maintain order and ... hold on! Was that the real reason they'd stayed at the cabin? Was he ashamed to let others know he lusted after her?

"Olivia!"

She turned toward him, blinking, unable to focus for a few seconds. From his concerned look, she knew he'd been calling her name more than once.

"We have to abandon the copter and we need to move now!" Collin jerked his head toward the opening.

Her eyes and nose burned from the smoke now

billowing into the cabin. She jumped to the ground and darted toward the thick brush. Behind her she heard the other men following and then several loud pops echoed around her. The snapping of leaves and tree limbs around her confirmed what she'd thought. They were being fired on.

As soon as she found cover on the opposite side of an enormous fallen tree, she looked around. No one was there. Taking a chance, she peeked over the trunk. A pilot was down. The other one struggled with helping Collin who was dragging his leg. Oh, hell no. It better be a flesh wound. Jumping back over the tree, she ran to Collin's side.

"Dammit! Go on! He's got me!" Collin shook his head.

She ignored him, almost panicking when her hand touched his shoulder and came away wet with blood. How many bullets had he taken? Out of the corner of her eye she noticed movement near the downed helicopter. The gunman pressed his body to the cockpit, his rifle against his shoulder, aiming at Collin's back.

Without thinking it through she grabbed Collin's MP5. "Go!" She pointed to the fallen tree. "Go on!" As she pressed forward, she muttered, "I'll take care of the asshole that shot you."

Ignoring the shouting behind her, she kneeled and fired. The man went down. She turned to leave, happy to see that Collin and the other pilot were out of sight, but then the humming of ATVs brought her back around. About twenty of the larger four-wheel vehicles came out of the surrounding forest. Each one had two operatives and their weapons pointed at her.

With no other choice and needing to give Collin more time, she threw down the submachine gun and raised her arms, waving them as if she wanted them to come to her.

She counted on them believing she'd been alone with the dead pilot and that Collin had jumped out elsewhere. Not since she was a little girl in the orphanage praying for new parents to love her had she ever prayed so hard.

Theo would certainly kill her now. And she prayed Collin would live through the ordeal, but any thought of praying for the leader of OS to save her ... well, she would be beyond crazy to believe that.

She wasn't worth saving.

<<<>>>

"We've got to go back. They'll kill her!" Collin struggled as Rex held him down. They were in another OS helicopter and this time no one was shooting at them.

He'd passed out from loss of blood after the pilot hid them in the tree trunk's hollowed end. When he'd regained consciousness as they loaded him into the copter's cabin, he'd expected her to be there waiting, shouting curses at him for getting shot. But when they lifted him inside and she was nowhere nearby, he demanded to know where she was. They'd told him she'd gone willingly with The Circle operatives.

"Who?" one of the men holding him down asked, shaking his head in confusion.

"They'll kill Olivia!" Grabbing for the tubes attached to his arm, he jerked one out but Rex stopped him before he could do more damage.

"They won't. She's the fucking Circle's top eliminator. She probably gave them your whereabouts. I told you, you can't trust her." Rex cut away Collin's pant leg.

"Fuck you! Turn this son of a bitch around!" They hadn't seen her face when she yanked his gun out of his hand. Her beautiful green eyes had been filled with love and worry. She'd saved his miserable hide.

Damn! He didn't get a chance to tell her he'd lied.

Sure he'd hoped their time away from the OS brought out the traitor, but he'd wanted to be alone with Olivia too. He wanted to show her how much he cared, probably more than he should. Not until he dealt with Theo could he tell her how he felt or even promise her a future. That was, if she wanted one with him.

Chapter Twenty-Four

"Hello! Anyone out there?" Olivia pushed the unbruised side of her face against the bars inset in her cell's door, trying to see around the corner. While keeping her eyes on the outer steel door, she listened for any sound from the other cells.

From what she could tell, counting meals, she'd been in The Circle's dungeon for four days and Theo hadn't deemed it necessary to come and see her. Not that she looked forward to the conversation, but she hated to be left in the dark. Her chuckle bounced against the stone walls. In the dark? What a riot. Except for the light shining through the small grate in the steel door, they didn't feel it necessary to turn on the lights in the cells.

For meals, a tray was pushed through a long thin opening at the bottom of her cell door. She'd quickly learned to return the tray through the opening or they wouldn't feed her the next meal.

The last time she'd visited the cells beneath the Main Sector, it had been to interrogate prisoners, and only two of the six cells had been occupied. After questioning the first man, she'd ordered them both released. He'd supplied all the information they'd needed without her even talking to the other one. Knowing Theo, the cells had been refilled several more times since. At least she had thought he had until she tried to communicate with the other cellmates. So far she hadn't met with success.

A groan drifted to her cell. Thank goodness, finally a sound. She was beginning to believe she was alone. She wanted to talk, maybe find out the chances of getting out of here. Anything to break up the monotony.

"Hey, I hear you," she said in a stage whisper. "How long have you been here?"

Amazing how a person could crave the sound of another human's voice in such a short time. She just knew she needed to escape before Collin tried something stupid to get her out. The thought of anyone risking their neck to rescue her brought a grin to her face. Just having someone care enough to want to save her made her happy.

Ouch! She cupped her jaw as she moved the lower half back and forth. She counted herself lucky it was still intact. One of the guards had hit her when she insisted on seeing Theo. While she nursed a bruised face, he probably still couldn't stand up straight.

Again, she tried to get a response from her cellmate. Nothing.

When she heard the beeping of the guard punching in the code on the main door's outside panel, she returned to her bunk and waited to see what happened next. Boot heels thumped toward her cell and then more beeping filled the air before he opened her door and turned on the light.

Showtime!

Squinting, she placed her hand above her eyes. Behind him stood six more guards dressed in black, less likely to show blood, holding MP5's and they all possessed square jaws and determined stares. Either they expected and hoped for a confrontation since they were probably friends of the guard who now could sing soprano, or Theo was no longer playing nice.

"Well, isn't this a wonderful surprise? Such a handsome escort. Theo shouldn't have." She slowly stood. Wouldn't want to alarm the deadly crew with any unexpected movements.

"Theo didn't." One of the guards motioned her toward the door.

From his tone and the evil stare he gave her, she felt it best to keep her mouth shut.

At an even pace, she walked out the cell door and through the space the guards made for her. Once they exited into the large hallway and up some steep stairs on the other side of the steel door, the men surrounded her and marched toward a new section she'd never visited.

After they'd passed the third code panel and no less than a dozen more guards, Olivia became worried. If she'd thought the dungeon heavily guarded, it was nothing compared to this section.

Maybe in this area they eliminated the operatives who betrayed them. Like incinerators lined up to burn the bodies, no fuss, no muss. Christ! She needed to get her mind off such gruesome thoughts.

Finally they reached an ordinary looking door and the guard entered another code. After a series of clicks, a beep sounded, signaling it unlocked. She stood in front of the opening staring inside. The huge room appeared to be all glass and steel. The high ceiling and tall windows made her think of a New Age church. The sun was so bright she found herself squinting again. One of the guards becoming impatient pushed her hard in the back. She stumbled inside but kept her footing.

The door behind her closed with a swoosh and the clicks and beep repeated. She looked over her shoulder. None of the guards had followed her. She turned back around and took a step toward the windows and then stopped. Standing off alone was a familiar silhouette. Collin? Motionless, he stared out across the Main Sector's exercise yard. He looked grim and didn't acknowledge her presence.

She wanted to go to him and pester him about his wounds and not coming for her sooner. But something about his stance held her back. She remained near the door, thankful his wounds hadn't been severe.

Although she'd known the pilot would protect him and Rex probably wouldn't be far behind, she'd worried about infection and everything that could possibly go wrong for Collin while she was locked up. Odd that it had been only four days and his hair had grown and curled around his collar. He looked as if he'd lost weight even though his shoulders were as broad as ever. Could she be mistaken? Had she'd been in the dungeon longer?

"Sit there," he ordered in a deep voice she didn't recognize as he faced her. A black patch covered his right eye, while his left glared at her from its light amber depths. Deep grooves carved around his mouth provided clues to a hard life. This man was not Collin but was similar enough to be his twin.

What the hell?

"Who are you? And where's Theo?" Forehead wrinkled, she forced herself to remain standing as a small ache in her head warned of a coming migraine.

"Olivia, do as Ryker tells you or I'll order him to use

force. And he loves to be forceful." Theo walked out of the shadows in full kingly red velvet regalia and sat on a throne-like chair at one end of the room. "Isn't that right, Ryker?" He crossed his legs as he picked up a cup from a small gilded table, and sipped the brew as he watched her over the rim.

The silent man remained quiet and still.

She ignored Theo and his role-playing psycho behavior. After living with him so long, she'd learned if she laughed, her punishment would be worse.

"Ryker, huh? What's your first name?" she asked, daring them to protest her question as impertinent. Without taking her eyes off the man with the patch, her hands searched for the chair and then she collapsed into the seat.

The man scowled at Theo and then returned to staring out the window as if answering her question meant nothing to him.

"So Collin never told you. What does that say about your lover, huh?" Theo's lips twitched. He enjoyed her surprise too much. "Ryker?" Theo drew the silent man's attention back to him. Those shark-like cold eyes shifted to Theo. "You can leave us for now."

The man stepped toward the shadows, where Olivia guessed was another door in the darkness, but he hesitated. "You sure?" he asked in his deep raspy voice.

"I'll be okay. She's quite familiar with how deadly I can be." Theo grinned. "Aren't you, my dear Olivia?"

Oh, God! She was going to throw up. Yes. She knew how dangerous he could be when pushed and betrayed. Collin's doppelgänger looked scary but she really wished he had stayed. Maybe she wanted to fool herself. Having Collin's face, sort of, wouldn't necessarily mean he would protect her.

Small tremors raced through her body reminding her of the horrors she'd escaped before and never wanted to return to again. She wanted to close her eyes and pretend he wasn't looking at her as if she was a long forgotten lollipop he planned to bite.

Though it was useless and, yes, she was crazy for even wishing it, she needed Collin to rescue her. She wasn't sure if she could stand up to the monster from her past.

Please, Lord, let him know I need him. Prayer was becoming a daily thing for her since meeting Collin.

Her need to know overriding her fear, she said, "Ryker isn't a common name. Are you any relation to Collin Ryker?" Reckless and stupid of her but the words were out of her mouth.

Theo glowered at her and then looked at the man as he ordered him to leave. "Now!"

The guy didn't budge. He had big balls not to be bothered by Theo's evil stare.

"Yeah. He's my brother," he said in a detached tone. Then he nodded at Theo and left the room.

Looking down at the floor as if she could find the answer, her headache grew a little stronger. Collin had never mentioned a brother. The two men looked so much alike they had to be related. But a brother? He appeared several years older than Collin.

"Such a shame. Now the cat's out of the bag," Theo said with his dramatic flair.

Rubbing the spot between her eyes, she leaned over and placed her elbows on her knees, lowering her head in the hope she wouldn't throw up.

Theo stood and walked around to the back of her chair. She felt his hands smooth down her hair. Shivers of disgust ran through her body. Feelings she'd ignored most of the time slammed into her. She hated this man and no matter how often she worked at holding back the fury running through her, she struggled to keep her hands away from him. So she concentrated on irrelevant things. Like how it had be around five days since she had a bath. She hoped her smell disgusted him and her hair had to look like a pile of pine needles.

He grabbed a handful of hair and jerked her head back until she was certain her neck would break as she looked upside down into his face.

"Ryker doesn't remember Collin like he did before. For the last ten years I've kept him in service at the New York sector, training, preparing him for when I'd need him. He only knows the man that would call him brother will try to kill him. But Ryker will kill Collin first. That asshole has no idea his brother's alive. I hope the surprise is frozen on that bastard's face when he dies. I would love to see it. The little twit has been a thorn in my side all his life."

Theo bent down and kissed her. She struggled and he bit her bottom lip until blood flooded her mouth.

He moved away from her mouth and she spit at him. Blood spattered across his face. With his hand still in her hair, he pulled her up and over the chair. Trying to relieve some of the pain, she held onto his wrists, kicking and twisting in his grasp. He released his grip and backhanded her on the already bruised cheek. She landed a couple feet away.

She spit again and this time on his teak floor. Her teeth felt like they would fall out. Every bone in her body rattled as she rolled to her knees. The thought of tackling him and beating him to a pulp was quickly forgotten when the six guards rushed inside.

"Are you all right, sir?" The one with the markings on his wide shoulders inquired.

"Yes, I'm fine. But I do need your help. Pull her off the floor and hold her." Theo snatched a tissue from a drawer in the coffee table and wiped at her blood sprinkled across his face and shirt.

Two of the men lifted her to feet, holding her tight by the arms. She probably could force them to let her go, but the other four, not counting Theo, would object with hard fists. She wasn't sure how much more she could take of the abuse.

"I have to say Collin had a good influence on you in one small area. You don't talk as much or make smart comments like you did before." He made sure to keep his distance from her feet.

"Where did he put the sword?"

She wondered why it took him so long to ask the question.

"I don't know."

Theo slapped the other cheek and then smoothed his hair from his face. A ringing in her ears matched the bright lights she was seeing over his head. Oh, well, both of her cheeks should match now. After he asked her the same question a few more times and she gave the same answer, her ribs and stomach followed suit. She had the satisfaction of throwing up on his beautiful floor and snazzy Gucci shoes.

The thought raced through her mind that she felt relieved he used his fists and not his favorite weapon of choice, the knife. Then a flash of light crossed her face.

Only one eye opened all the way but she quickly grasped the reason for the brightness. Theo's switchblade caught the sunshine streaming through the windows as he swung it across her chest. Liquid fire followed in its wake. She screamed. In seconds, a thin line of blood soaked her T-shirt.

The maniacal pleasure on Theo's face warned her of what else was to come.

She hoped to pass out before he killed her.

Chapter Twenty-Five

Two hours later, she remained sprawled across her cell floor with one cheek pressed against the cool cement, hoping to relieve some of the heat from her swollen face. She groaned when the chill seeped in. As she relaxed, she quickly remembered the numerous cuts on her chest and arms. They stung but none were deep enough to continue bleeding. Theo had planned for her to live a little longer it appeared.

"You're back," a croaky female voice said.

Olivia hated to move her jaw, but she needed some answers.

"Yeah. Who are you?" she asked, cringing from the pain shooting across her face and down her neck.

"How soon we forget." The person coughed up a lung and then said, "A. J."

"Shit!" Olivia found if she placed her other hand on top of the opposite cheek off the floor, the pain wasn't so great when she talked. So Theo had put A. J. down there too. "I'm sorry about this mess."

"I don't regret it," she coughed again, "much."

"When Collin breaks me out," Olivia's stomach rolled with the pain, "I'll get you out too."

Again, when did she become a helpless female who expected a man to pull her out of a jam?

"You're kidding, right? You're in here because of him. Men look after themselves. I learned that five years ago."

The sadness in A. J.'s voice conveyed a lot of what was left unsaid.

Olivia had always believed the same before meeting Collin so she understood it completely. True, Collin had disappointed her before, but for some reason she felt deep inside this time would be different. Those days in the cabin had been special to both of them, even if he never admitted it. While Theo alternated between beating and cutting her, she realized she needed to believe in Collin to survive.

"Is there anyone else in the other cells?" Olivia forced herself to move, standing on wobbly legs. She slid her feet on the cement floor so not to jar any area of her body.

"No." A. J.'s voice was nearer. She probably was looking out the small barred window in her cell door. "The day before you showed up, they moved a guy out of the last cell. I heard the guards mention something about transferring him to the New York sector."

"Did you know Collin had a brother and he worked for The Circle out of New York?" Even saying it out loud sent chills down her back.

"You're kidding. I heard his brother died in the car explosion with his parents. I guess that explains why Theo handled problems out of that area." After another coughing fit, A. J. asked, "How did you hear about it?"

Olivia tested a loose tooth. Hopefully it would tighten up if she wasn't hit again anytime soon. Funny. Most likely she would be dead. "For some reason, Theo had him waiting for me when I was brought into the room. He's near enough the spitting image of Collin to be his twin, except he had a lot of scars on his face and wore an eye patch." She still couldn't believe Collin had a brother and hadn't told her.

"Not a twin. Arthur Ryker's just nine months older."

"Shit. I had hoped Theo was jerking my chain. No wonder I thought it was Collin at first." Olivia thought of the man's harsh features, a man who'd lived through an explosion and probably watched his parents die a horrible death. With Theo as a guardian who probably perverted every memory he had to ensure he hated his own brother enough to kill him. "What do you think¾"

"Shut the fuck up! I'm tired of you two gabby females!" The guard pounded on the outer door.

Not wanting to press their luck and needing a little time to form a plan, she stretched out on the cot this time, tenderly resting her aching body. As A. J. had said, she couldn't depend on Collin, though deep inside she knew better. In fact, Theo probably hoped he would try to rescue her.

She closed her tired and grainy eyes. Talk about mixed emotions, she wanted Collin to prove A. J. wrong and show up as the hero. But then Theo would kill him. Her throat tried to close up with the thought. Every inch of her body ached as she fought the desire to curl into a ball and cry.

With her track record, Collin most likely had moved on and chalked her up as a good way to spend a few days in hiding. She shivered.

She sure missed his warm body.

<<<>>>

Collin struggled into a pair of loose-fitting woodland camos, forcing the left leg, bandage and all, into the pant leg. He'd already worked up a sweat from pulling on a black T-shirt over his bandaged shoulder.

Six days had gone by since they were ambushed and who knew what was happening to Olivia? No matter how self-sufficient she thought of herself, Theo was on a rampage, ordering the death of five OS operatives and even three of The Circle's. It was only time before news came in about Theo eliminating his top assassin.

Rex still hadn't discovered what they meant by secret weapon. It could be anything from a nuclear device to chemical or biological weapons or even a person inside the OS. His top personnel worked furiously for an answer and in the meanwhile they'd stepped up security. Collin had decided not to wait around until hell broke loose. He needed to save Olivia as he would any OS operative. At least that was what he wanted to tell himself.

"What the hell do you think you're doing?"

Rex stood over him with hands on hips, scowling as Collin gingerly lifted his foot and pulled on a sock.

"What the fuck does it look like?" He finished with the last sock.

"It looks like I'll have to kick your ass if you think you're leaving this room." The big guy kicked Collin's boots across the room, out of reach.

He lifted one eyebrow at Rex's childish behavior.

"How will that stop me?" With careful movements, he slid off the bed and stood, clutching the back of a chair.

"Collin. Friend. I've got bad news." Rex shuffled his feet.

So it happened. Theo killed her. He crumbled into the chair.

227

"When?" Collin saw the folder. "Fuck, man. What did Theo do? Send pictures of her dead body?"

Rex shook his head. "Photos. Yeah. I wish I had killed her." Then he handed the brown folder over.

His hand shook as he took the folder. He'd seen some of Theo's work and usually the body would be unrecognizable. In this type of work death was a big possibility. So he'd never allowed himself to become involved with another operative to the point he had with her.

He flipped to the first picture. For a split second his face felt cold as if all the blood had drained away. Then a rush of heat followed when he turned to the final five shots. In a rush of black rage, he threw the folder across the room. The photos landed haphazardly on the floor, pictures of Theo and Olivia kissing taunted him with his gullibility.

"They came in the mail today. I guess Theo wanted to make sure you knew she'd been playing you all along."

"Not only their top assassin but a damn good actress," Collin said vehemently under his breath.

"Before you ask, we checked. They haven't been tampered with. They're real." Rex moved to block his view of the photos. "Listen, I hate this for you. I won't say I told you so, instead I'll say we need to kick ass."

Collin breathed in deep, pulling himself together. When had he become a wimp? Had Olivia taken his balls along with his heart? He didn't want to believe the pictures were real. She'd always turned a little green when she mentioned Theo as if he made her sick.

Coming to a decision, he headed for the door, panting from the exertion, taking one step at a time. If Olivia was guilty of betraying the OS, the truth would eventually come to light. He didn't trust Theo's reasoning for sending the photos. Too convenient in his opinion. Then again, he could be deluding himself into believing she had some honor.

He refused to think of how he felt as he stared at the photographs, seeing Olivia's mouth covered by Theo's. Accepting one betrayal at a time was all he could handle. If it was true.

"Get back in bed. Killing her can wait. For that matter let me do it." Rex hovered nearby, hands out as if Collin might fall any second.

"I need to talk with Anne." As soon as Collin could return to the OS headquarters he'd ordered the doctor to be thrown into a holding cell.

"She can wait. You need to give yourself some time to heal." Creases divided the big man's forehead.

Collin could tell his friend wanted to put his mind to rest, but no matter what was said, he had to start pulling his organization together. Theo was up to something and Dr. Shelton was part of it.

Their plan to bring out the traitor worked with the help of their Romeo operative. A couple weeks earlier, Lucian Reilly had visited the doctor about a nasty scratch he received from a knife during an assignment. While stitching the cut, Anne quizzed him about The Circle. In itself, he found nothing odd about her curiosity. People often asked him about his time there, and like most women, she felt comfortable around him, one of the reasons he was so good at his work. When he was about to leave, she said, "You know I wonder if all this fighting between the two organizations isn't just a big misunderstanding. If Collin spoke to Theo, this could be all cleared up."

He'd liked the doctor but he knew the danger in her way of thinking. When he questioned her, she mentioned she'd met Theo once. He recognized Theo's method. He always worked through the weakest link. The Circle's leader could make a Democrat vote Republican and be proud of it. Lucian visited with Rex and repeated what she'd said and voiced his apprehension.

So they'd decided to test Lucian's concern by having Rex mention to only the doctor of their whereabouts in the mountains.

The attack had proven Lucian's fears to be correct.

Collin's knuckles whitened as he held on to the handrails in the elevator.

"No." He continued in a firm and steady voice. "I've waited long enough. I'm tired of waiting for our people to extract the information. Anne may not know much, but even an insignificant detail may help us understand what in the hell is going on."

But by the time the elevator reached the holding cell level, Collin hated to admit he needed help. Knees stiff and hands shaking, he allowed Rex to silently grab his arm and walk him to a chair in one of the empty interrogation rooms. Collin swiped his forehead with his sleeve and waited until his leg quit throbbing and his heart slowed down. His shoulder was better and caused only a few twinges when he moved too quickly.

With a nod of his head, Rex left and a few minutes later brought in Dr. Shelton. Dark circles surrounded sunken blue eyes as she looked at him with horror. Her beautiful blond hair gone, shaved from her head as part of a prior interrogation technique.

"You should be afraid, Anne. I personally oversee the punishment for major offenses, especially when it's betrayal." He leaned back in his chair, keeping his trembling hands beneath the table. Even as light-headed as he felt, he managed to stare her in the eye without wavering.

"I'm sorry, Collin. I'm so sorry." Tears streamed down Dr. Shelton's face. She rocked back and forth in the metal chair, looking up at Rex and then back to Collin.

"If you're so sorry, then you'll answer truthfully a few questions." His hands fisted. The need to shake the woman and make her talk was one he needed to suppress.

He'd seen people like her before. Strong as long as they were undetected, but once caught they'd fall apart. Force would only make her clam up or fall off the edge of reason. Then he wouldn't receive his answers. Thus, they shaved her head, stripped her, and threw her in a cell for a few days. Most cracked and willingly told all.

Leaning forward, he whispered, "Anne, I'll make sure they set you free if you tell me why you betrayed us."

"But you said you were here to punish me."

Spittle collected at the corner of her mouth. Her need to believe him filled her face, softening the lines around her eyes.

"I have to set up a front for the fellows," he jerked his head toward where Rex stood outside the interrogation room's door.

She leaned forward too. "I told them you would understand. They wouldn't listen."

"I'm here now." He finally trusted his hands to stay steady and he placed one over hers. "Tell me why."

"Theo promised if I helped him that when the OS returned to The Circle's fold, I would have free rein to experiment on live subjects. I could work in my favorite field, DNA research. No restrictions, he told me. You have any idea what I could accomplish? He would supply me with anything my heart desired. I could produce the perfect human being. My creation. I could become famous." With each word, her voice became higher pitched with excitement.

A perfect human? At the cost of hurting or killing others? She had sold her soul to Theo to become the real Dr. Frankenstein.

"What information did Theo ask for?" he asked. Her hand clasped his tight.

"Nothing much at first. Just wanted to know the number of wounded coming in from different raids. Every once in a while they would ask how you reacted to your people being unsuccessful." She pulled his hand up and pressed it to her cheek. "I always gave them useless information about you."

What she didn't know was that even useless information could be used against him.

"Can you tell me some of the things you told them?" he asked.

He turned his hand and brought hers to his mouth, rubbing her knuckles against his lips. The puppy look she gave him hurt as he hated what he was making her believe.

"Nothing really until that woman showed up. I waited a couple of weeks before I told them. I was certain you would kill the slut. But when I saw how she was using you, I knew I needed to get rid of her."

The half grin on her face showed how she expected his praise. He dropped her hand and sat back. Her face paled. He wiped his hands on his camos. His hands felt oily with her sickness.

"Did you communicate with anyone else in The Circle?" he asked.

She shook her head, tears splattered the table.

"Did anyone in the OS help you?" His chest tightened as he worked at remaining unmoved by her tears.

She shook her head again and sobbed. Red-faced and trembling, she rested her head on her arms. He wouldn't receive any more information from her.

Standing, he held onto the table. "Rex, take her to room 999. Rick will be waiting for her."

"No! I saw what you did to that Mason fellow! You killed him! I'm not like him. I'm not a terrorist," Anne screamed and reached across the table for Collin but Rex had already grabbed her arm. "You said you would set me free."

The taste of bile filled his mouth. He hated this part of his job.

"You will be."

Her death would be one more mark on his soul. When he was growing up, his brother had been the heir trained to take over The Circle. Collin had been happy with the position of the spare heir, never expecting to be more than a valued operative, most likely in logistics, never involved in the decision of sending someone to their death.

"You'll be free," he turned away and murmured, "while I'll stay in hell."

Chapter Twenty-Six

Olivia scanned the area outside the Main Sector's perimeter. Waving A. J. to the strip of woods beyond, she followed close behind. Running between swaying trees and bushes and jumping over the occasional fallen tree, they were fortunate the interstate snaked near The Circle's property on this side.

When she nearly tripped, she bit back a whimper. Her body shouted its protest at every jarring step and leap. Every inch of her body had a cut or bruise on it but she pressed on. Theo, being the persistent bastard, interrogated her weekly, never allowing her body to fully heal. Now that she'd escaped, if caught, her immediate death was guaranteed.

They squatted behind a bush near the five-foot steel fence. What little traffic zoomed by was on the opposite side going away from Atlanta. Not more than twenty feet from them was a faded beat-up silver Ford 150 with the tailgate missing parked off the side as if the owner had abandoned it. Just like they were told by Jason.

"I still can't believe it," A. J. muttered next to her and coughed.

"That Jason's a double agent?"

Another swipe at a mosquito urged Olivia to hurry out of the tall grass.

"Yeah." She coughed into her sleeve. "Do you think Collin ordered him to release you?"

"No. He told me he'd heard about me saving Collin's butt in the mountains. That's the only reason he risked detection."

Olivia shivered. Somehow his plan worked. When Jason sliced the guard's neck, she almost threw up. Looking at death through a scope had helped her maintain an unreal quality to it. Distance made it appear to be part of a violent action-thriller movie. But the victim was within a few feet and she could smell the blood; it was too up close and personal. Then when he shot another man in the back, he'd said he wanted to make it look as if one of the other guards had helped. That he'd come upon the escape and shot the betrayer, killing him instantly, but the women had gotten away.

Knowing Theo, he would believe Jason. Hadn't she believed for years that Jason was a loyal operative? The man was a better liar than she'd ever imagined. How many times had he lied about her targets? He knew they were Circle operatives. She squeezed her eyes shut for a couple seconds. That meant Collin knew too. Would Collin ask her to kill for him? Would she? Was she so needy for his love and approval?

Pulled down by the depressing thoughts, she pushed it away. Now wasn't the time for a girlish pity party. Then she heard shouting behind them. "Let's go!"

They climbed the fence and dashed for the truck.

Within seconds of jumping inside, Olivia scrambled for the keys hidden in the folds of the driver's seat and jabbed them into the ignition. She grinned big. The truck looked like crap but cranked like a charm.

About a mile down the interstate she found a cutoff through the median and turned, heading away from Atlanta.

"Where're we going?" A. J. asked after another bout of coughing. She'd pulled out the money Jason had promised to leave in the glove compartment.

"To Birmingham. I've got a safe house there The Circle doesn't know about." At least she hoped they didn't and she also hoped the OS hadn't discovered it. A. J.'s cough turned into choking. Olivia slapped her on the back, watching her with concern. "Are you sure you're okay?"

"Yeah. Just a little cold. Once we get somewhere less dank than that cell, I'll be right as rain." A few more miles down the road, A. J. said, "I thought you would want to return to the OS." Her voice quivered.

Olivia's gaze darted to A. J. and then back to the road. "Collin used me to get to the sword. I'm of no use to him now."

Tears welled up, blurring her vision, as her throat hurt from trying to remain stoic. If she'd meant anything to him, Collin would've been the one to release her from the cell.

Five weeks. Jason confirmed she'd been in that dungeon for five weeks. Her gut told her, Collin hadn't even attempted to save her. She'd learned years ago to not depend on anyone but herself. Expecting the best from a man only led to disappointment.

"We're a pitiful duo, aren't we? Men either betray us or go off and die." A. J. stared straight ahead and then coughed until her flushed face beaded with sweat.

Olivia didn't have anything to add to that. She'd decided they would first stop at a local twenty-four–hour Walmart to pick up drugs for A. J. and any supplies and food they would need. The popular store would be best in order to meld into the crowds and be near to invisible.

By the time they made it to the house near Edwards Lake, the sun was over the horizon. She parked the truck in the back.

The door key remained where she'd last hid it and they let themselves in. Without hesitation she punched in the alarm number and then made a quick call to the neighborhood's security office. Last thing she needed was for a rent-a-cop to come snooping around.

"Nice place." A. J. held up a fist full of tissues to her mouth as she coughed.

The Cape Cod–style home had an open floor plan with two bedrooms upstairs and two downstairs. A spacious kitchen with everything a gourmet cook would want.

"Go ahead." She nodded to the kitchen. "Get some medicine in you and go to bed. There's a bedroom through the third door on the left you can use. If you need me, pick up the phone and punch one. It'll ring in the master bedroom. I'm taking a shower and going to bed too."

An hour later, it felt good to be clean and her teeth brushed. Like an automaton, she wasted what little strength she possessed by blow-drying her hair. The everyday routines helped her to keep moving until she fell into bed without bothering with pajamas.

When her body softened and went limp, another concern floated to the top. Collin. She missed his lovely hard body and talented thick fingers. Her usual nightmare from so many years had all but vanished. Even in the dungeon, expecting to die, her dreams were filled with her time at the cabin and Collin teasing and filling her body.

Now she often woke to tears either from reaching a climax or wanting one so badly. Her body remembered how no other lover had brought her to climax so quickly and thoroughly with only his fingers and mouth.

She drifted off to sleep planning how to reach her hidden bank accounts and hoping The Circle or OS hadn't cleaned them out. Any effort to stop her dreams of Collin was hopeless.

The dream started like it always did, Collin licking and sucking on the nub between her legs as he had the first night. His chin rasped the tender skin of her thighs. She tried to move her hands. She wanted to touch his hair, feel the warm strands glide between her fingers, to hold him closer, but he had her wrists held tight in one hand. If it had been anyone but him, she would've fought him. Yet she expected and wanted it. Only in bed could she trust him.

He moaned as if he'd tasted a sweetness he missed so much. She liked how he savored her, his pleasure mounting with her own. He bobbed his head, tonguing and nipping until she pressed against his face wanting more.

Then her dream Collin slid his strong hands up her arms and cupped her breasts, pinching her nipples until she arched against him in the pleasure-pain he knew she liked. If only he could be real.

"Oh, Collin," she sighed.

"Yes, lover," his deep voice whispered in her ear.

"Collin!" Her eyes opened. Even in the dark room, the face she loved and feared was visible above hers.

He covered her mouth and moved his body over hers. "Shhh! No need to shout. I'm right here. You and I have some unfinished business."

The way he was looking at her warned she was in deep shit. Clasping him with her legs, she tried to flip him over, hopefully dislodging his hold.

He chuckled.

"I know all your little tricks. You're thinner. Is The Circle not feeding you enough? We wondered how long before Theo tired of you again and kicked you out of Main Sector."

If her eyes could kill, he'd be ashes by now. His dark clothes were rough against her tender bare skin. A large hand covered her tender mons, not the pressure of a man trying to excite a woman but to warn her of what he could do to her. Instead of panicking, she arched into his touch as her body recognized his feel, his scent. She moaned despite the pain of wanting him, her need to have him inside her overriding all else.

"You're going back to headquarters with me. But first I want to see if you're like I remember."

His gaze remained on her face. He moved his hand from between her legs. A second later, she heard the rasp of his zipper opening.

She felt his cock, hard and hot, on her thigh. He clasped her hip and jerked one leg up and plunged into her. She squealed, though the sound was muffled by his fingers. My goodness, he was bigger than she remembered or she was swollen from wanting him so badly. The sensation of her nakedness against his fully clothed body was such a turn-on and he knew she liked it.

She rejoiced when he removed his hand from her lips and brought his mouth over hers. His teeth pressed so hard against her lips she expected the taste of blood, maybe even craved it for what it represented. He'd lost control. She grinned. He hated that he couldn't be around her without the need to fuck her overcoming his good judgment. She understood how he felt. He only needed to walk into the room for her to want to touch him, unzip and taste him.

Each thrust brought a grunt like he wanted deeper and more of her. What was another bruise? She preferred his bruises, his scent all over her. Her nails bit into his back.

"Bitch!"

His tongue thrust into her mouth proving to her he loved having her marks too. Before morning she would make sure she wasn't the only one with new tender spots.

"Collin!" Rex shouted on the other side of the bedroom door. "Rick's got the other woman wrapped up and in the van. We need to get going before The Circle shows up."

"Just one fucking minute!" Collin said, startling her with his vehemence.

She hooked her heels around his legs. No way would he stop before they both got what they were working toward. He pounded into her and she sucked on his neck, certain to leave a love bite. Determined he would have as many marks on him as she could leave before he was finished, she reached between them and pinched his nipples hard. He howled and they shuddered together.

Instead of collapsing on her, he held himself off her. His eyes closed, and he fought for every breath. Then he looked down at her in the half light. She wished she could tell if those eyes were flaring amber or not. The dark room showed only different shades of gray. His large hands clasped her face as his thumbs rested beneath her chin. With his strength it wouldn't take much for him to snap her neck. She wasn't sure if he could see it but she lifted her chin as much as he would allow and challenged him to do it.

"Does Theo still have to spank your ass to get it off? Or

do you spank his?" he asked in a tone conveying his hatred for her and Theo and maybe for himself.

Even with all the cuts and bruises on her body, she sensed Collin would claim she asked for them. Maybe it was the wild combination of an intense escape, lack of sleep mixed with torture topped with an explosive climax, but all she wanted was for him to leave her alone or kill her.

"Go to hell."

She wished he would go ahead and end it all. Loving him was slowly eating away at her sanity.

"Oh, we're going eventually, baby. And I'll make sure your lover gets there first."

He moved off her and straightened his clothes and then zipped up his pants.

She flipped him the bird as she wrapped a sheet around her. He actually believed Theo was still her lover.

"You're an idiot," she sneered.

He merely raised an eyebrow at her. With her chin up, she was proud of how she strolled over to the closet without betraying one ache or pain.

"Get some clothes on."

Collin opened the bedroom door, hitting the lights and said something to Rex.

By the time he turned back to her, she wore jeans and a red silk blouse she'd always liked. Most of the cuts and bruises hidden beneath the clothing. The blue, green, and black bruises on her face would tell their own story to Collin. She refused to accept his sympathy if he had any.

He grimaced on seeing her face but still held out the handcuffs. "Hold your hands out."

"You've got to be kidding." She waited for him to back down. Now who was kidding who? "I don't understand.

What's your problem? I'm not going to let you put those on me."

"Rex! Come in here and hold her." Collin's eyes narrowed.

She didn't like this.

"Okay! I don't want Big Foot touching me." Proud that her hands remained steady, she held them out for Collin to place the stainless steel bracelets around her wrists.

Rex grabbed her arms from the back.

"Tell him to let me go!" What was happening? This was all wrong. She fought to keep herself steady and not panic. Her throat tightened with a need to cry.

Collin's cold gaze stayed on her. Not one spark of regret softened his face.

"When we get to headquarters take her to room 999."

During her time at the OS, she'd heard horror tales of people going into the room and never coming out the same. Either they were mentally impaired by the treatments or dead.

"No fucking way!"

Before she even thought it through her foot kicked back and she heard the big guy yowl.

A blur caught her attention before Collin caught her around the waist, lifting her and squeezing. Normally the move would only immobilize her for a few seconds but with all the damage her body had endured the past few weeks, pain shot through her body from all directions and she saw stars.

As she sunk to the floor, her legs refused to cooperate, she mumbled, "Oh, shit, not again."

Chapter Twenty-Seven

Every cell in his being screamed that he was wrong. She would never betray him, but all the evidence proved the opposite. Another betrayal in a long line of betrayals. He felt as if he was standing on a cliff, teetering near the edge of madness.

He forced himself to watch Rick work on her. The sterile all-white room with huge overhead lights resembling the type in an operating room was enough to scare any normal person. But Olivia wasn't normal, that he was already aware of.

The bruises on her face, he'd assumed Theo had gotten rough as he reminded her who was boss. Theo was never known for his gentle touch. And when they cut her clothes off, he saw the numerous blue and green bruises and more cuts than could be counted on her torso, he was certain Theo had gone over the edge of reason and taken Olivia with him.

How any human could do this to another was beyond him. Theo was a sick individual. Her long body stretched across a hospital bed looked unnaturally small. Tied down wearing only a simple hospital gown, she'd fought them until Rick shot her with a truth serum mixture. She looked around the room with eyes that appeared not to focus too well and a crooked grin.

Besides the feeling of euphoria, another side effect of the serum was numbness to any pain, causing torture to be unproductive. So for now, he would be spared the ordeal of watching Rick torture the woman he loved. No matter what she'd done, he hadn't rid his tender thoughts toward her. He had hundreds of OS personnel depending on him for protection. What happened in his personal life couldn't affect his decisions. Theo had changed the directive of The Circle and must be stopped.

"Hey, man, why don't you go and get some rest and I'll keep an eye on things here?" Rex leaned against the observation room's wall next to the glass.

"I'm fine. Have you checked on the other Circle operative we brought in?"

"Nah. Henry's taking care of her. Good thing you hired him. What with Anne being gone now." Rex shuffled his feet and stood straight. "He said the woman has a bad case of bronchitis and good thing she was brought in before it went into pneumonia."

"I don't want to give her over to Rick yet. He's busy with Olivia. Go. Ask questions. See how well she cooperates."

When did he start making war on women? He remembered how strong his mom had been, but she been gentle too, especially with him and his brother. She'd taught him that women should be respected and handled with care. She'd also been from another generation.

"Okay¾" Banging on the door interrupted Rex's agreement.

Rick looked toward Collin for guidance.

Should Collin continue or wait to see what the disturbance was about? He held up his hand for Rick to wait. "See who it is, Rex."

The big guy stepped over to the door and punched in the code. A whirlwind of dark hair and fury stormed into the room. Rex's gasp caught Collin's attention. His friend was staring at the woman standing in the middle of the room with her hands on hips. When Collin looked the woman in the face, he couldn't be any more amazed than if a ghost walked through the walls.

In fact, she'd come through the door.

"Abby!" Collin stood. For a dead woman, she looked pale but rather healthy.

"Abby?" Rex asked at the same time and reached out to touch her hair. "You're real."

"Rex?" She stumbled back and landed butt first hard on the floor. "You're dead."

He kneeled in front of her. "I thought you were. The Circle told us every gruesome detail about how they killed you."

"They told me you went berserk when they captured me and OS had eliminated you a few days later." Abby shook her head in disbelief. "I should've known they were lying." Tears streamed down their faces.

Rex reached out for her but she scrambled to her feet. "No. Don't touch me. I need to let this sink in. I ... I ..." She looked lost.

"Abby?" Rex held his hands out as if he was afraid she would bolt.

"Call me A. J. That's what they call me now." Tears flowed down her face.

Collin heard tapping on the window and dragged his

attention to Rick on the other side of the window. Rick nodded toward Olivia. Though the glass prevented him from hearing her, she shook her head, laughing and chattering away. So unlike her. A sign she was fully under the serum's control.

"You two leave." Collin wanted to know the details of how Abby ended up being an operative for The Circle but duty called. "I have work to do."

"No way am I leaving without Olivia." Abby used the hem of her blouse to wipe off her cheeks. "She's never had anyone to look after her." Her accusing glare pointed straight to Collin.

With his hands clasped on top of his head, Rex stared at Abby in disbelief. "How did you get here?"

"That guy." She pointed at Rick. "Wrapped me in a sheet and brought me here. I was running a fever and had taken so much antihistamine, I was out of it."

"You're a Circle operative? You're the one with bronchitis?" Rex glanced over at Olivia. "How did you get involved with her?" he asked Abby with distaste evident in his voice.

Without waiting to hear Abby's reply, Collin entered the interrogation room, closing the door behind him. Time for everyone to come to terms that greater things were in play and a woman's life could be forfeit. He was glad Olivia would have a friend to mourn her.

"Helllllo! Handsome!"

Her eyes rolled in her head and drool formed in one corner of her mouth. She looked so young and helpless.

"What has she told you so far?"

He hadn't cried since his family died, and his voice cracking surprised him. A couple deep swallows stopped the trembling in his throat.

"Nothing important."

Rick shook his head, his hand covering his mouth in effort to stop his grin. Collin glared at him. The man was a sick fuck for thinking any of this was funny.

"Hey, Col'n, com' here." She licked her lips as he stopped next to the raised hospital bed. "Com' closer." He leaned over. "Get me outta here. Pleeaasse."

"Answer our questions truthfully and we'll let you go free."

Nausea rolled his stomach. The thought of her cold and lifeless body being carted out of the room made him unwell.

"But you don't un'erstand. I tried to protect you because I love you." A sad look crossed her face.

Her words slammed into his chest and he struggled to keep his breathing steady. He glanced at Rick. The man had the sense to look busy with the gauges and buttons on the machinery in the corner.

The drugs worked by making the person feel euphoria. So in this case she believed she felt love, but it wasn't necessarily true.

"What were you protecting me from?" he asked, curling his fingers into his palm.

Her hair had fallen across her eyes and she blew noisily to push it away but the strand returned. He wanted to stroke her hair and ask her to tell him again that she loved him. But he needed to keep his mind on business.

"The shooters. They came. You were hurt," she slurred.

"You knew they were coming," he said accusingly.

"I did?" Her forehead wrinkled. "Yes. I did."

So she admitted it. His shoulders slumped.

"How did you tell Theo where we were?" he asked.

"I didn't tell Theo squat!" Her outburst dislodged the strand of hair, and he could see her hot emerald eyes glaring at him

247

"You just said you did." When he caught the confusion on her face, he added, "You said you knew they were coming."

"No." She furiously shook her head. "No. You told me they were after us. That's why I knew they were comin'." Her bottom lip poked out like a petulant child.

She had him there. He had told her they were being chased by Circle operatives.

"What did Theo tell you when he saw you again? The night we stole the sword, was it with Theo's knowledge? Were you setting me up? And for what?" Time was running out, the truth serum lasted around eight minutes.

"You're funny. A. J. got in trouble for helping me. I hate Theo. He threw me into the dungeon and forgot about me for days. Well, 'cept the times he wanted to ask me about you. He hit. He cut. But I didn't tell him nuthin'. Where did you put A. J.? Is she okay?" She looked hard at him as if she was trying to figure something out. "I've got an important question to ask."

"What do you want to know?" he urged.

A. J.? Was she talking about Abby?

"Is he only nine months older than you?" she whispered.

"Who?"

"Your brother. He looked like you but he had a mean look. You can be mean too, but you look serene even when you're mad. It's scary." She yawned and blinked.

Collin held his breath. He'd seen the look of a deadly woman or a sensual playmate on her face but never a sleepy innocent.

"I can shoot her with some amphetamine to keep her awake, but it might make her heart explode." Rick held a hypodermic needle, waiting for Collin's decision.

"No!" he bit off. After taking a deep breath, he calmly said, "You can leave. I'll let you know when I'm finished."

The pity in Rick's eyes was hard to take. Collin wanted to snap at him to leave now but waited while the man stored the needle away, typed in some data into the computer connected to the machinery surrounding her, and exited the room.

"Why is your brother working for The Circle instead of with you?" She opened her eyes wide and blinked.

"Olivia, my brother died in the blast with my mom and dad when we were kids." Could Theo be trying to pull a fast one? Maybe he had a surgeon cut a person to look like Arthur. But for what reason?

"Well, he's the most solid ghost I ever saw. He even talked to me. Theo said your brother hated you enough to kill you."

Her eyes closed and when he believed she'd drifted off to sleep, she opened them again. "Collin?"

"Yes."

He gave into the desire to touch her hair. The silky softness reminded him of their first time together. He never could remember feeling anything as soft as her and probably never would.

She licked her dry lips as she blinked up at him.

"Are you going to kill me now? I think I rather have you kill me than Theo."

"Why's that?" he asked. This had to be the most surreal conversation he'd ever had.

"Because you wouldn't make it hurt. Theo likes to dish out pain and not the good kind." She smacked her lips. "I bet your brother likes pain too."

Chapter Twenty-Eight

Olivia wanted the image of Collin imprinted onto her brain. Then she could haunt him later. Damn, these drugs screwed with her mind even though the effects had finally dulled. She was a fighter and he hadn't injected her with anything to kill her yet that she knew of. For over two hours he'd drilled her, wanting to know when Theo planned to attack the OS again.

The look he gave her whenever she mentioned his brother clearly said he didn't believe her.

"Collin, I'm not going to beg you to believe me. He's your brother. Ask A. J. If you don't trust her, ask Jason. He got us out of the dungeon." She swallowed deeply. Her throat burned as if she'd drunk acid. Thank goodness, she no longer sounded drunk.

"I find it hard to believe Jason released you."

A thousand nails pounded into her head. Talk about a hangover; this was so much worse than any all-night binge could produce.

"Why is it, since I've met you, I've found myself in several beds about to throw up and not from having a good time?" She eyed him and realized she wasn't making her case. "Listen, I know Jason is your double agent, so why is it so hard to believe he helped me and A. J. escape?"

Unmoved, he continued his silent treatment.

Frustration curled her fingers.

"For Christ's sakes! Do I have to pull every word out of your mouth? Tell me! Are you going to kill me or not?" If her hands were unbound, she would be pressing the heels of her palms into her temples.

He blinked. For him to show that little bit of emotion meant something had happened.

"We received news after we brought you in that Jason turned on us. He's the reason three more OS operatives are dead now," he said as his dark eyes waited for her reaction.

"What?" Circle operatives and now OS. Had Jason been sniffing too much hair lightener? She continued to stare back as she waited for Collin to say more.

"What did you say to him?" he asked finally.

Did he believe Jason's betrayal had something to do with her? Tired of trying to prove herself to him, to everyone, she shuddered.

"I had nothing to do with Jason's deceit." She shook her head. "Kill me. Put me out of my misery. I never believed in happily ever after until I met you, but then I don't deserve it."

She closed her eyes for a moment unable to believe what she'd just said. Besides she couldn't stand looking at the man who refused to see the real Olivia. The drugs in her system had dissipated more and she could think clearly.

"I understand. Your seduction was all a sham to get nearer to Theo through me. You wanted to steal his sword and drive him further into insanity so you can take over." She opened her eyes, hoping he couldn't see her pain.

"Well, I got news for you, dickwad! You're just as evil as he is and I hope your brother kicks your ass when he takes over OS!"

That was one way to burn the bridge she'd hoped to cross with him. Love, marriage, white picket fence, and two point five kids were a pipe dream anyway, especially for people like her. Who would want a wife and mother with the issues she had? Shit! What had she just thought? Love? Marriage? *Kids?* Where did that come from? She couldn't have kids anyway. Besides she wasn't the marrying type.

Panic tightened her chest, wondering how he planned to eliminate her. Then she looked at his face as he'd been quiet an awfully long time. His dark eyes flashed amber.

"I believe you. I don't know why or if I can trust you completely, but I believe you. Jason's betrayal colors a lot of what he's told me," Collin said so low, she barely heard each redeeming word.

Her limbs suddenly felt weightless. She wasn't sure what convinced him she'd been telling the truth, but she felt he no longer planned to kill her. But something about the way he held his shoulders, all straight and tight, had her suspicious about why he was finally believing her.

"I see. So none of my actions before today told you that I can be trusted?" Her voice trembled on the last word.

She fought the desire to hope. Hope and optimism were the ingredients for becoming the man's pawn to be used and abused.

As Collin opened his mouth to answer, Rex returned and rattled the glass with a fist. Then he motioned for Collin to return to the observation room.

Collin stepped away and then Olivia said, "You got to be kidding, right? Tell Big Foot you're busy with setting me free."

She hoped she hadn't misunderstood his sentiment. He'd looked at her funny when she'd said the last sentence. What was up with that?

"Just give me a few minutes. He wouldn't interrupt unless it was important," Collin said before he strode over to talk with Rex. That small explanation was the first one in the entire time they'd been together.

She shut her mouth with a click and shook her head in amazement.

The minutes dragged by until about a half hour later. Collin returned and yanked off the Velcro strips holding her down.

"There's an emergency and we need your expertise."

While Collin helped her to a sitting position, Rick rushed in and after slamming a few drawers pulled out a wicked-looking needle. The fluid inside the cylinder was a different color from the one earlier but no less intimidating.

"What's that for?" Her head was floating a foot off her shoulders with the sudden movement. The drugs they'd given her were revisiting her with each movement.

"We need to sober you up, you could say." Rick stopped next to her and without cotton swab or warning jabbed her with the needle.

"Shit! What's your problem? Give a girl a heads-up." If not for Collin holding her, she'd have kicked the guy as the medicine zipped through her veins, leaving a trail of fire. "That's some evil stuff."

"We need you alert and ready to kill," Collin said. Red-hot anger flowed in waves from his body, his flushed face warned the amount of effort he exerted holding back his emotions.

"So it's going to be like that? No, 'I trust you, Olivia,' or 'I can't live without you?'" Before he could respond with an explanation that would disappoint her, she asked, "Who do you want me to kill?" Maybe he planned to use her again before he ordered her death. What did it matter? She was alive for now.

Calmness blanketed her, focusing her attention on what he would answer. Theo would be a good answer. Even she was surprised how quickly her old killer mind-set returned.

If it was his brother, she wasn't sure how right she was for the job. Despite how angry Collin made her, she worried she couldn't do it. He had Collin's face, scarred but nevertheless his face. Eliminating him felt wrong.

"Jason Kastler," Collin said as he tossed a duffle bag to her.

<<<>>>

Collin watched as she dressed. Her wounds would need to be seen to later. Several areas of her body were different shades of blue and green. Theo had worked her over good.

She didn't act sore, but considering the amount of drugs in her system that didn't surprise him. He wanted to make sure she was steady and the shot had diluted the truth serum's effects. Her reflexes and sight must be in top condition for what he needed her to do. But perversely he found watching her lift one long leg and then the other to pull up a "barely worth it" thong to cover herself with a scrap of silk to be so sensual he hardened like a steel bar. When she bent over and cupped her breasts, slipping on her bra, he forced his gaze away before he exploded in his pants.

Christ! This wasn't the time to let his body rule his mind. He had to set the wheels in motion. They had only one crack at making sure his plan followed through.

From what Rex relayed, Theo's latest decision had pushed up their plan. Jason had gotten word to Lucian that Theo had ordered a hit on Collin. Rex had said there was more and had taken him to another interrogation room where Lucian sat with worry creasing his handsome face. Lucian who was one of the calmest operatives Collin knew was shaken by what was coming down.

"I know how sick Theo can be, but this goes beyond ..." Lucian, pale as his white shirt, stabbed his fingers into his thick hair. "Jason said Theo was salivating with anger on realizing you had stolen not only his sword but his lead eliminator. Theo told him to kill you and every OS operative he came across. If he returned without the job being done, he'd cut off his dick and then start on his limbs, piece by piece, and if he still lived, he would cut out his heart, but for each body part he took, he would kill a female operative in The Circle." When Lucian finished, he dropped his hands into his lap, holding them in effort to stop their shaking. "The man is really a sick fuck."

Lucian was right. Theo had finally reached the end of his sanity.

Collin returned his attention to Olivia on hearing the rustle of denim. He'd believed her about Theo but he still was using her again. Once she realized that, and she would find out the truth, he wasn't sure if she would forgive him again.

She snapped her jeans and then dipped her head into a T-shirt. As soon as her head popped out she asked, "Where's he located?"

She had her professional face on, almost robotic, well trained by The Circle to do her job. One moment, he threatened to kill her and then next she prepared to follow his orders. Like a good little soldier. Though he admired her talents, it bothered him deep inside. Maybe when all of this was over, he'd ... what? Help her be a normal person? How would he help her if he couldn't help himself?

He heard a tapping sound and looked down. Arms crossed, she patted her foot, waiting for him to answer.

"He's in the garden and he's got Nic," he stated.

"How did that happen?"

"He told Rex he had valid information to share. Nic went with Rex to make sure he was clean of bugs or cameras. He grabbed her and shouted he wanted to talk with me. He has her in the courtyard, holding a knife to her throat."

"It almost sounds like he wants us to kill him."

"Probably. He's been ordered to eliminate me or others will die. So the only way to stop him is to drop him in his tracks. So we're going to oblige him." Collin headed out the door with Olivia catching up and walking alongside him.

"There has to be another way."

"There isn't." Collin swallowed. Damn, he hated this.

"There's more, isn't there?"

"If we don't kill him, Theo will, slowly and painfully, kill others unless we kill him. He knows he's a double agent. Theo believes I don't have the balls to have him killed."

"That doesn't make sense. Why didn't Theo kill Jason?"

"You know as well as anyone Theo loves using people's natural tendencies against themselves. Jason will kill me to protect those at The Circle. Theo wants to see how far I'll go to stop him. In his own crazy logic, he believes if I let Jason to live, I'm weak. If I'm weak, he won't negotiate with me. He will only meet someone as strong and deadly as he is. I need him at the negotiation table. I've tried for years to get the old man to meet me and discuss a truce. This is the only way." Collin hated he had to give the order to end his friend's life. But they had no other alternative.

In less than five minutes they walked into the office she'd searched so long ago. Out the window a crowd of OS operatives gathered in one corner of the courtyard, while Jason's tall form holding Nic in front of his body stood in the opposite corner. She looked like a doll dangling in his arms, her feet hanging a foot off the ground.

"Is the glass bulletproof?" She tapped the pane with a fingernail.

"Of course, but it won't be a factor." He pulled open a drawer in the desk and pressed a button. The hum of small motors filled the room as the window lowered and a strong breeze ruffled their hair and sent loose sheets of paper flying to the floor.

"Well, isn't that just nifty?" her tone full of sarcasm. He guessed she remembered how her escape had been stopped by no openings in the windows.

"Your rifle is over there." He pointed to several boxes lined against the wall.

"Oh, my baby!" She tore into them as if it was Christmas morning. Each piece she lifted and caressed with loving care, murmuring sweet words, even kissing the micro-computer before assembling the rifle and placing it on the tripod. By the time she'd keyed in the coordinates, he'd decided she was as sexy handling her rifle as she'd been putting on her clothes.

"Are you ready?" he asked. His thoughts shifted back to the hard decision at hand. Their months of planning coming to an end and he'd hoped it wouldn't come to this, but Jason had known something like this would happen. He'd been right. There was no other way.

"Why hasn't he left?" she asked as she adjusted the rifle's sight, her expression all business.

"He's waiting for my answer." A chill clutched the back of his neck.

"And my rifle is your answer." The unfeeling tone she'd used saddened him even more.

Collin crossed his arms and widened his stance. Even though the words nearly choked him, he said, "Kill him."

Chapter Twenty-Nine

The quarter-sized red circle in the middle of Jason's forehead proved Olivia's supreme marksmanship. Collin leaned over the body and closed the operative's eyes. Rick had already placed Jason on a stretcher, while another man cleaned the mess sprayed over the sidewalk and rose bushes. Even knowing the physics, he always found it bizarre how such a large bullet made a comparable neat entry wound but a massive exit one.

"Sir!" Henry, the new physician to the OS, closed up the backpack he used to carry emergency medical supplies and waved Collin over. "Nic is okay. She wants to talk with you. I've given her a sedative to calm her nerves."

The small bald-headed man moved out of the way. Sitting on a bench near the water fountain, head bowed, the dark-headed security officer looked up, eyes sunken and face washed of color, she appeared to be the walking dead. A large white bandage covered the side of her neck, but otherwise, no other visible markings gave away her ordeal.

"If you're not feeling up to it, we can talk later this

evening." He sat next to her and placed a hand over her cold one.

"I'm fine. I don't know how he got in. My grid must be faulty somewhere." Her gaze shifted to over his shoulder. "Unless someone let him in."

He felt Olivia's presence. His body canted toward her before he was aware of it. "She's been with me."

Nic crossed and chafed her arms. "It's all confusing. I believe he's a Circle operative. He kept saying you had betrayed the OS and made a deal with Theo. I told him he was crazy and then Rex showed up and the guy went crazy. When Rex tried to reason with him, he grabbed me, threatening to slice my throat if you didn't come and talk with him."

By the look on Nic's face, Jason had put on a good show. Collin turned to check on Olivia. Maybe too good of a show. The plan had been to convince that bastard, Theo Palmer, into believing he really wanted to make a deal and Jason had been willing to sacrifice his life to see it done.

Collin still remembered the last words Jason had spoken to him. "Let me do this. Let me go out with a bang and not in a hospital bed hooked up to machines as they pump foul chemicals into my body."

Jason had been certain in Theo's warped brain he would see this as a sign that Collin was worthy of negotiating a truce between the two organizations. Collin only hoped the cancer and the pain pills Jason tossed down each day hadn't played a part in his reasoning.

Who would believe Collin sacrificed an operative just to set up Theo? Certainly not Theo. It helped to have the reputation of being a straight shooter and a bleeding heart when it came to his people, no matter how hard he tried to be cool and unfeeling like his father had taught him.

And Collin understood why the double agent had given his life to the plan. Dying of cancer wasn't for the faint of heart. The whole mess just pissed him off. Because of one psycho wanting more power, so many people he cared for had died.

<<<>>>

Olivia glued her gaze to Collin's back because she refused to look at Jason's face. Her programming had kicked in when he'd handed her the rifle. She remembered setting up the gun and shooting, but every step felt like a dream. Maybe it was her way of dealing with Jason's death. Not since her foster mother's brother had she killed a person she'd personally known.

When Collin glanced over his shoulder at her, she stiffened. His eyes were dull as if all his hope lay on the gurney mere feet away. She wanted to see his amber eyes flare again. She wanted him mad or turned on, not so lifeless.

He lifted his chin. "You remember where my rooms are?" She nodded. "Okay. Go and you can clean up. We'll talk then."

Olivia stared into his eyes until Nic spoke softly and he turned to look at the other woman. She remained frozen for a few moments, then she realized everyone had become quiet. What were they thinking about her being ordered to the boss's rooms? That she exchanged Theo for Collin? Why was she feeling as if she'd done something wrong? Jason had made the decision to die. He could have killed Nic or Collin. He could have taken his own life.

When she turned to leave, her gaze fell on a group of OS operatives hovering near the door. They jostled each other, trying to get out of her way.

Once she entered the air-conditioned hallway, she noticed one of her old guards standing to the side. She grabbed his arm and said, "Is my suite still intact and can you get the code?"

"Yeah, but the boss said¾"

She bunched up his shirt and slammed him against the wall. His hands opened and closed by his sides. He really wanted to fight back, but obviously had heard rumors about her and his boss. Face red, he lifted his cell phone and called the security desk and then relayed the code to her.

"When you see him, tell him where I'm at," she said and strolled away.

Relieved to reach the suite, she headed straight to the shower, peeling off her blouse, quickly followed by shoes and jeans. By the time she twisted the knobs and the water had warmed, she was naked and soaping up. As the spray massaged and stung the cuts and bruises, the release of tension was replaced by the realization of what she'd done. Chances were if the roles had been reversed, Jason would have killed her without a care or thought. But nevertheless, she'd killed her handler and friend.

She leaned against the tile and sobbed. A cool breeze warned her before strong hands pulled her out of the shower and into his arms.

"Shh. Baby. You followed orders. Did your duty. You saved a lot of lives." Collin rocked her back forth for a few seconds and then hooked one arm behind her knees, while pressing her wet chest to his naked one.

He placed her on the bed and crawled in beside her. Before her body could even shake from the cold, he flipped the sheet and comforter over them and wrapped his arms around her waist. His big body touched her from her shoulders to instep. She never remembered anyone ever holding her like this.

Moments drifted by as his breath tickled the top of her head and his hand skimmed her arm, up and down, heating the chill bumps, soothing her. She closed her eyes and shuddered.

"You're okay now. You're here with me." His voice calmed her. She wished he would continue to talk. Though he spoke softly, his voice had a thread of steel through it. A dangerous edge she appreciated and made her want him even more.

"Don't ask me to do anything like that again," she whispered.

He pulled her tight and squeezed. Her body finally relaxed as she struggled with the scene being replayed behind her eyelids.

"Shh. Don't think about it." He kissed the top of her head.

She nodded, closed her eyes, and fell asleep.

<<<>>>

It was morning. In the far reaches of OS headquarters, there were no windows to allow sunlight to reach her, but she knew. Even as a child she sought the rays of the sun to warm her skin. She'd never been the type of child or teenager to sleep until noon. That was, except for the time she walked the streets for Big Daddy. With a shake of her head, the memory evaporated as she sat in a chair near the bed watching Collin sleep. On the nightstand, the clock's red letters glowed five forty-five.

The windowless room's muted lighting from strategically placed lamps cast shadows across the bed. He slept partially on his side with one knee raised. Her eyes drifted from his sturdy foot, up his long legs, across a lean torso to his chin and mouth, while his eyes remained hidden in the shadows.

During their time in the mountains she'd become familiar with every inch of him, but she'd never had the chance to sit and stare at the whole package. Tanned skin broken only by a light sprinkling of hair down the center of his chest tempted her fingers to touch and follow the trail to his groin. The urge to kiss and soothe each circular scar scattered across his chest and legs almost brought her out of her seat to touch him. One scar in particular near his groin caused her to say a little prayer of thankfulness. If it had hit a little to the left, she would've missed experiencing more pleasure than she'd ever known.

A sardonic grin lifted one corner of her mouth.

"What are you grinning about?" he asked without moving.

Like she would tell him she admired his body and talents.

"You have no tattoos. So many guys ink their bodies now." One hand cupped her chin as her elbow rested on the chair's arm. "And I'm awfully happy to see your most recent bullet wounds are healing nicely."

He turned on his back and placed his hands behind his head. Light bathed his whole body and he was obviously pleased by her attention. Long and firm, his cock stretched toward his belly button. Ripples of muscles led to a broad chest sparsely sprinkled with dark hair. With his arms up, biceps bulged and showcased his masculinity even more. She could sit there all day and stare at him, but he had some explaining to do.

"What was the real reason you had me kill Jason?"

Chapter Thirty

"I'm waiting." She forced her eyes to look into his face. No flare responded to her inquiring stare. Her heart squeezed with disappointment. He would never trust her enough to tell her the truth, to be part of his life. She dropped her gaze and crossed her arms over her chest and shivered. What temp did they keep the thermostat on?

"He was dying of cancer." His voice soft as usual had an edge to it, almost a rusty sound. "I had offered to send him away for treatments but he'd waited too long and it'd spread through his bloodstream. He wanted to help me push Theo to the table for a truce. Theo's head is so wrapped up in the legends of King Arthur, he's twisted them to believe a man's worth is equal only to the hard decisions he makes. No matter how insane it appears, Jason sacrificed himself to provide Theo the proof that I was man enough and serious enough for him to meet with and discuss the future of our organizations. Theo will also believe he won by bringing me down to his level. Despite all of that, he won't expect us to take over The Circle."

Olivia bit the side of her mouth. Part of her preened at the thought he trusted her enough to tell the truth, but she'd never imagined this scenario. How could Jason make that decision? Preferring to die over finding a way to live? And how could Collin accept someone's decision to die at his hands? Well, actually at her hands. The burden would be on both of their shoulders. But for Collin to be in control of The Circle, she wasn't sure if that was best. The Circle had sectors all over the United States and several countries. She suspected it to be ten times the size of the OS. Would such power corrupt Collin as it had Theo?

She shook her head. Cool strands brushed her bare shoulders reminding her she was still naked. Her movement caught his attention and the amber flared. That little spark almost had her pushing all concerns to the side. Almost.

"Why such extreme measures to meet with Theo? Why not just send an invitation to meet at a mutual location?" Why did men complicate everything?

His hand rubbed his chest and then slid down his stomach to a firm thigh. Her gaze followed as if a string was attached from his fingers to her eyes. Then his palm clasped the soft sac beneath his semi-hard cock. All the air left the room. Oh, he was beautiful.

Blinking, she shook her head and then her hand slapped the arm of the chair. "Stop that. You won't distract me. No matter how much I want to lick you like a lollipop." She sighed. "I'm here to stay. The best way I can help is for you to be truthful. That's the least you owe me after what you put me through."

No need for her to point out her time in room 999 by his orders or his instructions to kill her ex-handler.

When he flinched, she pulled her head back. He actually let her see an emotion besides anger and humor? The more time she spent with him, the more he revealed his true emotions. Then, bang! the stone expression slammed in place.

An echo of rolling thunder vibrated the building. At the same moment, Collin shot out of the bed and grabbed her around the waist, throwing them to the floor with him on top. As the thunder built momentum, the lights flickered and snapped off and she understood what had happened. The next set of explosions caused pictures and sheetrock to fall around them.

"It appears Theo has found us and wanted to say hello." He grabbed his pants off the floor and struggled into them as she did the same.

The thoughts of tons of cement and steel on top of them terrified her, but she trusted Collin. She threw on the rest of her clothes and grabbed a bag, filling it with anything she could reach. At the same time, he slipped on a T-shirt and in a slow unhurried manner tied his boots. He obviously wasn't worried. They opened the door and people rushed by but no one appeared panicky. Collin clasped her arm and marched down the hallway in the same direction as everyone else.

"Would I be right in assuming we're going to a bomb shelter?" She adjusted the bag on her shoulder. Everywhere they stepped glass crunched beneath their feet. Thankfully she'd thought to pull on her thick-soled boots.

Before he answered, another blast rattled the remaining light fixtures, white powder sprinkled from the ceiling. He wrapped his arms around her as he pushed her head down on his chest enabling him to hunch over her, protecting her from the debris. She had to fight the grin off her face as she felt so safe and now wasn't the time to get mushy.

"No. Not exactly," he said in his usual evasive way.

She sighed and shook her head. "Then where are we going?"

"To meet with Theo." They walked through a long hallway that continued along a downward grade.

For whatever reason he wanted to meet with the lunatic, she was willing to go too. She only hoped they wouldn't die in the process.

Four huge doors, the type in school auditoriums, opened into a large room the size of six football fields and the ceiling disappeared into the darkness beyond the hanging lights. People ran or walked with purpose in every direction. Huge diesels cranked up and the roar echoed in the room. Computer equipment, furniture, and boxes upon boxes marked with every item imaginable were being loaded into the trailers.

All the organized activity enlightened Olivia. "You were planning on moving. Did you expect Theo to try to blow up your building?"

His stride continued across the expanse of the room, operatives nodding at him or waving, but no one stopped him and he ignored her question as she matched his pace.

Tired of his silence, she did the only thing she could think of. She tripped him. If he hadn't been concentrating on the activity around him, she'd never been able to do it. She had to say it was a great feeling for about three seconds. Then he regained his balance and swung around to stop Rex from shooting her in the back of the head.

"No!" Collin pushed the rifle barrel into the air.

"The bitch tried to bring you down!" Sparks shot out of the big guy's eyes. Well, she guessed their ceasefire was over.

"She merely reminded me to pay attention to my

surroundings." Collin crossed his arms and stared deep into Rex's eyes. "I trust her with my life. Understand?"

All activity in the huge room came to a standstill, only a few whispers echoed in the room. It appeared she wasn't the only one surprised by his statement.

Confusion darkened Rex's face and then his black brows rose, creasing his forehead. "You got to be fucking kidding me! You and her ... no way!"

Olivia looked to Collin and then Rex and then back to Collin. Why couldn't Rex get over his hatred of her? Would Collin push her away?

Surprised when Collin took her hand, she watched wide-eyed as he raised it to his lips. His lips felt warm. Her limbs felt like they were melting.

"What was the question?" Collin's eyes were smiling at her even if his mouth wasn't. He was making a point.

"Did you know Theo was going to bomb your building?" She no longer cared what the answer was as a feeling of lightness came over her. The man holding her hand so gently trusted her despite his second in command's feelings.

"Yes. We hadn't expected it so soon." He nodded to an operative pushing a large cabinet on a hand-truck. "Everyone knows what they're expected to do. About fifty miles outside of Atlanta is our new Main Sector. No more living underground."

"But what about me? What should I do?" Did she sound as pitiful as she thought?

Rex had heard her questions and had released a "Humph!" in disgust.

Then she remembered something that had happened in room 999. She turned to him. "Where's A. J.?"

"You mean Abby?" Instead of giving her his normal glare, Rex shook his head.

269

Olivia's breath left her body. Had her friend been sicker than she thought? The thought of someone else she cared for dying brought a chill to her hands and face.

"Tell her, Rex. You've got her worried." Collin jerked his head toward her.

"She's better. We took her to a private clinic last night where she can recover," Rex said. He flipped his hair over his shoulders and then smoothed it down.

If she didn't know better she would swear that was a nervous gesture. Before she asked any further questions, Collin pulled her away from Rex.

"I have something for you to do. Let's move out of everybody's way." He headed toward a black truck hooked up to a long black trailer.

A door opened on the side and inside were computers screens streaming information and various pieces of equipment blinking every color of the rainbow in the confining space. About ten people stopped what they were doing and turned to stare when they stepped inside.

"Nic, come here and show Olivia what we plan to do," Collin jerked his head toward her.

Confused, Olivia wondered if the security officer had been in on Jason's decision until she noticed the stiff way she answered him.

"Yes, sir," said Nic in an all-business tone, pointing at a computer-generated reenactment of their strategy. Either he'd told Nic the truth and she was still angry or he hadn't said anything and she worried about what he was up to.

Olivia tried to stand back and not make the woman dislike her any more than she already did.

"We've located the exit tunnel you and St. Vincent came out of. The scout we sent has met with success and opened it from the outside. A small detail of our operatives should rendezvous in about twenty minutes and then fifteen minutes or less they will be through and have Theo's Atlanta Main Sector under control."

"With minimum fire?" he asked.

"If they meet no resistance as you expect," Nic glared.

So, he'd told her. Obviously Nic was as upset as she'd been about Collin's silence leading up to Jason's death.

"We're going in?" Olivia asked.

"No. You and I are meeting Theo at a warehouse." Collin nodded to another operative who handed them each heavy bags. "In the back is an area where we can clean up and change."

The floor beneath her feet shifted. The truck was moving.

"Where is the warehouse?"

She followed him into a small room with two bunk beds on each side. Throwing their bags on the bottom bunk, Collin pulled on a panel, and a sink and mirror were revealed.

"Theo wants to meet us and discuss our surrender." He wet a cloth and tossed it to her. She looked at the damp washcloth without really seeing it. "Wash up."

"But you're not surrendering." She wiped at her face and arms. Somewhere she missed part of their conversation. She felt so lost. "When did you find out he'd agreed to meet?"

"Before I pulled you out of the shower." One side of his mouth lifted. "We were a little busy or I would've told you sooner." He pulled off his shirt. She worked at looking anywhere but at his beautiful chest. Would she ever get tired of looking at him?

271

He dropped his pants, leaving on his boxers. She turned her back. Too many people around to contemplate doing anything though, Lord of Mercy, she wanted Collin again.

His chuckle behind her frustrated the hell out of her.

"One thing about Theo," he continued, "he's been so successful he's beginning to feel invincible. When a person feels that way, they make mistakes, and he's making some humdingers."

"I hate to say it, but Theo doesn't make mistakes." She pulled out a T-shirt and black pants. As she pulled off her cement dust–coated shirt, she felt his eyes on her.

"He let you live," he said in his usual low tone.

Eyebrows raised, she turned as he wiped the cloth over his chest.

"You did too." For some reason it bothered her to hear him refer to her life as a mistake.

Maybe he was right. Her mother had meant for her to die in that trash bin after she was born. Obviously she'd been a mistake to her.

The next few minutes were quiet as they dressed and she fought back the ache in her chest and throat. No way would she let him see her cry over anything he said to her. The stress was getting to her. Before she realized what he was doing, he wrapped his arms around her and carefully squeezed.

"Quit," he whispered. "Your life is important. I'm glad I let you live and will never believe you're a mistake. I was saying Theo made the mistake because you're strong and a danger to him."

She rested her head on his shoulder and squeezed him back. Warmth and relief flooded her body. He might portray to the world a façade of coldness and single-minded-ness, but to her he'd allowed the shell to crack and let her see inside. Maybe her own shell had cracked too, allowing him to see the little girl needing love.

Her lips to his neck, she muttered, "Thank you." God, he smelled musky and male, sex and desire wrapped in one.

Their tender moment was broken by a knock on the door.

"Sir, we're five minutes away."

Shifting her body from his, she looked into his face.

"What conditions did he give you?" she asked.

One dark brow rose. "He's allowing two bodyguards each."

"So me and Rex?"

"Yes." His barely there grin had her smiling back at him.

"Who do you expect to be at Theo's side?" Dread filled her throat.

"He's lost so many people. Could be anyone."

Would he listen to her now? She pressed her lips against his. She wanted one more kiss before they started fighting again. He tasted so good, his heat drew her in, wanting more, anything he was willing to give. He pressed her against the wall, his body hot and hard.

"What's wrong?" he asked as soon as he pulled away.

She opened her mouth to deny it and then shook her head. "Listen. About your brother¾"

"Stop it." He stepped back. "Whoever you saw at Theo's Main Sector, he was an impostor and his purpose was to shake up my authority at the OS." He opened the door and nodded to the control room. "Let's go and see what they've found out so far about Theo's plans and the layout of the warehouse."

She pursed her lips and raised her eyebrows as she

walked by him. Now wasn't the time to argue and she had a feeling Collin would have no option but to believe her when harsh reality slapped him in the face.

Chapter Thirty-One

Olivia craned her neck looking around. The warehouse was nothing special; one large room with a three-story high ceiling and metal stairs in a corner that led to several glassed-in offices. Besides the steel double doors they entered, a single door on the back wall appeared to be the type to slide open. No other exits to the street.

In the middle of the empty floor sat a strange large round oak table with six high-back chairs, three facing the other three. The tabletop was beaten and scratched as if a sharp object had been slammed against it in several places.

From what she could see, there was nowhere for anyone to hide; the ceiling was solid without the expected skylights. Glaring lights did little to heat the area and Olivia hated how she felt like she was missing something important.

"You would think Theo could be a little more original in his choice of meeting places." Rex muttered as his gray eyes scanned the area for the hundredth time.

"He always said there was safety in doing what's been done before. Something about knowing all the hiding places and the mistakes," she stated as Collin examined every corner.

She dug her hands into the pockets of her lightweight trench coat. The MP5 beneath the material pressed against her side, giving her the reassurance she could protect Collin. Not that he needed protection as he carried at least two pistols and a knife, all hidden on his body. Watching him strap them on earlier had made her wet. Just thinking about it now, she squeezed her legs together and struggled to keep her mind on keeping an eye out for Theo and his thugs.

She hated to even think what Collin's reaction would be when Arthur Ryker showed up. It didn't take a genius to know Theo planned for Collin's brother's emergence from the grave as a way to throw Collin off. He hoped to make it easier in taking back the OS.

Over her dead body.

What worried her even more was that she knew Theo and he never did anything halfway. So who would be his second guard?

In Theo's dramatic timing, the large sliding metal door in the back of the building screeched open. Theo walked through first. Was he brave or crazy for taking the chance of an ambush? Olivia didn't have to guess. The man was certifiably nuts. He wore all white and the robes looked to be from medieval royalty. His white hair brushed his collar. Some strands blew across his face as the wind outside whipped through the open door. Those piercing blue eyes cut over to Collin and stayed. Theo obviously had counted on Collin not believing her tale of seeing his *dead* brother.

She also watched Collin. Her heart drummed faster and faster. How would he feel to discover his brother alive after all these years? And the man responsible for hiding him¾Olivia had no doubt that Theo had a hand in it¾loving every moment. When Collin's usual passive face bleached white, she stepped nearer to him.

"What's the asshole doing here?" Rex asked in his deep voice behind them.

Rex knew Ryker was alive and hadn't told Collin?

When she looked at the big guy, she noticed his gaze wasn't on Collin's brother but the other man walking in to stand next to Ryker. Nearly as tall as Rex, the guy had a shaved head and his eyes were such a light blue that they looked almost white. His bottom lip was pierced with a gold loop and his sleeveless shirt revealed one arm covered with tattoos. He sneered at Rex.

"Someone you know?" she asked in a low pitch.

"Yeah. My turncoat asshole of a brother."

Jack Drago? Why had Theo brought him out of New York? Was he as crazy as she heard? Well, he was with good company if that was the case. She shook her head and looked over to Collin. He'd regained his composure, but couldn't take his eyes off the other man with the eye patch.

"Let me introduce my two guards." Theo stretched out his hand to the left. "Jack Drago." And then with a kingly flip of his wrist, indicated his right. "Arthur Ryker."

Ryker stared at Collin as if he wanted his heart for dinner. Such hatred rolled off him in waves. Olivia moved a hand beneath her coat, touching the gun, calming her nerves with the knowledge she could protect Collin. This did not bode well for the meeting.

"Hello, brother. I thought you were dead." Collin remained still.

"I'm sure if I had been, it would make life simpler for you."

Collin frowned. "Theo, how long have you known he was alive?"

"I've known from the beginning. Ryker understands I saved him. I was there to pull him from the fires of hell. I've protected him from the enemies of The Circle. If not for me, he'd be dead." Theo's tone said more than the words.

Then it struck Olivia, had Theo set up Collin's parents' death? It certainly would've been a win-win situation. Kill his partner and raise the child in his image.

Her gaze darted to Ryker. Was he brought up in the pervert's image? Did he prefer young girls too? Theo's cutoff was fourteen. What about Ryker? Would his be younger? Shit! She hoped not. To have to kill Collin's brother would be difficult but not impossible.

Theo swept his arm to the table. "Thought it only right to sit at the table that represents our organization."

"Organizations," Collin corrected.

Theo nodded his head and then sat in the middle of three chairs nearest him.

Collin opened his long wool coat and lifted Excalibur and placed in the middle of the table.

Theo's eyes glowed and his fingers twitched with a fanatic desire to grab the sword. His belief that it represented his authority to rule The Circle and the OS held him in its grasp.

After Rex and Olivia sat on the chairs across from his brother Jack, Collin took his seat across from Theo. The way everyone watched each other and moved without any sudden movements, the tension reached out and held each person in its grip.

"So you've decided to not only bring the sword back to me but bring the OS back into the fold. I'm glad to see you've come to your senses," Theo smiled in a fatherly way and then looked over toward Olivia.

She really wished the old man wouldn't do that. His every move was being analyzed by those around them and they could easily judge her as an accomplice. Rex leaned over and glared at her as he growled. She shook her head and rolled her eyes. The big guy knew they were setting up Theo but either he was a better actor than she thought or he had forgotten.

"As my message said, I'm willing to discuss the possibility," Collin said in his usual soft voice.

Sitting with his hands folded on top of the table as if he had all day long to chat, Collin started the discussion of the pros and cons. Their conversation became a buzz in the background as Olivia watched the other players on each side of Theo.

She caught the hate-filled looks Ryker shot at his younger brother. Jack's frown deepened the furrows in his forehead, and instead of looking angry, he appeared concerned about his older brother.

Minutes passed and twice Collin had to speak to Rex to calm him down. Each time he did, Ryker made a smart-ass comment. All the family squabbling brought a gloating look to Theo's face. As any good leader would say, know your enemies' weaknesses and exploit them in every way.

In a split second, Rex's chair clattered to the floor as he hollered at Jack, "You betrayed us, you bastard!"

Ryker stood, pointing as he shouted at Collin, "Jack did what was needed. You're the traitor to everything our father had built!"

Then they all were screaming over each other, shaking their fists and pounding the table.

Worried the men would begin swinging in any minute

and really she had enough of their arguing, she pulled the trigger on her MP5 and sprayed the wall to her right.

The room fell quiet. She cleared her throat. "Okay. We understand. Everyone hates everyone here. Let's hammer out this treaty and move on."

Theo's grin spread wide and he stood, slowly clapping his hands. "That's my girl. She has the brains of a man and the taste of a two-dollar whore."

Collin's chair screeched on the cement floor as he stood, pushing it back. "Leave her out of this."

She wanted to place her hand on his arm but Theo would interpret it to his advantage. Just by taking up for her, Collin had already given Theo an edge.

"You always had the white knight syndrome, my boy." Theo smoothed the front of his robe. "That's why you will never lead The Circle. Do you really think it was coincidence that Olivia was in Seattle at the same time as you? And that you were fed her location? It was all planned. She knew just how to play you. I knew you would see her as a challenge even though she's so easy to fuck."

Theo returned to his chair and leaned back, his smug grin ate at Olivia. Collin wouldn't believe Theo, would he? She had no part in the meeting. Unless Theo had set her up. Would he take a chance on Collin killing her?

"Actually, Olivia was in Seattle to kill an OS operative. Did you think it was coincidence that Ned Grandly died the day you met her? She's very good at her job. No mess considering the body landed in the water. No fuss, no muss." The old man tented his fingers in front of his mouth, probably to hide a grin.

Numbness spread through her limbs. Once again Theo proved he'd lied about everything. All this time she'd thought with each kill she rid the world of another psycho. How could Theo do this to her?

She reminded herself, this was Theo and he did enjoy playing God.

<<<>>>

"I'm aware you'd set her up. As I've set you up today." Collin remained standing, watching Theo as realization sunk in the old man's brain. "By now, the Main Sector of your empire is now under my control." He hoped their plan had worked.

Tired of all their maneuvering for position, he glared at the old man.

Theo stood and turned to Arthur. "What are you standing here for? He's taking your legacy from you again!" Theo's whole body shook.

Arthur's face flushed in anger.

"Actually, you took it the first time along with everything else of value in my life." He leaned toward Theo, baring his teeth as he continued, "I've been doing a little investigating myself. You're the one who had the explosives set in the car. You had hoped to kill us all. No sooner than when you pressed the button you received a call. You were told my brother was nowhere near the accident. Then and only then did you decide to pull me out of the wreckage. You took me and destroyed everything normal and good in my life. You used me in ways no human should use another."

Arthur's face darkened as he grabbed Theo by the shoulder.

"And I refuse to let you use me anymore. I'm not your

slave to do as you say. Go to hell, you bastard!" Spittle whitened the corners of his mouth with hatred.

He stretched across the table and wrapped his hand around the sword's pommel before anyone could move. The thump of flesh and sharp scratch of bone being hit vibrated through the deathly silent room. Theo grunted and his eyes widened, staring at his killer in disbelief. Arthur whispered into his ear and then pulled the bloody sword from his body.

"I thought of you like a son," Theo groaned and collapsed into his chair. A shiny, dark red stain on his tunic spread across his stomach.

Collin stared at his brother. No one moved for several seconds. Then Jack leaned over and closed Theo's eyes. No one protested the man's death.

The room returned to focus as his breathing resumed. Theo no longer threatened his life, no longer controlled how he looked at the world around him. He was free. Seeing the man dead would never bring his parents back, but Collin could close the door on the past and move on. His big brother he'd loved so much as a kid was alive. That was what he needed to concentrate on for now.

"What now?" Collin sounded cold-hearted, but the bottom line was he needed to be careful in dealing with the brother he no longer knew. Though he didn't completely agree with the method of Theo's death, he admitted the end result was needed.

His brother leaned over and wiped the blade on Theo's sleeve, leaving two red stripes as if they were marks of rank. Then Collin spotted a slight tremor of his hand. Good. He wasn't as unmoved by what he did as he appeared. Maybe there was hope for them to work together.

"You understand that the sword is now mine," Arthur challenged him.

Collin dipped his head. "I truly never wanted it."

He stared at the older brother he wanted to know. Such pain stared out of those familiar eyes.

"We stopped your people from entering Main Sector. They're safe. No one harmed," Ryker said, his tone not reassuring.

Before he could question him, Olivia asked no one in particular, "Are you sure he's dead?"

Jack pressed two fingers against his neck. "Yep."

"Good. The son of a bitch deserved to die." Rex folded his arms and watched his brother.

"Arthur, what do you plan to do now?" Collin's hands hung at his side, not taking a chance any move could be interpreted wrong. The way Arthur eyed him and Olivia, Collin wasn't sure what to expect.

"Ryker. Call me Ryker." His brother pulled out a cell phone and pressed a few buttons. "Let the OS operatives leave. It's done. Come and pick us up."

Their dad always preferred to be called by his last name.

"You took a big chance we wouldn't attack you after you killed Theo," Collin stated.

Forehead wrinkled, Collin had a hard time coming to terms that the scarred man standing in front of him was his brother. He remembered Arthur as a jokester who looked after him. From what he could tell, his brother had achieved the level of impassiveness his dad always claimed was needed for the job. Arthur ... no, Ryker appeared colder and more ruthless.

"I didn't worry." Ryker looked at Olivia. "She wouldn't

attack me. He deserved to die. She understands." Then he handed the sword to Jack.

Collin glanced at Olivia. Had she planned this with his brother? He would ask later. For now, they needed to work at settling the war between The Circle and OS.

"Maybe we all do," Collin said as he stared at the blood on Theo's robe pooling and running down to the floor. He had a hard time wrapping his mind around the fact Theo would no longer cause trouble.

"I can help you with that if you want," Ryker offered.

His blank face told Collin more than he wanted to know. The man who was his brother had no conscience and would have no problem killing him.

"Would you?" Trying one more time to reason with his brother, Collin spoke in an even tone, hoping he would listen. "Don't you think we need to work together to bring the OS back into The Circle and to regain the good reputation our dad had worked so hard for?"

"I'm not Theo. When you parted with The Circle, you proved you no longer deserved to be part of the organization." The last of the words came out of Ryker's mouth as a growl and he placed one hand on the table as if he was about to attack.

Collin grabbed Rex before he met Ryker head on. The click of a gun bolt being pushed alerted him. Not loosening his grip on Rex, he turned. Olivia held her submachine gun to her shoulder and pointed at Ryker.

"I don't care if you have half his face. I'll blow it all off if you move another inch." She stood with legs apart and elbows out.

"You need to call off your woman." The look Ryker gave Olivia said he found her actions titillating and Collin didn't like it one bit.

"I believe we've all had enough," said Collin.

He saw no way to come to terms with his brother at this time. He needed to get his best friend and his woman under control. Yeah. His woman. He liked that. He looked at her holding the dangerous weapon and a stirring below his waist warned him he needed to get *himself* under control.

With a push he released Rex and turned to watch Ryker walk away, going out the same door he'd entered, leaving it open.

Jack fell in behind Ryker until Rex shouted, "Hey, stay. We're brothers. We can talk it out. I'll forgive you."

Rex's brother stopped. Head down, he stared at the floor and smoothed a hand over his tanned scalp.

"There you're wrong. I've done things you'll never forgive," he said as he lifted his gaze.

Such anguish on his face brought an answering one from Rex's. Then Jack stepped into the alleyway and the shadows beyond.

Rex probably felt like Collin did, unsure what to do next. Seeing Theo's body draped over the throne-like chair brought the realization an era had ended. His dad and Theo had created an organization to fight the evil elements and protect the weak. Except his dad had been killed by his best friend. Remembering what his dad had quoted to him one time, he murmured, "Power corrupts; absolute power corrupts absolutely."

"Maybe your brother learned from Theo's mistakes." Olivia stepped closer and asked, "Are you okay?"

When his gaze fell on her hand resting on his arm, she pulled away. He let her. They had a lot to discuss and he needed to decide if what he felt for her was lust or something more.

"I'm fine. I need to get back to my people and check on

our new facilities," he said as he tried to avoid the tears shining in her beautiful green eyes. Relief loosened the tension in his body when she looked away.

"Well, I guess it's goodbye." She cleared her throat.

"What the hell do you mean goodbye?" he shouted. The tension tightened around his chest again. He wanted her in his life.

"Listen, you got what you want. Theo's dead." She gave him her back. "He can't ... oh, God, he's gone." Her body shuddered as he grabbed her and pulled her into his arms.

"Shhh. Be happy that you didn't do it and won't have that on your conscience. Every time he ordered someone's death, his was assured to happen in the same way." He pressed his mouth to the top of her head as he squeezed her. She vigorously shook her head. "You know I'm right."

She pulled away and faced him. "No. You misunderstand. I wanted to be the one to kill him. I hated him!" she hissed. "I hated what he did to me and made me do." Fat tears rolled down her face. Her eyes red and skin botchy.

Knowing the eccentric bastard, Collin had a good idea the degradation and misery she'd suffered until she found a way to escape death by the old man's hands. There was nothing he could say to help her forget. So he tightened his hold and brought her against him. She wrapped her arms around his waist, resting her head on his shoulder.

Minutes passed and Collin heard Rex call their cleanup crew. By the time they showed up, Olivia had regained her composure.

<<<>>>

"Collin," Olivia said as she rubbed her cheek against his chest.

Dry eyed, she soaked up his undivided attention even with all the activity surrounding them. The cleanup crew had arrived and was doing their job. Before the sun rose again, the place would be cleaned of blood and fingerprints, bullet holes would be repaired, or any sign that anything lethal happened would be gone.

"Yes, sweetheart?"

His eyes had been closed when she'd moved her head from his shoulder. Now he looked down at her with a tenderness she'd never experienced from him. Could he have feelings for her? Real feelings? If that was true, what she must say would extinguish any chance.

"I'm leaving and returning to The Circle."

His arms fell away from her. All activity around them stopped.

"Why?" he asked.

How could she tell him she wasn't good enough for him? How could he look at her knowing she'd killed so many OS operatives? She only hoped some were common psychos like Theo had told her. Theo's taunts reminded her of what she really was. Collin deserved a good woman without blood on her hands. She needed time to think.

"Ryker will get you killed," he simply stated.

"As you mentioned before, I'm too valuable to your brother."

She wished she could lie to Collin and tell him it was for the common good. Only one reason existed. She was scared. The man in front of her had become too important in her life. He may care for her, but he would never love her. And she never believed in all that martyred shit people tried to feed each other. Just being around him and seeing him every day was not enough. A piece of her would die each day. Since she wasn't fit to live with regular folk, she would return to what she knew best. Killing for The Circle.

"You know the OS will continue to work at stopping The Circle if he continues Theo's policies." His jaw shifted.

Good. His being mad was better than acting as if he didn't care. He would never beg, not that it would change her mind.

She looked around, swallowing the lump in her throat, determined to act as if they discussed her resigning from a job and nothing more. An unreal quality had her reaching out to touch his cheek. He jerked back. Yeah. The sum total of their relationship, they didn't trust each other. No. That wasn't quite right. She trusted him completely. He trusted her not at all. He believed she was betraying him by leaving.

"Goodbye." She waited for his response.

His lips remained closed. She placed the MP5 on the table and walked away, leaving through the same door Ryker and Jack had hours earlier.

As soon as she reached some distance from the warehouse, she wandered aimlessly down several streets. The few people she passed gave her a wide berth as tears soaked her reddened cheeks and dripped off her chin. She came to a bus stop and sat on the bench as she stared off into the air. Thankfully people on this side of town never meddled in weeping women's affairs. Some days she hated being a woman with churning emotions popping up no matter how hard she tried to hold them back. She wished she could be as cold and unemotional as the men in her life.

She wiped the tears onto her sleeves and stood straight. Being a wimp wouldn't get her what she wanted. There was no way she could go back to The Circle. Ryker would make her think of Collin too much. She had to think of something else.

She needed a new direction in her life. New experiences would be great too. Being alone as an orphan child and adult had never bothered her.

She snapped her fingers.

The orphans at St. Vincent! She'd never felt comfortable around children, but falling in love had made her realize she wanted children. Even though she couldn't physically have any of her own she had an orphanage full to call her own. Helping them would help her move on. Give her the experience of doing something right. She could do it.

In a cloud of exhaust fumes and screeching brakes, a bus stopped in front of her. She blinked. The street name on the sign flashing above the driver happened to be two blocks from St. Vincent. She'd never been on a city bus. She laughed. A sign. A real sign. Someone up there agreed with her decision and had provided her transportation.

Maybe afterwards she would see a new sign for how to teach a hardheaded man a lesson.

Chapter Thirty-Two

Collin stalked down the hallway of Olivia's house. By the time he reached the last room, sweat beaded on his forehead and his heart pounded against his chest. Had he missed her? Where could she be?

Despair drew him to the window overlooking the small garden in the back. He held back the curtains with shaking hands. How many nights had he stared at his ceiling wanting her and wishing he'd gone after her?

Sheets of rain poured from the heavens. An old-fashioned two-seater swing hung from large oak tree's limb and swayed. His gaze moved to the other side of the yard. That was when he saw her. She stood on a moon-shaped cement patio about ten feet from the back door. He'd thought at first she was a statue as she stood in the middle with her hands reaching toward the sky. Her long nightgown stuck to her body and water flowed off the white folds of cloth.

By the time he reached the backyard, he'd expected her to disappear like the dreams he grabbed for each night since she left two months ago. The downpour had slowed to a drizzle. She remained in the center but now with her arms held out to the sides and her head thrown back as she let the mist wash her face. A willing sacrifice to the night.

He couldn't bring himself to touch her and break the spell she weaved around him. Beads of water decorated the tips of her eyelashes. From the outside corners of her eyes, thin streams ran down her temples. She looked as if she was crying. Was she as unhappy as he'd been?

"Olivia?"

He leaned over her body, almost touching, his lips a breath away from her moist ones. Her eyes drifted open and more water flowed from their depths.

"Collin?" she said his name as if she couldn't believe her eyes.

"Yes."

"I've missed you."

She brought her arms around and clasped his shoulders. Her body trembled against his. He licked her bottom lip, savoring the taste of her mixed with the cool moisture.

"Are you cold?" he asked.

His hands covered her breasts and lifted them as he placed a kiss on the cloth cupping each taunt nipple.

"No. But I ache for you."

He dropped his hands to her hips and pulled on the cloth, but the wet material clung to her body. Impatient and wanting to see the body he missed so much, he slipped out his knife and sliced the front of the gown from neck to knee.

"You realize you owe me for two gowns now." Her words brushed his neck as he leaned forward to tear the material off her body.

He inhaled, enjoying the way her cool breasts warmed against his chest. The fragrance of vanilla brought back memories of their time together. An exotic scent mixed with the familiar. He pulled her into his arms and his hands slid down her back.

"I've missed you," he repeated.

His mouth covered hers and met coldness. He looked down to see lips made of chiseled stone. Stumbling back, he realized he'd been making love to a statue. What happened? His eyes searched the area surrounding the patio and then caught movement in the window he'd peered out earlier.

Then a strange sensation pulled his gaze to the front of his shirt. A small green spot danced across his chest.

"No! Olivia! It's me!"

He lifted his hand, signaling to her to stop. The sounds of the computer on her sniper rifle winding up reached his ears. With a jerk, his body was sailing through the air and everything around him turned red.

With heart pounding, he woke as lightning lit up his bedroom. A shadow moved near the window, at the same time, thunder shook the bed. He tried to sit up but his wrists remained near his head. Manacles chained him to the headboard. When he shifted his feet, he felt the same around his ankles.

"Olivia?"

<<<>>>

Olivia loved thunderstorms. When she was little she remembered the nuns warning her of how dangerous it was to stand near the windows. Considering the numerous ways she'd come close to dying over the last few years, she wasn't too worried about lightning.

Just then a bright line divided the sky for a few seconds, quickly followed by thunder echoing above her head. Rain pelted the window as the wind shoved drops sideways. On the radio earlier, she'd heard tornado warnings would hang around until the early morning hours. A sense of anticipation dangled in the air.

"Olivia?"

"Finally, my Prince Charming is awake." She climbed onto the bed and straddled his big body, her face above his. "I thought I would have to start without you."

The chains holding the manacles rattled as he tried to reach for her. She didn't move. It would take two thousand pounds of pressure to break the chain holding him. Only the best for what she had planned.

"Did my brother send you?" he asked as his eyes flared when her naked body rested onto top of his.

How convenient that he slept in the nude. Though she had to admit she would enjoy tearing his clothes off.

She chuckled.

"I can promise you, your brother had nothing to do with this."

His gaze darted to her breasts. Oh, yeah, he liked what he saw as she felt him lengthen and become thicker. Torturing herself was not in her plans, so with a slight shift of her hips, she sank down on him. The thickness filling her brought a sigh to her lips. He felt so good.

"Dammit. Get off me."

His body told a different story. He arched and then followed with a thrust of his hips.

"What fun would that be?" she whispered and groaned.

She closed her eyes and lifted and lowered her body. How many nights had she stared at the ceiling wishing he rested between her thighs doing this?

Not once had the thought of taking another lover into her bed crossed her mind. The man beneath her was unique and matched her perfectly. She would never be able to control him, glancing at the chains she amended that thought, except with a little help and for a short time.

He jerked on his shackles.

"You're going to regret this."

She laughed.

"That's rich. I believe I said the same thing when you handcuffed me."

Every taut masculine muscle in his chest shifted when hers came to rest on top.

She nipped at his ear. "My only regret is the last few months we wasted time with our hardheadedness. We could've been doing this."

Her mouth covered his. Satisfaction heated her body as his mouth responded.

When their lips parted, he said in the soft voice that sent shivers of lust through her body, "Let me go so we can do this right."

Oh, she was tempted. He was the only man she'd ever made love to that she allowed to take control. Her body shivered in remembrance of their time in the cabin. Her mouth dropped to his neck and licked the place where his heartbeat pumped so strong. The tart smell and taste of Collin drove her to a frantic pace. His groan reassured her that he wanted this as bad as she did. In seconds, rolling waves of sensation pounded in every direction from where he filled her. Then Collin arched against her and moaned.

She moved off him and the bed, stepping into the bathroom. Moments later, she returned with a warm, damp cloth. She took her time cleaning the part of him that provided so much pleasure as she ignored his angry stares.

"Now, Olivia, release me."

Her nipples tightened. Was her body ever satisfied very

long around him? His low, harsh voice commanding her was such a turn-on.

"No."

She almost giggled when he narrowed his eyes. Maybe she should be afraid of him. He'd shown her several times how dangerous he could be, but during their time apart she'd realized how much she missed him. He'd gotten under her skin and she wanted to prove to him how much she loved him. Every time she said that to herself, she couldn't help but smile. Such a unique experience, loving someone else.

Sure, he could turn her down, but she had to try to make him understand. In her business lying was expected. So she doubted he would believe her. Showing would have to do the trick. If she released him, he would only send her away. She wanted to show him all the ways she loved him.

"This is crazy. Okay. You've paid me back plus some. Let me go."

When she continued to wipe a well-muscled thigh with special care, his cock began stretching, recovering from their little romp.

"Dammit! Stop now."

She threw the cloth on the floor and swept one hand up his length. "You don't mean it."

"Watch me."

He jerked and pulled on the chains. The metal dug red marks around his wrists.

"Stop it! You're hurting yourself."

"Then let me go!"

"If you really wanted me to let you go, you would've already called out for help. Rex is down the hall and your guards are alive. I didn't hurt any of them." She moved her hands away and stood. "I'm only trying to make you understand that I love you."

His cold look told her so much. She'd been wrong. He didn't want to hear about how much she loved him. She'd never told a living soul that before. Her greatest fear was realized, she was unlovable. Nausea bubbled up from her stomach, almost to her throat. Even when he hadn't followed her out of that warehouse or checked on her all these weeks, months, she'd thought it had been only his pride. She'd thought if she put him in a position of … oh, Christ! Her logic was all screwed up. You don't chain up someone you love.

She walked over to the nightstand and pulled out the top drawer. Her hands were steady. The numbness that always fell over her as she prepared to kill someone pulled her into the near trance she hated. When she unlocked the first ring, he snapped the key out of her hand and made short work of the other manacles.

He moved off the bed and stood in front of her, his fists clenching open and close. The fury radiating from his body popped her back to defensive mode.

"Go ahead and get Rex, you crazy bastard. I love you and I refuse to force any man to love me! Go ahead and kill me. But you'll always wonder what you missed out on."

Not caring if she was about to die or not, she stood and reached for her blouse at the end of the bed. Collin snatched it from her hand and threw it on the floor. More thunder shook the walls, rattling the window.

"It was driving me nuts, not being able to touch you as I've dreamed about for so many nights, for so long." He kissed her. The power of the kiss left no doubt in her mind what he had on his. "I love you, you crazy bitch." His hands roamed all over her body until he cupped her butt and lifted, throwing her on the bed. "Now it's time for me to do what I've wanted for a long time."

Her breath was short and she barely asked, "What's that?"

"Fuck your brains out!"

She wrapped her arms and legs around him. Her laughter bounced off the walls as Rex and the guards probably heard Collin's every word. Her soft-spoken man had expressed his and her feelings plainly and loudly.

"Finally," she whispered in his ear.

<<<>>>

"I don't care how many times you suck my dick, I'll talk with him when I damn well feel like it."

From where Olivia kneeled at his feet, she watched as he tucked his semi-hard cock tenderly back into his pants with shaky hands. She loved flustering him.

Two days earlier, she'd found out from Rex that Arthur had left a message for Collin to call him back. Rex had shaken his head in disgust. "He's being hardheaded and won't tell me when he plans to return the call."

They hadn't heard from Collin's brother in several months, not since he walked out of the warehouse after killing Theo. Rumors trickled into the OS that The Circle had moved its headquarters into the mountains of east Tennessee where no one could find them and besides a few Circle missions that had gone sour, nothing else had been heard from the large and dangerous organization. Collin believed they were regrouping, getting used to the new order of things. Still, it worried her.

She grinned. "Am I so predictable now?"

He grabbed her hand and pulled her into his arms. "You're many things, but never predictable."

"How old were you when your parents died?" she asked the question before thinking it through. In their time together, they rarely spoke of the past.

"Ten."

"Poor baby." She smoothed his hair and kissed his cheek. A muscle near his mouth twitched. Was he trying not to smile or was he bothered by her compassion? Even after all this time, she still couldn't read him. Maybe that was why they were so good together. They didn't take each other for granted.

"You'd told me once there were nine months between you and your brother. So he was around eleven. That had to be a horrible time."

She unbuttoned his shirt a couple of notches and slipped her hand inside. The feel of his hard chest and the sprinkling of hair against her hand sent a tingling through her body. Touching him was such a turn-on.

"Dammit, Olivia. I'm not your scratching post." He pulled away from her and walked back to his desk and sat.

"Oh, but you like this little pussy cat so much."

She purred and laughed when his eyes flared amber. Seeing that look in his eyes always reassured her he was still fascinated. Not since that stormy night together had he told her he loved her again. But she understood he wasn't the type to say it often, if at all. That one time would have to be enough.

One side of his mouth arched up. Oh, yeah. There was that smile she rarely saw but loved so much.

"You got me there." He typed on the keyboard as he stared into the monitor. "Be a good little kitten and come over here and look at this."

"You're sure you want me that close to you during your *working hours?*" The last two words she emphasized by doing air quotation marks. Not long ago, he'd set ground rules that she must behave herself during certain hours of the day. Otherwise, she shot his concentration to hell and back.

"Yeah. You know you'd better behave."

"But I love it when you get all manly and try to boss me around." She moved behind him and looked over his shoulder. An aerial view of buildings surrounded by razor wire and towering trees appeared on the monitor. "Is that what I think it is?"

"The new Circle's headquarters."

"It's huge. No way could he build all of that in just a few months." From what she could see, parts of it literally spilled out of mountain and the mountain sat in the middle of ten thousand acres.

"We've learned Theo had started building it a few years ago. His plan was to move into it next year."

"Do you think Ryker is treating Marie okay? She did help us." Olivia had been surprised to learn the young girl's true age was twenty-one. When Marie was sold to Theo by her parents, she been small for her age, probably from malnutrition, and looked nine. In actuality she'd been twelve, almost thirteen. Olivia had been right. Marie was a good actress to hide her real age from Theo. He would've killed her for lying.

"He's not the brother I remember when we were kids."

Olivia fingered a few strands of his hair. She didn't like hearing the sad tone in his voice.

"What now? You don't intend to blow up your brother."

She wanted to feel confident he wouldn't kill Ryker, but

one thing she'd learned about Collin, he did whatever was necessary to protect the OS and his people.

"No. When I spoke with Arthur yesterday, he was having trouble with someone killing women in his area."

She punched his arm. "You sneaky bastard. You wanted those blow jobs." When she hit him again, hard, he pulled her into his lap.

"You're so good at it," he whispered as he held her face and stared deep into her eyes. How could she complain when he looked at her like that?

A wiggle of her butt brought an answering hardness in his lap. She closed her eyes and rested a cheek in the crook of his neck. Never had she'd been so content. She felt like she lived in a beautiful erotic dream now. With a sigh she squeezed him around the waist and he returned the sentiment.

"Collin, are you sure¾" Nic stopped in mid-sentence as she walked into the room. She lifted her gaze from the papers in her hands, her eyes widened as she stared at the pair cuddling behind the desk.

Olivia worked hard at getting along with the dark-haired woman. In fact, she avoided her whenever possible. At first, she'd tried to be friendly, but Nic refused all over-tures of friendship. Just as well, as A. J.—she could never get use to calling her Abby—told her the woman followed Rex around like a little puppy. And like most men, he didn't see it. A. J. tried to ignore Nic as she struggled with Rex's never-ending questions about her life in The Circle. Olivia had pointed out she needed to talk to him, that she had nothing to be ashamed of. She had done what was necessary to survive because she'd believed Rex was dead and he'd believed the same of her. What A. J. had done with Jack,

Rex's brother, was over and done years ago. A. J. ignored her advice, as she did Nic's crush on Rex.

"Sure of what?" Collin pressed Nic, pulling Olivia out of her thoughts.

The woman blushed and cleared her throat. "Ah, that Ryker believed it was someone in the OS?"

He nodded with one eyebrow lifted.

Olivia stiffened as her face flushed and then she twisted, turning her back to Nic and shooting Collin a look he couldn't misinterpret. Anger didn't cover how she felt. He'd told Nic before telling her he'd called his brother. Hurt churned her stomach. No matter what his intentions were, good, bad, or sexual, she should be first. She pushed off his chest to stand and he grabbed her wrists, stopping as he gave her a cold stare.

"Let go of me," she whispered. He was boss and she refused to embarrass him in front of one of his people.

"Nic, I'll talk to you later." He cut his eyes over to the other woman without releasing Olivia.

"Sure. If you don't mind, I'll leave these over here for you to look at."

Nic slid the stack of papers onto one of the empty chairs in front of the desk. With a wrinkled brow, she took one last glance and then closed the door behind her.

Tremors started at Olivia's chest and traveled down until her hands shook like a person in twenty degree weather without a parka. She kept telling herself she was overreacting. It didn't mean he suspected her of betraying the OS.

"Olivia, do you have something you want to tell me?" His hands dropped from her wrists.

Before he could grab her fingers, she slapped him. As his cheek turned red, she understood her anger was more from jealousy than anything to do with his distrust. This business rarely allowed anyone to be naïve for long and it had been years since she trusted anyone until she met Collin. Just because she trusted him didn't mean he returned the sentiment.

His eyes flared amber as he captured her hands, stopping her from doing more damage.

"So, you didn't have anything to do with sabotaging The Circle's missions," he said more as a statement of fact than a question.

Her growing anger burst free when she broke from his hold and jumped to her feet. He followed in a synchronized move as his big body covered hers, pressing her back to the wall. He clasped her wrists into one hand and slammed them over her head.

"Let go of me," she hissed.

"You're fucking hot when you're mad." He nipped her earlobe.

"You said that just to make me lose my temper." Frustrated but happy to know he still trusted her. She wiggled, showing her willingness to play along.

"And you're more dangerous than any firearm you love so much. You're my sniper rifle. I would let you slap and beat me every day of the week as long as you return the favor."

"Let you beat me?" she asked.

He never acted like pain was his forte before and it sure wasn't hers. She might enjoy having it rough on occasion, but never for the pain. Olivia shifted her hip. His hard cock pulsed against her groin and she melted into him. No man ever made her feel like this. Soft and feminine.

"No. Let me love you." His mouth took hers.

She moaned and sank into the kiss. She loved this man

who wasn't afraid to let her be herself. Leaning her head away, she touched his cheek.

"What about your brother and The Circle?" she asked.

He gave her a crooked grin.

"Let him get his own woman."

She giggled.

"Do you want to get the handcuffs or should I?"

Circle of Danger Excerpt

The story of The Circle Organization continues in Circle of Danger. Marie and Ryker's story.

After four local women are found dead from a new designer drug, Arthur Ryker orders his mercenary organization, The Circle, to find the source, a mysterious figure called the Wizard.

As a child, Marie Beltane was sold for drugs by her parents to a madman. Now that he's dead, she's determined to prove she's worthy of more and goes on assignment to stop the killings. But things go wrong when she's injected with the same drug.

Scarred inside and out, Ryker struggles with his failure to protect Marie from the world as well as himself. He becomes reckless during his search for the antidote and is captured by a new evil. Now he must become the monster he always feared to save the woman he always loved.

Read on for a sneak peek at the thrilling sequel to *Circle of Desire* and prequel to *Circle of Deception*. Available now!

Excerpt of Circle of Danger

Arthur Ryker sprang out of bed and immediately stood at attention, feet apart, his scarred hands in the ready position at waist level. One hand cupped by the other, restrained but prepared to kill. He shook his head and sighed. Just once he wanted to leave his bed like a regular person and not like a trained monkey.

"A bad dream?" a deep voice asked from the bedroom entrance. With one pierced black eyebrow lifted, Jack Drago leaned against the door jamb.

Ignoring the question, Ryker walked naked into the bathroom. When he returned to grab some clothes out of the closet, Jack hadn't moved but his gaze had most likely inspected every inch of the room. There wasn't much to see. A king-sized bed sat in a corner, while a mirror-less dresser was centered against one wall, no pictures or the usual bric-a-brac to give away the occupant's personality. Then again maybe it did. Rather stark for a man who owned enough properties and businesses to keep his organization in the best covert weapons money could buy. He didn't care what Jack thought about his bedroom. Except for a few hours of sleep and a shower and shave, Ryker rarely spent time in the room.

"What do you want?" he asked, glaring at his second in command.

With cold blue eyes, Jack studied him and then his gaze shifted away.

Ryker grunted. Not many people could deal with looking at the thick scars down the side of his body, but it was his blind eye that bothered most. White from the scar tissue damaged in a fire so many years ago, he normally hid it beneath a patch. But he'd be damned before he slept with one on. So if Jack decided to make a habit of waking him in the morning, he could fucking-well get use to the sight. Considering the man had four visible piercings and who knew how many hidden, along with tattoos covering one arm, he shouldn't have a problem with his scars. The man understood pain.

With sure, quick movements, he thrust his legs into jeans and yanked on a black T-shirt. After tugging on his boots, he strapped a small pistol at his ankle. With his patch in place, using his fingers, he combed hair over the strap securing its position. Hell, he needed a haircut again. Maybe he'd shave his head like Jack. A simple enough solution. If only the rest of his problems could be so easily solved.

"She's in trouble," Jack said in an even tone as if his voice could defuse a bad situation.

Ryker's stomach and chest tightened as if he'd been hit. He knew who Jack referred to without adding a name. She happened to be part of why his life was so complicated.

"Did you hear me?" Jack straightened his stance.

"Yeah." Desire to break someone's neck raced through his body. "Where is she? What happened?"

With a sharp snap, he inserted a snub-nose into the shoulder holster hanging at his side and jerked on his leather jacket. He gritted his teeth for a few seconds to regain his composure. Then he took a deep breath, squared his shoulders and exhaled.

"Last time Bryan heard from her, she'd entered the

target's house in Chattanooga and was downloading information off a laptop. He lost communication with her." Jack quickly stepped out of the way for Ryker to move into the dark hallway. "They believe she's still in the house. If the Wizard sticks to his M.O., we'll have about three hours before he takes her away or kills her."

Ryker wasted no time in reaching a massive room with mirrors from ceiling to floor. When the mansion was built in the 1800s, the room was used as a ballroom. It was empty now, except for a Steinway covered with a white sheet, and the high-sheen hardwood floor sounded hollow as he tramped across it. He only used the room for one purpose—to reach the stairwell hidden behind one of the mirrors.

"Took you long enough to spit it out." Ryker glanced at his second in command.

Jack remained quiet, staring straight ahead. Ryker didn't really expect an excuse. The man knew how he felt about that. No excuse for failure, especially when it came to protecting Marie.

Four months earlier, Ryker moved The Circle compound from the suburbs of Atlanta to an area near the Smoky Mountains. The mansion was situated in the middle of almost ten thousand acres, which included a large mountain filled with a network of tunnels and bunkers perfect to house the facility he needed. Last year, the final phase of the project was completed and now they were training new recruits in the underground Sector. The nearly fifteen square miles provided the privacy he needed. In a world filled with evil people, his covert organization of assassins came in handy.

Their footsteps echoed in the long, well-lit tunnel. A semi could pass through the passageway without scraping the side mirrors or the tips of muffler stacks.

"Who was her backup?" Ryker asked.

When a few seconds passed without an answer, Ryker stopped and faced Jack.

"They're handling it."

Ryker continued to stare.

His second in command sighed. "She went in without a backup."

Jaw clenched, Ryker strode to the iris scan next to a large metal door. A buzz sounded and he slammed the door against the inner wall.

The gripping pain in his belly grew and reminded him of the fear he lived with for years before he took over control of The Circle. She could not keep doing this to him. He refused to allow anything more to happen to her. She knew this and still didn't listen.

The noise level in the basketball court–sized room almost broke the sound barrier with printers running, people shouting or talking to those sitting next to them or to others on the Internet or satellite phones along with the clicking of keyboards. Each wall covered with large screens captured a different scene of people living their lives in various parts of the world. In the center of the room, faces bleached white by the monitors in front of them, the supervisors and handlers communicated with their operatives.

Ryker stopped in the middle of the bullpen, searching for his prey.

The balding, whipcord-thin Bryan Tilton stood over a handler shouting instructions and pointing at the screen. Maybe a sixth sense alerted Bryan. He looked up and his eyes widened.

Ryker charged toward him, ignoring the people ducking for cover behind partitions and beneath desks.

"You son of a bitch!"

His fist clipped Bryan on the chin, sending the man sliding across the floor. Desire to flatten the asshole's pointy nose almost overrode all of Ryker's control. Good thing Bryan remained sprawled out on the linoleum.

Standing over the man, Ryker opened and closed his fists. The temptation to punish him further for his stupidity warred with the fear of jabbing the cartilage of the idiot's nose into his brain.

"I swear, sir, I told her to wait until I could get backup in place, but she wouldn't listen." Bryan cupped his jaw and shifted it from side to side. "Two of our operatives are held up in a traffic accident about twenty-five miles from her last location."

"Last location?" Ryker gritted his teeth.

"The target's house, off Riverview Road." Bryan scooted back when Ryker took a step. The man's head bobbled on his skinny neck. "As soon as Phil and Harry reach it, they'll extract her."

Afraid he would crack the man's chicken neck, Ryker turned away and pointed at the nearest handler.

"You! Sal?" Mohawk trembling, the pale man nodded. Ryker said, "Tell Phil and Harry to call me on my cell as soon as they reach the house. Do not go inside! Jack and I will be there in twenty minutes. Have them wait for us." He turned back to Bryan. "Have the Spirit ready in five minutes." His helicopter could cover the miles quickly and land almost anywhere.

Circle of Deception Excerpt

The story of The Circle Organization continues in Circle of Deception. Abby and Rex's story.

The hot Circle series continues as the team of sexy spies and assassins goes undercover—under the covers.

After disappearing days before her wedding to fellow Circle agent Rex Drago, Abby Rodriguez discovered that trying to reclaim a life—and a love—lost is a whole lot harder than she thought. When her family's safety is threatened by an arms dealer, Abby must go undercover with the one man who sees right through her as they play the scariest roles yet: husband and wife.

Mission or no mission, Rex Drago wants answers from his ex-fiancee. Forced to play along as a rival arms dealer and the husband he once wanted to be, Rex is finding it hard to stay professional—especially since Abby is just as hot as ever. And when they find themselves in a very intimate position, Abby and Rex must act the part—or risk blowing their cover entirely.

Read on for a sneak peek at the thrilling sequel to *Circle of Danger*. Available now!

Excerpt of Circle of Deception

The naked man swayed back and forth, his ankles bound by duct tape and rope to a massive hook suspended from the ceiling. A bare light bulb at the end of a long wire swung in the opposite direction, casting drunken shadows across every inch of his sweat-coated skin.

Abby Rodriguez's gaze followed the movement of Rex Drago's body as if watching a tennis match in slow motion.

"Enjoying the view?" His bored and resigned tone barely hid his sarcasm. Even upside down, his eyes taunted her.

"Yeah. Actually, I am." She sat cross-legged a few feet away on the warehouse floor, her favorite Sig in one hand, resting on her knee. "You've been working on your abs. Got them looking good. Almost an eight-pack. Maybe you could get a job modeling for romance novels." With his big arms tied behind his back, she admired how the muscles expanded each time he struggled with the tape. A sparse swirl of hair rested between his pecs and trailed to a thin line down his abs toward his groin.

"Funny. Real funny." He cleared his throat. "Get me down."

"Having a problem with your sinuses? I guess hanging like that"—she waved in his direction—"bottom up, could cause a problem. Kind of chilly in here too."

"Where's Jack and Nic?" His coal-black hair, cut high and tight, almost brushed the floor with each pass. She missed his long hair but the military style gave him a more deadly look. Heaven and Hell knew he already intimidated enough people with his six-foot-five height.

"Nic is monitoring the silent alarm, making sure it's off and no backup wired in. Jack's somewhere nearby, probably taking out the guard we spotted in the back that Savalas left behind."

Tilting her head, she looked a little harder at the tattoos running across each of his biceps. She never remembered seeing them on him before. Motivated less from curiosity than from her attempt to avoid staring at what dangled from his groin. Oh, yeah, that appendage had always been worth admiring, but the man already had an ego the size of...well, of his cock, and he needed no one stroking— For goodness' sake, her mind refused to stay on the problem at hand. Hand? Her gaze darted to his gorgeous penis and then away.

She sighed. Every time she worked with Rex, her libido revved up at the most inappropriate times. The man oozed sex appeal. With cheekbones to die for and eyes of a clear gray ringed by darker gray, his looks were saved from being too perfect by the scar that ran across his nose and near the corner of his lip to a point on his left cheek. Then again, the scar only added to his aura of danger.

He growled. "Are you planning on cutting me down anytime soon?"

She grinned big, knowing how much he hated depending on anyone's help. "Well—"

"Abby, dammit! Quit playing around." His body began swinging harder as he fought the ties.

"Is that any way to talk to a friend?"

313

"Some freaking friend," he muttered.

"What did you say?" She looked a little harder at one of the tattoos. Tiny writing around a delicate Valentine heart appeared to move as he flexed his bicep. Was it for a current girlfriend? Weird, he'd never been into visual displays of love. Even when he'd asked her to marry him years ago, it had been during a private moment and more of a statement than a proposal. Things changed. People changed.

Gunfire echoed through the large warehouse. What trouble had Jack stumbled across? Time for her to quit teasing the big baby swinging frantically in front of her and let him go.

"If I ever get down from here, I'm going to spank that sweet ass of yours red."

"Ha! That's no way to talk to the person who's saving you." She almost flinched when his glare turned to ice. Those beautiful eyes used to be filled with love when he looked at her, but no longer. Years ago, she'd made sure of that.

The jingle of a gun strap caught her attention. In a smooth move, she twisted, aiming her gun at the person behind her.

"What the fuck!" Jack Drago, Rex's brother, jumped out of her Sig's sight, clutching a M4 rifle across his torso. "Quit being a pain in the ass and cut him down. Savalas has more men coming and we don't have time for you two to reminisce." He glanced over his shoulder, checking the perimeter.

"I don't need help, especially hers." Rex continued to glower at Abby.

She wanted to laugh, but at the same time, the thought of Rex being killed scared her more than she wanted to admit. No way would she ever let him know that. She'd broken his heart once and he'd done the same to hers. She planned to never let it happen again.

"Fine, then! I'll put you out of your misery." She raised her gun and pointed it at Rex.

"Wait! Hold on! Abby, dammit!" He twisted and struggled with the binding around his wrists, causing his body to flop around like a hooked trophy fish.

The shot reverberated in the large warehouse and cut off Rex's shouting as he fell to the floor. She'd always been an excellent shot, and the little bit of duct tape and rope never had a chance.

"For Pete's sake, what the hell's going on here? Rex?" Nic ran to the big guy moaning on the floor. Her ball cap flew off, releasing a short ebony braid. "Oh my gosh, oh my gosh! Did she shoot you? Tell me where you're bleeding."

"Abby, dammit! You could make a preacher cuss. What if he'd cracked open his skull? We don't need to be slowed down dragging his big ass out of here." Jack nudged Abby to the side and stood over his brother while Nic cut the rope and tape off his wrists and ankles.

"My last name is Rodriguez," Abby said, arms folded over her chest. She secured the Sig in her shoulder holster. Frustration stiffened her back and lifted her chin. She refused to let the men browbeat her.

"What?" Jack squinted at her in confusion.

"You and Rex obviously think my last name is dammit." She concentrated on staring back at Jack while Nic rattled on about Rex's cuts and bruises. She hated seeing the other woman fussing over him. For some inane reason, she wanted to be the one to do it.

Rex stood, drawing her reluctant attention as he rubbed the marks left behind by the bindings. He towered over Nic. Abby wanted to push her out of the way and run her hands over his hard body, checking for broken bones, making sure he was okay.

"You're crazy," he said, glaring at her.

That snapped her out of the mushy feelings. One eyebrow lifted, she said, "Yes, I am. And don't you forget it." With a flip of her hair, she sauntered off.

About the Author

CARLA SWAFFORD loves romance novels, action/adventure movies, and men, and her books reflect that. And on top of all that, she's crazy about hockey, and thankfully, no one has made her turn in her Southern Belle card.

So, it's no surprise she writes spicy romantic suspense filled with mercenaries, motorcycle one-percenters, and southern criminals. And in the last few years, she's included sexy hockey players in books without suspense, except for the kind that asks, how will they ever find their happily ever after?

Married to her high school sweetheart, she lives in the Southeast U.S.

To find out more about Carla, be sure to visit her Facebook and TikTok pages or join her newsletter on her website. www.carlaswafford.com.

Also by Carla Swafford

Brothers of Mayhem Trio

Hidden Heat

Full Heat

Above currently published by Loveswept, an imprint of Random House in ebook only

Naked Heat

The Circle Organization

Circle of Desire

Circle of Danger

Circle of Deception

Above previously published by Avon, an imprint of HarperCollins.

Circle of Dishonor (novella)

Circle of Defiance (novella

Kidnapped For A Day (short story)

Above novellas and short story available individually in Ebook and in paperback together

Atlanta Edge Hockey Romance

Crossing The Line

Fake Play

(more to come)

Southern Crime Family

Jake

Sen (coming soon!)

Ethan (coming soon!)

Small-Town Duo

Loving The Small-Town Preacher's Son

Loving The Small-Town Hero

Milton Keynes UK
Ingram Content Group UK Ltd.
UKHW010846280324
440101UK00001B/23